Shame burned  veins.

Matthew thought once he had her with child nothing else would be important to her!

'How little you know of me if you think your children would be enough to replace my brothers in my affection,' she flared at him, jerking free of his embrace. 'You have the legal right to Winterbourne, of that there is no dispute. But do not think I will accept you in my heart in place of my brothers and my father. . .I am not so complaisant!'

Dear Reader

We have a romp of a Regency for you this month, in the second book by Stephanie Laurens. Max Rotherbridge, rakehell par excellence, finds himself guardian to four beautiful heiresses. . . We introduce new author Francesca Shaw, who uses the English Civil War for her first book. Henrietta is left penniless and homeless by her father's will, and her only recourse is to marry the inheritor, Matthew — but he fights for Parliament. How the impasse is broken makes for a lively tale!

The Editor

Francesca Shaw is not one but two authors, working together under the same name. Both are librarians by profession, working in Hertfordshire, but living virtually side by side in a village in Bedfordshire. They first began writing ten years ago under a tree in a Burgundian vineyard, and, although they have published other romances, MASTER OF WINTERBOURNE is their first historical novel. Their shared interests include travel, good food, reading and, of course, writing.

MASTER OF
WINTERBOURNE

Francesca Shaw

First published in Great Britain 1993
by Mills & Boon Limited

© Francesca Shaw 1993

Australian copyright 1993
Philippine copyright 1993
This edition 1993

ISBN 0 263 78051 1

Masquerade is a trademark published by
Mills & Boon Limited, Eton House,
18–24 Paradise Road, Richmond, Surrey, TW9 1SR.

Set in 10 on 10½ pt Linotron Plantin
04-9304-86013

Typeset in Great Britain by Centracet, Cambridge
Made and printed in Great Britain

CHAPTER ONE

'IT'S as well black becomes you so, mistress,' Alice murmured as she coaxed the last wayward tendril of soft brown hair into a knot at the nape of Henrietta's neck. 'I forget the last time I saw you in colours.'

Henrietta Wynter made no immediate reply beyond stretching out her hand to pick up the oval miniature portrait which lay on her dressing-table beside the crystal lotion bottles and the jewellery she had chosen from the worn blue velvet case which had been her mother's.

'There is no one left to mourn, Alice.' She lifted her eyes from the painted likeness and met the compassionate blue gaze of her maidservant. 'By the year's end I will be quit of my weeds. . .perhaps by then I will also be quit of some of this sorrow. It seems never-ending.'

'He was only a child,' Alice offered in clumsy consolation. In her large family deaths in infancy were too common an occurrence to be mourned for long. 'And you had not seen him these past five years.'

'Francis was all of my family left to me—and the future of Winterbourne.' Henrietta's eyes filled with tears as she looked at the painted likeness she held, the unformed baby face of the five-year old, the tumble of light brown curls on the big lace collar, the rosebud mouth and wide brown eyes so like her own. 'This is how I remember him, just an infant. And he was only ten years old when he died, so far from home.'

Alice put down the comb and lifted a single string of pearls from the lace cloth, allowing the heavy smoothness to settle against Henrietta's bare throat. 'Your lady mother's good-sister would have loved him well; it was only ill chance that he caught the fever. And he wasn't alone: he may have been far from Winterbourne, mistress, but the Low Countries give harbour to many loyal

5

subjects of His Majesty. He would have had English friends his own age to play and study with.'

'Study to what end?' Henrietta asked bitterly, sweeping aside the heavy black silk of her skirts and rising from the low stool. 'If he had lived, when would he ever have been free to take up his inheritance? The King is in exile, his sovereign father murdered, and his assassins rule in London. Francis would have had to pledge his allegiance to the Council of State — and no Wynter could ever do such a thing.' She sighed, brushing one hand across her forehead in a gesture of hopelessness. 'When will Winterbourne ever have a master again?'

Alice clicked her tongue impatiently as she followed Henrietta across the room, smoothing the broad, lace-edged collar encircling the white shoulders. 'It has a *mistress*,' she said firmly. 'You have guarded it well and one day soon you'll find a man worthy to be master here.'

'Worthy! Where are all these worthy men?' Henrietta demanded, the colour high in her cheeks: it was an old complaint. 'Dead on the battlefield lying alongside my father and my brother James, or so compromised with Parliament they must skulk abroad. All that are left are mere children, old men or equivocators who have compounded to keep their lands.' Then, incurably honest, she added, 'But if it were not for the influence of my godfather with those in authority now I would have had to swear allegiance to Parliament or pay dearly to keep that which has been in my family for years. From now on *I* must be Winterbourne! I am accountable for the estate and its people — you are all my family now.'

Restless, she moved to the window, sinking on to the cushioned seat. With an impatient movement she unlatched the casement, sending it swinging wide, scattering the fragile pink petals of the dogroses bunched in a pewter pot on the oak ledge.

Alice came and knelt beside her mistress on the broad seat, leant her elbows on the ledge and looked out over the expanse of lawns and orchards to the ruined Tudor gatehouse beyond. With the inrush of soft spring air, the green scent of growing things, their sombre mood lifted, no longer mistress and servant but two eighteen-year-old girls exchanging smiles at the sight of the perfect May morning.

After the wet of early spring the grass was so lush and green that it seemed to scintillate under fruit trees bowed down with blossom. The air was clear and still, so still that they could hear the sheep folded on the slopes below the beech woods that sheltered the house and Home Farm to the north and east.

'On a morning such as this,' Henrietta murmured, picking up a slim vellum-bound volume from the cushions, 'we should be dressed in muslin and ribbons, waiting for our suitors to ride up and woo us with pretty phrases. . .but instead,' she finished with a laugh, 'we must put on our aprons, go down to the laundry-room and see how severity will serve with that flighty new girl.' But despite her down-to-earth words she didn't move, except to put down the book of poetry again. 'And, although I would like nothing better than to spend the morning reading this new volume Lady Willoughby so kindly sent, it will not get the laundry seen to!'

'It is not severity that girl needs,' Alice replied crisply, although with a regretful look as Henrietta laid down the book. Both girls had a passion for love poetry not shared by a disapproving Aunt Susan. 'What she needs is wedding and bedding, or we will find ourselves with a love-child to provide for.'

'Is it any lad in particular?'

'If only it were.' Alice was dour. 'But she rolls her silly sheep's eyes at anything in tight breeches! A hasty marriage is one thing; a child with no name is quite another, and a burden on the parish.'

Henrietta glanced slyly at Alice's heightened colour and indignant eyes. 'Why so hot for morality all of a sudden? Is the silly wench casting her lures at your Robert?'

Alice tossed her head, loosing a quantity of blonde

hair from the confines of her starched linen coif. 'He is not mine, and I am not his until I choose to accept his suit,' she stated with dignity, promptly spoiled by adding, 'And he has more sense than to take notice of a chit who is any lad's for the asking!'

'Why keep him dangling so? He is a good man, steady and true, and now he's my steward he can keep a wife and family. You would have a fine house at the Home Farm, and a position. It cannot be because he lost an arm fighting at my father's side?'

'He is no less a man for the loss of an arm.' Alice glanced at Henrietta, assessing her mistress's mood. 'I can vouch for that. . .' Her mobile lips quirked with secret memories.

'Indeed, miss!' Henrietta struggled to be severe with her beloved maid. 'And just how, may I ask, have you been testing his manhood?'

Alice shook her head with sudden discretion, her eyes sparkling with the reflected morning light — or perhaps her secret.

'Alice!' Henrietta was suddenly exasperated with her maid. 'Why are you and Robert not betrothed yet? I know he intended to ask you — he told me so when I gave him the position of steward here at Winterbourne. If you are sharing his bed without a promise before God, you are being sinful, and if you are teasing him you are being unkind — and I believed you neither.'

Alice reached out a hand and touched Henrietta's white fingers as they lay on the silvery oak. 'In truth I do not tease him, and he knows why we cannot be betrothed.'

'Why not?' Henrietta looked at the girl's flushed face keenly. 'He is a good man, you could not hope for a better, nor a more loyal. He stood over my father's body at the battle of Newbury, despite his own grievous wounds, and he has run the estate for me faithfully — I owe him a greater debt than I can ever pay. And you must know,' she added softly, 'the very special place you have in my heart.'

added thoughtfully, 'my father trusted him with his affairs.'

'Well, this time he's expended some crowns on an escort,' Alice remarked as the coach with a rider behind clattered through the gatehouse arch, frightening a flock of white doves into wheeling panic.

'Perhaps he's carrying a money chest, although I can't imagine why. I knew he must come soon; there will be papers for me to sign and we have known of Francis's death these six weeks past.' Henrietta got to her feet, smoothing down the heavy silk with care, suddenly the mistress of Winterbourne again, no longer a carefree girl. 'Alice, do come in!'

Alice, leaning dangerously over the sill, was exposing an indecorous amount of freckled cleavage and still more golden hair tumbled free from her cap in her eagerness to inspect the new arrivals. 'That is no hired outrider, not astride such a fine mount,' she commented, running a shrewd country eye over the strapping grey gelding pacing behind the carriage.

'More a war horse,' Henrietta agreed, looking over Alice's shoulder from the discreet shadows of the room. But even as her eyes took in the powerful hocks and roman nose of the mount she became aware of the rider astride it. The tall, erect figure on the grey rode easily, one hand on the reins, the other resting lightly on his thigh. He was all in black, relieved only by the white linen bands fluttering at his neck. His cloak was strapped behind his saddle and his high boots were powdered with the fine white chalky dust that, in dry weather, covered every road in this part of Hertfordshire.

The face under the broad brim of the hat was shadowed. Alice, taking in the plainness of his garb, the modest plume in his hat, let disapproval tinge her voice. 'A Puritan — although a fine figure of a man for all that.'

'Another lawyer, by his bands.' Henrietta ignored the latter part of her maidservant's observation, but something about the figure on the horse prompted her to lean forward and tug at Alice's shoulder. 'Come in, Alice! It is unseemly to stare so.'

The sharp urgency in her tone must have carried on the still morning air to the courtyard below: the man reined in the powerful grey and looked up to the open casement, his eyes meeting Henrietta's with the directness of a touch.

Blushing furiously, she stepped back, one hand to her throat. To be caught gaping like a serving girl at an inn window, and on the very day when she expected to have her legal right to Winterbourne affirmed! Scarlet-cheeked, she snapped at Alice, 'Get down to the kitchens and order refreshments for our guests. Tell Martha to prepare the Spanish chamber for Lawyer Stone as usual, and a room for his clerk and that other man as well. Quickly, girl! I will tell my aunt they are here.'

Hurt, Alice gathered her skirts around her with an affronted sniff and swept out of the room in a passable imitation of Henrietta at her most dignified. Despite her embarrassment and irritation at being caught in such an undignified attitude Henrietta couldn't resist a smile at Alice's injured dignity.

Hurriedly she turned to her dressing-table, lifting the lid on her dressing-case to reveal the soft silvered mirror inside. She bent down, patting the curls in front of her ears into order, checking with a turn of her neck that the knot at her nape was still confined in its ribbon net. She tugged gently at the upper edge of the collar, arranging it more becomingly across the swell of her bosom, then on impulse tilted the pink liquid in one of the glass phials on to her fingertips, filling the cool air of the room with the fragrance of rosewater. Henrietta traced her wet fingertips behind each ear and at each pulse-point at her wrists, then caught herself in the action.

Why go to such trouble for old Lawyer Stone whom she had known all her life? Provided she was dressed neatly and decently she very much doubted he could say five minutes later *what* she'd been wearing. No, the impulse behind this sudden toilette was the tall, dark

man on the horse. Cross with herself, Henrietta snapped
down the lid of the dressing-case. Indeed, she must be
seeing a surfeit of young sprigs if the prospect of
conversation with a mature man, even a sombre lawyer,
had this effect on her!

Impatiently she waited for Alice to return, listening to
the sound of voices from below and the stirrings of the
household as it prepared to greet the unexpected visitors.

Alice returned after a while, breathless and flushed.
'Your aunt is receiving them in the long gallery,' she
reported. 'Mary is bringing refreshment to them there
and Kate and Martha. . .' she paused to catch her breath
and rattled on '. . .are preparing the Spanish chamber
and the red bedchamber.'

'Good.' Henrietta nodded in satisfaction that her
household was rising to the occasion.

'You were right,' Alice added slyly as they walked
down the panelled corridor to the long gallery. 'The
rider is no clerk. By his bearing and his clothes he's a
gentleman, and a fine one at that.'

'Your hair is loose,' Henrietta chided, trying to ignore
Alice's gossip; she needed to collect herself before meet-
ing him. 'Tidy yourself before we go in to our guests!
Do you want them to think we are country bumpkins?'

The door stood open and from within they heard the
soft tones of Henrietta's widowed aunt offering drinks.
'A glass of Canary, Mr Stone? Or perhaps some of our
own cider you enjoyed so much last time we had the
pleasure of your company?'

'Thank you, madam,' the lawyer's rich courtroom
voice filled the big room, 'a draught of cider to wash
down the dust would be most welcome. I cannot recall
such a dry spring for many a long year.'

'And you, sir?' Aunt Susan was saying as Henrietta
entered the gallery, Alice a correct two paces behind her.
'Will you have cider or wine?'

'A glass of Canary, if you please —— ' The stranger
broke off and turned at the sound of Henrietta's footstep

on the polished boards. Lawyer Stone heaved himself to his feet from the fireside chair and beamed as he always did at the sight of her.

'My dear child!' He came and took her hand, kissing her on the cheek with the familiarity of a man who had known her from the cradle. The shrewd old eyes scanned her face, noted the smudges of sleeplessness under her brown eyes, the only flaw in the smooth, pale complexion. Yes, she'd grown from a girl into a woman in the short time since he'd brought her the news of her brother's death. 'You are in fine looks,' he said softly. 'And the grief will pass in time.'

Henrietta was touched by such gentleness from a man usually bluff and businesslike. She returned the pressure of his hand and smiled her thanks.

'You are right, sir. Hardly an hour passes without my thinking of Francis, but I can remember without anger for his death now—and without doubts as to the rightness of his being an exile in the Low Countries.'

Stone patted her shoulder, and walked heavily back to his chair, pausing as he suddenly remembered his silent companion. 'But I am forgetting my manners in my pleasure at seeing you, Henrietta! Allow me to present your. . .my colleague in law, Matthew Sheridan. Sheridan, Mistress Henrietta Wynter.'

Henrietta kept her eyes modestly lowered as she dropped a slight curtsy to the stranger, aware only of the long, booted legs, the elegance of his bow in contrast to the plainness of his dress.

'Madam?' The deep voice turned the single word into a question.

'Sir,' Henrietta replied coolly, but when she raised her eyes to his face the question was still there in his eyes. What he was so silently asking she had no idea, but she felt the colour rising in her cheeks, the breath constricting in her throat.

Without the shadowing brim of his hat she could see his eyes were green beneath brows as dark as his hair. His face was tanned, lean and serious, the face of a thinker. Yet Henrietta could not deceive herself that here was a scholar, locked away in his study from the world: those green eyes spoke of experience and action.

Haughtily she held out her hand, maintaining a formality at odds with the reaction he was evoking in her. Matthew Sheridan took it in a light grasp, bent his dark head, briefly brushed her knuckles with his lips and as briefly released her, stepping back to accept the glass of Canary from the maid.

Illogically annoyed at his punctilious behaviour, Henrietta crossed to stand beside her aunt's chair. Despite the range of windows down its length the gallery was darkened by heavy brocade hangings and old oak panelling. Listening politely to her aunt's enquiries about the journey, she became aware of a figure waiting at the far end of the long room.

'You have your clerk with you, sir?' The man did not look like her old acquaintance Adam Wingate.

'Not mine.' Lawyer Stone nodded in Matthew's direction. 'He's Sheridan's man.'

'There is refreshment in the kitchen for him,' Aunt Susan offered hospitably.

'Thank you, madam, I prefer he stays here.' Sheridan was almost brusque, but Henrietta noted how the green eyes sought out the shadowed figure, sending what seemed to her a silent message.

Intrigued, Henrietta longed to ask why Lawyer Stone had brought these two strangers to Winterbourne. Too well-bred to ask directly, she waited, one hand on the carved back-rest of her aunt's chair, listening to the conversation. No doubt the reason would emerge in time.

'Fetch a footstool, Mary.' Mistress Clifford ordered, as the old lawyer winced and rubbed his knee. 'Why do you travel in that old carriage if it only serves to aggravate your gout, sir?' she scolded with the familiarity of long acquaintance.

He groaned as he lifted his foot on to the stool, but

replied with a chuckle, 'It's not the draughts in my carriage, madam, it's old age and good living.'

Aunt Susan sniffed disapprovingly. 'Your housekeeper should look after you better.'

'She tries, but what I really need, madam, is a good wife!'

Unaccountably Aunt Susan blushed deeply, but replied with spirit, 'You have been too long a bachelor, sir, to settle to the married state!'

'I know.' The lawyer sighed deeply. 'And where would I find a wife to take me with all my manifold faults?'

Glancing between the two of them, Henrietta was suddenly struck with a startling new idea: so *that* was how the wind was blowing! Aunt Susan and Lawyer Stone—how had she been so blind not to see it before? She suppressed a smile of satisfaction at the thought of her gentle aunt finding happiness after all these years of widowhood and looked up to find Matthew Sheridan's eyes on her again.

Flustered, she broke in to the conversation. 'Is this your promised visit to read my brother Francis's will, sir?'

'Henrietta!' her aunt protested. 'You are too hasty! Let the gentlemen finish their wine at least before you press business upon them.' She had never approved of the role Henrietta had been forced to assume in the absence of male relatives, and she was constantly shocked at her niece's unseemly interest in the business of the estate.

'I am sorry, Aunt.' How could she explain that the presence of this silent stranger was making an already painful occasion even more of an ordeal? 'I want this matter behind me. I do not relish the discussing of it, but it cannot be postponed. I must know how matters stand with Winterbourne.'

Both men seemed to recognise the anguish in her tone, but it only served to sharpen her aunt's annoyance at her bad manners. 'It can certainly be postponed until the gentlemen have rested from their journey!' Henrietta might be head of the household, but Aunt Clifford had been her guardian since her mother died, and, although a gentle woman, never forgot her duty to bring up her niece as a lady.

Stung, Henrietta dropped her aunt a small curtsy and moved in a rustle of silk to the window-seat in the central bay window. She stared blankly at the glass, her eyes unfocused on her own blurred image. She must not disgrace herself with tears, not in front of this austere stranger whose silent presence was unnerving her enough to deserve her aunt's reprimand. Was she so unused to the company of mature men that she was robbed of conversation? No, it was Matthew Sheridan himself; he was the cause of her unease.

A second image appeared in the glass, a tall black reflection overlaying her own. As if her thinking about him had conjured him up, Matthew Sheridan stood behind her, a glass in either hand.

'You are upset. Take this; drink it slowly.' It was an instruction, not a question, and she took the glass without argument. Their fingertips brushed and she was very aware of the warmth of his hand, the male scent of leather and warm linen. She sank down on the window-seat and gestured to him to sit beside her.

That was better; she didn't need to look at him. Sipping the sweet wine, she gathered her composure, once more mistress of herself and Winterbourne.

'Have you come from Hertford this day, sir?' she asked politely.

Matthew Sheridan crossed one booted leg over the other and half turned to survey the view from the long window. 'From London yesterday, then overnight at Mr Stone's house.'

He was obviously uninterested in discussing his journey. Piqued that he would not make an effort at conversation, Henrietta cast round for another neutral topic but failed to find one. Nor was the silent presence of the clerk watching her from the shadows a help.

'Mr Stone introduced you as his colleague. . .?'

'A courtesy only. We are both lawyers,' he responded indifferently, his attention apparently still on the view outside.

It was like pulling teeth! Henrietta gritted hers; she was used to more attention than this from gentlemen! Had the man *no* conversation, or was he deliberately trying to unsettle her? No such constraints afflicted her aunt and Lawyer Stone, who were talking animatedly, her aunt almost flirtatious, at the other end of the room.

But she couldn't pretend he was ignoring her; she could feel his eyes on her profile, longed to tug the edge of her collar higher so that the heavy lace and crisp linen concealed the swell of her breasts. The skin prickled with the awareness of his look and she gripped the stem of her glass as she felt the blush start to stain her throat.

However severe she'd been with Alice, there was no denying the girl had been right: Matthew Sheridan was a very attractive man, disturbingly so. She could cope with the likes of Marcus Willoughby, indifferent to the reams of passionate poetry he quoted, his mannered wooing. He excited nothing within her — yet *this* man, who couldn't even be bothered to exchange social pleasantries, was stirring emotions she'd only ever tasted in the poems of Marvell and Donne.

Without realising it her lips silently framed the opening phrase of her favourite poem. '"Had we but world enough, and time. . ."'

Their eyes met and she realised with a shock that he had read her lips for he completed the second line softly, '"This coyness, Lady, were no crime".'

Henrietta stared back, too taken aback to cap his quotation, turn this into a harmless, if flirtatious game. This was all she had ever dreamed about, sitting in a secluded window-seat with a handsome man quoting exciting words of love to her. Why was the reality so unsettling, so different from the dream? In her reveries the man pressed heated yet respectful kisses on her hands, she accepting his devotion as her right. This was altogether more dangerous, yet all he had done was quote one line of poetry. Why was she in such a tumult?

'You have another visitor.' He had turned his head from her as though nothing had passed between them, the sharp eyes focusing on the horseman swinging through the gatehouse arch on a showy chestnut.

Henrietta turned quickly, then sank back with an audible sigh. 'Oh, not again!'

Matthew said nothing, but his expression grew mocking as he took in the details of the young man's appearance, the negligent way he sat the horse, the length of his blond curls, the extravagance of lace and plumes.

'Marcus Willoughby!' Henrietta exclaimed, unable to conceal the impatience in her voice. 'And *another* new horse. Let us hope this one will not unseat him on the carriageway like the last!' Despite her annoyance she couldn't resist a smile at the memory of Marcus's dusty discomfiture.

'Aren't you going to greet your guest? Or should I say suitor? He looks like a man who has come a-wooing, although it's a pity he cannot manage both that horse and a nosegay at the same time.'

'Mary will tell him I am engaged,' she said dismissively, too much in agreement with Matthew's assessment to resent his familiarity. Marcus and she had grown up together, almost brother and sister; his recent transformation into ardent suitor was too sudden for her to take seriously.

Marcus had reached the front door and was using his spurs to make the horse caracole showily on the gravel. The watchers from above were treated to a fine view of his enormous plumed hat and bunches of ribbons as the chestnut plunged and cavorted.

'A very handsome young sprig,' Matthew commented drily. 'A neighbour, no doubt.'

'Indeed yes.' She felt more comfortable now his attention had shifted from her. 'And *young* is precisely the term for him!' Henrietta sighed as Marcus was turned away, a crestfallen expression on his young face.

'You must have many suitors to dismiss such a fine one without a trace of regret.'

'Too many—and all cut from the same pattern!' Encouraged by the amused quirk of Matthew's brows, she elaborated warmly. 'My older brother's friends are either dead or in exile for their loyalty to our sovereign King; only their little brothers are safe at home—youths like Marcus Willoughby. And all have ambitious mothers, all see Winterbourne dropping into their hands through an alliance with me!'

There was a moment's silence then he said carefully, 'You are a young woman: surely a young husband should not be displeasing to you? Or perhaps there is one among them you favour most?'

'Marriage is a duty, sir,' Henrietta responded coldly, not liking the implication in his words that she might look for passion in marriage. 'I must marry to provide Winterbourne with a strong master, and a father for its heirs. These are troubled times; no inexperienced youth will serve my purpose.' She turned to face him, quite unconscious in her vehemence of the magnificent picture she presented, her eyes alight, the colour high in her cheeks, the heavy pearls rising and falling with her breath.

'My mother died ten years ago; I had to learn young to control a household. My father was killed in '44, James four years later. For the last three years I have been Winterbourne, trustee to my little brother for this house, these lands, his people! Now they are my people, and I will not abdicate this heavy responsibility easily to some fortune-hunter!' And I want a man to love and cherish me too, she though wistfully. But that was something a well-bred girl could never express.

Matthew Sheridan heard her out in silence. 'The country is at peace now. You are wrong in thinking there are no men capable of shouldering your burden, sharing your bed. Good men of family and experience, honest men who want nothing more than to put this division and bloodshed behind them and rebuild the country for their heirs.'

'*Honest* men!' Henrietta was on her feet in a swirl of black skirts. 'Parliamentarians, you mean! Turncoats and traitors! Scavengers on the lands of those who would be true to the King. . .'

Matthew was on his feet too, his voice low with anger. 'The King is dead, madam! And many thousands of good men died too for his intransigence. Parliament and the rule of law govern England now and Winterbourne and every estate like it in the land will suffer until the Royalist party accepts this truth.'

Furious brown eyes parried his adamantine stare. 'King Charles the Second lives, sir! In shameful exile perhaps, but he is no less the King for that, nor for the fact he became King because of the unlawful killing of his father. Preach not the law to me, sir! Reconciliation will come when our King is restored and the traitors punished—only then will I accept the sacrifice of my father and brothers!'

Henrietta's hands clenched into small white fists at her side, her arms aching with the effort of keeping them there and not striking the harsh, judgemental face before her. Matthew's chin was set and grim, all the mockery that had lightened the taut features gone. They had kept their angry voices low but some quality of the exchange must have reached the seated figures at the far end of the room for both had turned to look in their direction and Aunt Susan was half out of her chair.

There was an abrupt movement in the shadows and the clerk moved from the concealment of the brocade hanging and into a shaft of sunlight. Henrietta turned and saw him clearly for the first time, a wizened figure in rusty black cloth, his lips above the severe white collar forming the word 'strumpet' as clearly as though he'd spoken it aloud.

The master might not be a Puritan, but his clerk most certainly was, and his scandalised gaze on her low-cut gown and dishevelled curls left her feeling stripped to her shift.

"Sir!' Henrietta drew her small figure up haughtily. 'Your servant is impertinent and I would be obliged if you would keep both him and your opinions in their place in my house.'

'Nathaniel——' Matthew gestured briefly and the man stepped back into the gloom. 'I suggest, Mistress Wynter, you wait until your legal position is confirmed before you lay down the law.' His voice was even, but there was an edge to it which made a shiver pass down her spine.

It took Henrietta a moment to recover, then she gathered up her skirt with one hand and turned to join her aunt and Lawyer Stone. 'Legal nit-picking! Mr Stone did not see fit to tell me why you are intruding in my affairs, but since you *are* here I suggest it is time the will was read.'

As she reached his side the old lawyer got up with more than his usual show of reluctance at leaving a glass of wine. 'Perhaps we should sit at the table, my dear. Cobham, the box!'

The weasely clerk sidled up and placed a battered document case on the glowing Turkey carpet that covered the long table. Lawyer Stone sat at the head, gesturing the women to take their places either side of him. Under Henrietta's indignant stare Matthew took the heavy carved chair at the other end of the table, his clerk at his elbow. Well, if it was Lawyer's Stone's wish that this total stranger should be privy to her business, so be it. Tomorrow they would be gone and she would be confirmed mistress of Winterbourne.

As usual Lawyer Stone took several minutes to prepare himself. First he produced eye-glasses which he polished at length before hooking them over his ears, then he blew his nose noisily on a vast kerchief before sorting the red-taped documents into neatly aligned piles. Henrietta repressed an impatient sigh and sat, hands folded, trying not to fidget. Why were there nervous butterflies in her stomach? She knew this would be a sad and evocative occasion, but she was prepared for it and it would soon be over. Reading the will would finally lay Francis to rest. . .

Lawyer Stone cleared his throat portentously. 'The entail under which the estate passed from your father to your brother James, and from him in the absence of sons to your younger brother Francis still stands. You are of course aware of those terms, Henrietta; we discussed them on the melancholy occasion of James's death.'

Henrietta nodded. 'I remember. And I remember too how the threat of sequestration hung over us then because neither Francis nor myself would pledge our allegiance to Parliament. Does my godfather's influence with Parliament still protect us from the danger of confiscation?'

'Indeed, it would do so, if you still needed such protection.' The old man exchanged a sharp glance with Matthew then dropped his eyes to the papers before him. 'I am happy to say you no longer need Sir Andrew's influence.'

'If that means that this pernicious persecution of those whose only crime is loyalty to their sovereign lord the King is at an end then I am glad of it, although I shall always be grateful to my godfather.'

Aunt Susan stifled a slight yawn: it had grown warm in the long gallery and her mind was half on the preparations for dinner.

'So with that threat lifted I am free to continue to manage Winterbourne and its estate? There are many decisions I need to discuss with you——'

'Wait.' Lawyer Stone brought his hand down heavily on the table, making Aunt Susan jump guiltily. 'As you know, the estate is entailed in the male line.'

'Indeed, yes; when I have a son he will inherit,' Henrietta stated, surprised this needed repeating.

'No, what I mean is that the nearest male relative of your father inherits.' His eyes were fixed on her puzzled face, resolution and a strange pity in them.

'But there are none—my father had no brothers.'

'Your grandfather had.'

'But surely long dead; my father never spoke of one.' Henrietta smiled at him, wondering if the Canary wine or increasing age was affecting him, making him pedantic.

'Yes, but not without an heir.' The words fell like stones into a room suddenly silent.

'Then why have I never heard of these relatives?' Henrietta demanded. 'Are you telling me some impostor has emerged thinking to benefit from my bereavement?'

'My grandfather was estranged from his family over his choice of wife, so much so that he forswore the name of Wynter, moved to London and took up the profession of the law.' Matthew's cool voice was like a douche of water, knocking the breath from her lungs.

'*Your* grandfather,' she managed to whisper, although the room was tilting before her eyes. 'You are my *cousin*?'

'Yes, of a sort. My father's father was your grandfather's brother.' Suddenly there was concern in his look. 'Mistress Wynter, you look faint. Nathaniel, fetch wine quickly!'

'No!' Henrietta shot the clerk a look of loathing, ignoring Matthew as she turned vehemently to her lawyer. 'Be plain with me, sir! What does this mean?'

'It means that Matthew Sheridan — Sir Matthew Sheridan — is heir to Winterbourne.' The old man was obviously shaken by Henrietta's violent reaction; he removed his eye-glasses and patted her hand. 'When you have had a moment to compose yourself, my dear, you will realise what a relief it will be to have this heavy burden of responsibility lifted from your frail womanly shoulders.'

CHAPTER TWO

HENRIETTA rose unsteadily to her feet, her fingers gripping the silken edge of the table carpet for support. 'Do you tell me,' she managed to ask between stiff lips, 'that this man, this Parliamentarian, is the true. . .the *only* heir to Winterbourne?' She held the old lawyer's eyes with hers, refusing to look at Matthew Sheridan, although she was aware he had pushed back his chair and made a move towards her.

'That is what I said.'

'You have seen the proof; there can be no doubt?' she persisted.

'I would not be here with him else.' Mr Stone's professional dignity was affronted. 'Here, read for yourself.' He pushed a small pile of papers towards her.

Henrietta waved them away. 'If you say so, then I believe you.' She hesitated, biting her lip as she sought for words, then burst out, 'Is there no way it can be set aside?'

Lawyer Stone turned sharply, ignoring his gouty leg in his indignation. 'Henrietta! Consider what you are suggesting! It would be exceptional for an unmarried girl to inherit in any case, and certainly not where there is an entail in force. An entail can only be set aside with the agreement of the adult heir in the lifetime of his father.' He subsided and mopped his reddened face. 'Think, child — as a single woman you could never have governed this estate; you should be thankful the Lord has sent a fit and worthy man to relieve you of this unwomanly burden.'

Seeing the stricken look on her pale face, he added more gently, 'You are now free for your proper role in life — marriage, the raising of children. And you will soon have a husband to govern and guide you in all these things.'

Only pride and a stubborn refusal to break down in front of Matthew Sheridan kept her on her feet and her voice steady. 'I shall leave you now, sir. You must have legal matters to discuss with the new master of Winterbourne. I thank you for your counsel. Please send for my. . .for the steward whenever you are ready for him.' She had to go before the last vestiges of control broke, before that man reached her side as he seemed intent on doing. Stiffly she curtsied to Lawyer Stone, then, head high, walked through the door, closing it with great care behind her.

Her dignity lasted for three steps beyond the door, then she lifted her skirts in both hands and fled pell-mell down the stairs, her high heels clattering on the wooden treads and then across the flags of the hall. She had the briefest impression of the look of surprise on Alice's face as she passed her, then she was out into the warm spring air.

Where to go? Henrietta paused irresolute on the gravel. She needed to be alone, away from the questioning looks of the servants, from Lawyer Stone's dry legal advice, Aunt Susan's fussing. There weren't even any household tasks she could immerse herself in: none of it was her responsibility now. The bunch of keys that always hung at her waist like a badge of office weighed like a stone. Impulsively Henrietta snatched it off and flung it on to the stone steps.

A bee bumbled past her cheek on heavy wings and she remembered one duty she could still perform. The bee skips stood in orderly rows in the orchard, their inhabitants busy in the sun-warmed blossom. The bees must be told of the change of master; it was one of the many rules she had been taught for looking after them. Country lore held that the bees were told of every death, of every major change, or they would die themselves or fly away to seek a new master.

Henrietta picked her way through the long grass under

back on him deliberately, hoping her cold formality would discomfort him.

'I had hoped you would show me both the house and the estate yourself.' He was not so easily dislodged.

Henrietta turned back, feeling her eyes fill with frustrated tears. 'You are cruel, sir! I have acknowledged you, a complete stranger, master in my brother's place. You cannot expect me to act as your guide when every room, every field and ditch holds memories for me of what I have lost!'

The tears were running silently, unstoppably down her cheeks, her composure in shreds. Matthew swore softly under his breath, ducking under the low branch to envelop her in his arms. Henrietta stiffened in shock and began to struggle against their strength.

'Hush, cousin; if you do not want to show me the estate I shall not force you. You have had a heavy burden to carry far too long. Weep if you must; there is no one to see you.'

Except you, Henrietta thought confusedly, then gave in to the comforting strength of his arms, as he pulled her head down to rest on his chest. No man had held her since the last embrace her brother had given her when he rode off to war, and now, her cheek against Matthew's heart, Henrietta ralised how much she'd missed that strength, how solitary she'd been in the company of women.

It must be the shock making me so weak, she thought hazily, as she let him hold her closer still, the warm cloth of his shirt absorbing her tears. Then his hand began to stroke her curls and his breath was warm on her forehead. Beneath her cheek the rhythm of his heart quickened and suddenly the embrace was no longer brotherly, her own responses no longer those of a sister. Henrietta pushed him away sharply, more angry with herself than him.

'Sir! This is not seemly!'

She saw laughter in his eyes, heard it in his voice. 'May I not comfort my cousin?'

'That was not. . .comforting.' Henrietta dropped her eyes in the face of the responsive twinkle in his.

'Hear me out, cousin; I would help you,' he said persuasively, still too close for comfort.

'What can you do to help me? Winterbourne is yours now. It was never mine at all. You heard Lawyer Stone; the entail cannot be broken.'

'With your help it can. My heir could break it.'

'Your son, if you have one, cannot yet be of an age to consent.' She paused, puzzled. 'And besides, what can I do?'

'My heir is as yet unborn.'

Henrietta's bewilderment deepened, then she saw the question in his eyes and understood. 'You. . .you want. . .you're asking me to. . .?'

'We can call the oldest boy Wynter if you like,' he offered.

'Do I understand you aright? You are asking me to marry you?' Henrietta could hardly get the words out in the face of this unexpected proposal, so against every convention.

'Any other arrangement would be highly irregular, madam; I am shocked you should suggest it.' The mobile mouth quirked with amusement.

Henrietta knew she had gone white; he was laughing at her! 'And I am shocked you should jest so! What makes you think your suit would be in any way acceptable to me?'

'You must marry someone,' Matthew replied reasonably, dropping to the short-cropped turf at her feet. 'Please, come and sit and let us discuss this while we have privacy. You were frank enough with me in the long gallery about your need for a husband. Why then are you now so coy?'

She stood for a moment looking down at his dark head, at the long booted legs sprawled easily on the bank. Perhaps it would be better to humour him, at least while she formulated her rejection. Henrietta did as she was bidden, sinking down in a billow of silk. 'Indeed I must marry, but I have no shortage of suitors, as you have seen. Why should I accept your suit?' She was pleased she sounded so calm when all she wanted was to dent that arrogant assumption that she was just another chattel of Winterbourne, his for the taking.

'You had no shortage when you were an heiress, although as I recollect you were not happy with the choice. You may find you are less troubled now.' Matthew crossed his booted ankles, apparently giving all his attention to his somewhat dusty toe-caps.

Henrietta shot him an angry glance, back erect. This was not how she had imagined a proposal would be. 'I may no longer be heiress to Winterbourne, but I still have my name and my portion.'

Matthew leaned back on his elbows, watching a fish rise between narrowed lids. 'I am sure that if your father and brothers had lived they would have seen you well endowed as befits your station,' he said smoothly, 'but there is no such provision in the will.'

'I have *nothing*?' Henrietta stared at him aghast.

'Nothing I do not choose to give you.' He swivelled on one elbow to regard her keenly. 'But if you are my wife you will want for nothing.'

For a long moment he held her eyes while Henrietta felt the unpalatable truth sink in. Then she announced defiantly, 'I shall go to the Low Countries, to my aunt and uncle. They looked after Francis; they will give me shelter.' She forced herself to smile at him with a confidence she did not feel. 'I am not without friends, sir.'

'And how do you intend finding the money to travel?'

'Surely you would not deny a kinswoman the means to establish a new life?'

'I am offering you a new life — as my wife. You can remain mistress of Winterbourne, and your children will inherit it in their turn. You told me this morning that was all you desired; why turn your face against it now?' There was a long, perilous silence. Henrietta let herself be drawn into the deep green gaze and be held there.

Her breathing slowed; time seemed to stand still. Matthew raised one hand and touched the back of it to her cheek. 'Am I so unacceptable to you?' he asked softly.

He was no fool, Henrietta thought indignantly. He knew the answer to that as well as she! He was eminently eligible — but he needn't think that by inheriting Winterbourne she was his for the taking.

She wanted wooing, she thought resentfully. Any young woman would! Marriage for people of their rank was a duty, the formation of an alliance, but it should not be a cold business arrangement! 'And what do you gain by this? You have Winterbourne already. And besides,' she added with spirit, 'why at your age are you not married? You must be all of thirty.'

'I am. And I was married; my wife is dead.' For a moment all the humour was gone from his face, and Henrietta recognised the memory of a grief as deep as her own. 'It is time I remarried, and you will bring me all your knowledge of this estate and its people. Besides, I know my duty as your kinsman, your sole male relation, and that is to protect and shelter you.'

So he loved his dead wife still; the remembered pain had darkened his eyes, his fingers twisted unknowingly a broad gold band on his wedding finger. What he's offering, Henrietta thought, is a convenient arrangement for him and a neat solution to the problem of what to do with me. Each of us needs to marry, of that there is no doubt, and this cold proposal at least has the merit of keeping Winterbourne in the family!

'If you wanted to do your duty as my kinsman you could give me my portion and let my uncle find me a husband,' she riposted spiritedly to hide the hurt. So much for her dream of a suitor who would love her for herself! All she was was an inconvenience to be tidily but honourably dealt with.

'One of those fortune-hunting Cavalier exiles who haunt the Continental courts? Oh, no, Henrietta, I have better ways to waste my money.' He watched her stormy face for a few moments then added quietly, 'I did not believe you so selfish as to desert your people.'

'What do you mean?'

'I would have kept on your servants, your steward, your farmworkers if you were my wife. But if you wish to leave I can find my own people to fill their places. There is no shortage of good men seeking employment now the country is at peace.'

Henrietta was shocked by his plain speaking. 'In effect you would coerce me! You are not doing this out of concern for a kinswoman or you would not be so cruel! Tell me plainly, sir; what do you want of me?' She hoped against hope she would push him into a declaration of affection, some sign that he intended to woo as well as wed her.

There was a long, long silence that hung heavy in the still air, Matthew's green gaze held hers with an intensity beyond all her experience, her knees felt weak; she was glad she was already sitting. She had told him that morning she wanted a man, not a boy to wed; now she burned with the knowledge that her immodest words had come back to haunt her.

Suddenly she knew he wanted her as. . .a woman, someone he desired in his bed, although he scarcely knew her and he still loved his first wife. She was an unrealistic fool to expect any sign of affection from him. Yet when he had held her just now he'd been tender and when his arms had tightened the beat of his heart had told her he was not indifferent to her. Henrietta cast down her eyes, feeling a shiver pass down her spine. In all her eighteen years she had never been conscious of a man's desire, and now, experiencing it for the first time from Matthew, she was totally confused.

'I will tell you what I want of you,' he said, and there was no sensuality in his voice now. 'I want a wife with a knowledge of this estate, a proven good housekeeper and an intelligent and educated mother for my children.'

Mortified to find her immodest thoughts had after all found no echo in his motives, Henrietta flung back, 'Any

woman of breeding would give you your last two quali-
ties, sir! And, as to the former, my steward knows more
of this estate than I ever will.' She scrambled to her feet
and stood over him, anger loosening her tongue. 'And
let us be frank, *cousin*, it is accepted on these occasions,
when a man seeks a wife, that he does so with at least
some show of affection or attachment!'

Matthew got slowly to his feet, giving Henrietta ample
time to regret her impetuous challenge. Standing before
her, he was disconcertingly close, dangerously male,
regarding her with heavy-lidded green eyes.

'If you are asking me to make love to you, Henrietta,
I will willingly comply. However, as we are not yet
betrothed, do you not feel this place is a trifle indiscreet?
I could come to your chamber later. . .' He stretched
out one hand, rubbing the ball of his thumb lingeringly
down the line of her neck until it met the heavy warmth
of her pearls.

'How dare you touch me?' Henrietta stumbled backwards, frightened at what she'd unleashed, the lightning
change from cool logic to explicit sensuality. She had
wanted fine words and dalliance, not dangerous reality.

'Oh, Henrietta!' His voice and eyes mocked her. 'You
play at being a grown woman, you manage your estate
and complain that your suitors are all callow boys. You
ask for a mature man and demand pretty speeches but
you cannot pretend you do not know what the right true
end of it will be. I will behave with restraint but you are
like a child with a stick stirring a beehive—do not be
surprised if you are stung.'

'You are offensive, sir—and arrogant!' The racing of
her heart and the flush staining her skin was not all anger
and embarrassment, and the recognition of her own
shameful excitement added a guilty vehemence to her
protest. 'I would not marry you if you were the last man
in Christendom!'

Matthew shrugged. 'As you will. I doubt you will
starve, but your people may—there are enough masterless servants in the countryside already.'

'I wish to God you were out of my sight, sir!' Henrietta stamped her foot, too angry now to heed his threat.

'We leave soon; we can stay at Winterbourne a day or two at most. I have too much important business in hand to linger here now. You have until tomorrow morning to change your mind; if you decide not to accept my offer of marriage I will provide you with passage money and escort to your friends in the Low Countries — but not a silver shilling more.' He swept her a bow that mocked courtesy. 'I wish you joy of your deliberations, Mistress Wynter.'

Henrietta stood watching the lean figure make its way through the orchard away from her without a backward glance. What had she done? He was not a man who made idle threats; that much she could judge of Matthew Sheridan. If she persisted in her refusal to marry him he would make her people destitute and their families with them. There were people enough living on parish relief in the Vale for her to know the harshness of life for masterless men.

And what of Robert who had fought at her father's side, had been maimed in the service of the Wynter family? Who would employ him? How could he ever marry Alice now? The weight of the responsibility weighed on her as it had never done before. Nor could she delude herself that her mother's brother could afford to support her people until she found a husband. 'If I could find one to take me with no portion to offer him.' She spoke out loud, knowing it was the voice of cold reason.

She regained her room without meeting anyone, for which she was profoundly thankful. One window faced across the entrance court to the master bedroom opposite; as she stood looking out Henrietta could see the housemaids at work, the flap of sheets as the great bed was made up, the casements pushed wide to air the long-disused chamber. Aunt Susan must have given orders to prepare the room for the new master of Winterbourne, as was fitting.

'Oh, mistress!' Alice swirled into the room, her face alight with excitement. 'What a day this is! Such good fortune, you could hardly hope for better! A kinsman, and such a fine-looking man. . .'

'What have you heard?' Henrietta demanded, knowing full well how the gossip would be spreading like wildfire through the household. A sensation of helplessness swept over her.

'That Master Sheridan and you are to wed. Oh, just wait until they hear the news in the village! They'll peal the bells for joy. . .what shall you wear, mistress?' She bustled over to the great clothes-press and swung open the heavy door. 'Your best primrose silk would look well. . .'

'I am not marrying Matthew Sheridan.'

'. . .it has never been worn. And the new kid slippers. . .' The sense of Henrietta's words cut through her excited chatter and she stopped, open mouthed. 'I heard wrong? He hasn't asked you? But he will, mistress, never fear,' she added cosily. 'After what Letty saw in the orchard. . .'

'Alice, be quiet! My head is splitting. He *has* asked me, and I have refused him. Now draw the curtains, and fetch me a tisane of lavender flowers for my head.'

'I'll need the keys for the stillroom.'

'I cannot find them.' Henrietta was evasive, shamed of the childish gesture. 'Ask my aunt for hers.'

Alice looked amazed. It was inconceivable that the mistress of the house could misplace her precious keys without setting up a hue and cry. 'Where did you have them last? Shall I look for them?'

'Leave it be!' Henrietta sat down on the bed and rested her aching forehead in her hands in despair; she couldn't think, her head was bursting. Alice opened her mouth to speak, thought better of it and left the room.

A few moments later Mistress Clifford bustled in. 'What's this, my dear? Dinner will be set on the table in a minute and you are all in disarray. What have you been doing to lose your keys? Alice told me some nonsense about your refusing Sir Matthew—you must take him seriously and not flirt; he's no man to be left dangling like your other suitors. . .and child, there's grass on your skirts and petals in your hair!'

'Aunt, please.' Henrietta put a hand to her throbbing temples. 'My head aches so. . .'

'It's the excitement.' Her aunt exchanged a knowing look with Alice who had followed behind. 'Come, tell me what he said!'

'Alice! Will you please fetch me my tisane?'

Her maid ignored her, turning in an indignant swirl of skirts to Mistress Clifford. 'I told you she meant it! She says she won't have him, Mistress; she says she turned him down.'

'Henrietta, can this be true?' Her aunt was horrified as she took in Alice's words and the look on Henrietta's face. 'How can you be so foolish? You must go to him this minute and tell him it was just a silly whim!' She softened her tone. 'I know it must have been a shock, my dear, but this is no time for maidenly reticence; he is not a man to be trifled with.'

'I do not like him,' Henrietta said mulishly.

'That has nothing to do with anything.' Susan was sharp. 'And what is there to dislike, miss? He is an educated man of affairs, with a fine house in London, so Lawyer Stone tells me. And a healthy, well set-up man of maturity and sense.'

'I won't have him! He's a. . .he's a Puritan!'

'He's no such thing!' her aunt responded robustly. 'You are pettish and wilful. I must go down to our guests and apologise for your incivility. Think well on what you are refusing, and what will happen to you if you do!' Aunt Susan swept out of the room, the colour high on her cheeks.

'I have never seen your aunt so angry,' Alice remarked a few minutes later when she returned with the infusion, cool from the stillroom.

Henrietta slipped off her shoes and climbed on to the

canopied bed, sinking back against the piled bolsters with a sigh. 'She doesn't understand.'

'Nor do I understand—what is there against him? Winterbourne will be yours forever, you will never want for anything, and you must marry *someone*. Why not him?' She watched her mistress sipping the aromatic drink as if weighing up her words. 'And he's a fine man; it will be no hardship to take him to your bed.' Seeing the blush staining Henrietta's throat, she muttered, 'So that's it,' under her breath and settled on the other end of the bed with a glance to make certain the door was shut.

'There's no need to be afraid. You don't want to heed those silly wenches gossiping in the laundry; where the man is gentle and knowing there's much pleasure in it for a woman. And that's a good thing, for the wisewomen say it makes for easier getting of a child. . .'

'And what do you know about it?' Henrietta knew she should not encourge such an improper conversation, but her curiosity overcame discretion.

'Enough to know that with the right man it's a very great happiness.'

'Alice! have you been bedding with Robert?'

The girl tossed her head. 'And if I have? You told me yourself only this morning we should be betrothed.'

'But you aren't! And what if he were to get you with child?'

There was an uncomfortable pause, then Henrietta said slowly, 'I saw you coming out of Mistress Perrott's cottage yesterday. Why were you there? We were not in need of any herbs, and no one here or on the farm is sick and needing her ministrations.' There was only one other reason for the women of the village to consult the wisewoman. Her eyes fell on Alice's slender waist as the truth dawned.

'It doesn't show yet.' The girl was quite matter-of-fact. 'Robert will wed me before it does.'

Henrietta was stunned. There was no way she could separate Alice and Robert, drag the girl off to the Low

'When you are betrothed, Robert and I shall be wed. Your mother would not have wanted me to leave you before you were betrothed. My mother was your mother's maidservant, we were playmates together — I cannot leave you now.' Seeing Henrietta's obdurate expression, she added firmly, 'And Robert understands.'

Henrietta doubted it, knowing how lovelorn her steward was, how his cold grey eyes turned soft when they fell on Alice's buxom figure as she bustled across the yard to the drying lawns or the stillroom. Touched by her maid's devotion, she found herself momentarily without words and sat tracing the striations in the greenish panes of window glass, watching the shadow of her hand as it fell across the plaited rush matting.

'I thank you, Alice,' she said at last. 'I need you now too much — perhaps I am too selfish — to let you go. Perhaps in a few months, when I am used to being mistress of Winterbourne in law, instead of just its guardian as I have these past three years, since James was killed. . .'

There was another silence, both girls sharing the memory of James Wynter, the plumes in his hat blowing gallantly in the wind as he rode out for the last time through the mellow red-brick arch of the old gatehouse to hazard his life for the King — and to avenge his father.

As if to echo their rememberings there was the faint sound of hoofbeats on the hard-packed Chiltern chalk of the lane leading to the village. The horseman must be coming to the house; there was nothing beyond but the Downs and the woods.

'Who can that be?' Henrietta cocked her head to one side to catch the sound on the clear air. 'No one from the house has ridden out this morning, and Robert is overseeing the roofing of the long barn.'

'One of your suitors, without doubt,' Alice suggested slyly. 'Perhaps you should have worn your pearl-drop earrings; they are very becoming. Let me get them for you.'

Henrietta sighed heavily. 'Surely not at this hour! Am

I never to be granted a moment's peace from these callow youths? They pretend they come to offer me sympathy on my brother's death, but I know better. All their mothers and aunts have been plotting and scheming since the moment they heard Winterbourne is mine! No doubt their cousins and widowed uncles from London will follow shortly, once the news gets abroad!'

'You must wed, mistress,' Alice pointed out practically. 'You need a husband to govern Winterbourne. And Winterbourne,' she added softly, 'needs heirs. You are eighteen. . .'

'And almost an old maid!' Henrietta finished wryly. 'Well, I shall find neither a strong governor for the estate nor a man to father fine sons from this succession of inexperienced puppies. I need a man who knows the world, a man older than myself — and the like of Marcus Willoughby —' she nodded dismissively in the direction of their nearest neighbour's lands '— is neither.'

'And he has pimples,' added Alice to seal the argument. 'But listen, I hear coach wheels. Surely Mistress Clifford would have told us if visitors were expected today?'

'She has said nothing to me.' Henrietta leaned over the sill until she could see the church tower, halfway between the house and the village. 'My aunt Susan may be scatter-witted from time to time, but she would never neglect the demands of hospitality.'

Both girls leaned out of the window, blonde hair against brunette, grey stuff gown against the dull sheen of black silk. Their curiosity was finally rewarded by the sight of a cloud of white dust above the untrimmed hawthorn hedge, then a glimpse of a large black carriage creaking up the track to the gatehouse.

'It's Lawyer Stone,' Henrietta announced, sitting back on her heels. 'No one else would drive such a dreadful old carriage; I am certain it must have been built in the late King's father's day. A very careful man with his money, is Lawyer Stone; he takes as much care of his sixpences as of his gold crowns. Which is why,' she

Countries, now she was carrying his child. And how could the steward support a wife and child with no position?

'Does Robert know?' she managed to ask, struggling to hide her dismay.

'No, but he'll be well pleased.' Alice's round face flushed with pride. 'He has great love for me, and I for him.'

'I know. I'm happy for you.' The weight of responsibility settled round her neck like a millstone. 'Leave me now, dear Alice, I will try and sleep.'

Henrietta lay on the bed watching the sun shift round on the panelled walls, the shadows gradually lengthen. The clatter from the great hall as the meal was cleared came and went and silence fell over the front part of the house as the servants went about their business in the stillroom and laundry.

The household routine was as familiar to her as her own heartbeat; she could follow the time by it and knew when she heard the cattle lowing as they were driven in for evening milking that it was almost suppertime. She would have to make a decision soon but she felt strangely sapped of both strength and will, as though she had been ill for a long time.

She moved restlessly against the banked pillows; her aunt was right, Alice was right, she acknowledged it. So why was it so difficult to say yes? Because he made no pretence of wanting her for himself? Because he was so obviously marked by the loss of his first wife? Or because she had lost even the appearance of choice in the matter? But struggle as she might she knew her duty lay in securing the future of her people. . .

At last she heard the sounds she had been waiting for: her aunt moving in the adjoining chamber as she tidied herself to meet their guests at supper. Henrietta smoothed out her crumpled skirts, splashed cold water on her face from the ewer that stood on a chest by the wall and pulled a comb through her curls. A glance in the mirror showed her a wan face and with a sudden

spurt of pride she touched rouge to her lips and cheekbones and hung her pearl-drop earrings in her lobes.
Matthew Sheridan was never going to guess the hours of
anguished thought he had cost her.

'Come in,' her aunt called when Henrietta scratched
at her door. 'You've decided to accept him,' she said
shrewdly after one comprehensive glance at her niece. 'I
am glad of it, you foolish girl!' She bustled forward and
kissed Henrietta's cheek. 'I am sorry to have had to scold
you, but this is no time for blowing hot and cold.
Matthew Sheridan is the perfect man for you, and I am
glad you've had the sense to realise it.'

Henrietta dropped a dutiful curtsy and kept her inner
thoughts to herself as she watched her aunt finish her
toilette. 'You are very fine tonight, Aunt,' she observed.
It was rare for Mistress Clifford to wear her best lace and
tonight she had added the diamond earstuds her late
husband had given her as a betrothal gift.

'Well, my dear, you must keep this a secret——' she
dropped her voice and looked almost coy '—but
Lawrence Stone has asked me to marry him. I have said
yes, but not until I see you safely married—I told him
so.'

It was the final feather settling on that millstone of
responsibility around Henrietta's neck and it brought
her to her knees. There was no way now she could refuse
Matthew Sheridan's offer; if she did so, insisted on going
to the Low Countries, her aunt's sense of duty would
compel her to go too.

'I don't mind telling you,' her aunt was prattling on,
apparently taking her approval for granted, 'when Lawrence read the will this morning I thought all was up
with us and we'd end our days in Bruges with your aunt
and uncle Walton. And I make no bones about it—live
with my brother's wife I could not!'

Henrietta looked at her aunt's sparkling eyes and saw
for the first time the shade of the lively young woman
she'd once been. 'I'm so happy for you, Aunt,' she said
simply. 'And I can think of no one who better deserves

the fruit trees, brushing aside the low branches heavy with flowers. When she reached the plaited straw skips she sank down and watched the worker bees buzzing in and out of the entrances, their back legs laden with pollen. Matthew Sheridan was master of Winterbourne, she told herself. If Mr Stone said it was so, it must be so, and all that which had been hers this morning, her home for eighteen years, now belonged to a stranger.

For five years the sole purpose of her life had been to keep Winterbourne alive and flourishing for her brothers and the household which was their responsibility. She hadn't wanted it when Francis had died for the position or the wealth that went with the estate, but because it was all she knew. There were no male Wynters left, but their blood flowed through her veins too; she loved the place as they had done. It was her life.

And she knew her duty. Resolutely she stood up, her back to the house, and addressed the hives clearly as if she were addressing her assembled household. 'Winterbourne has a new master. His name is Matthew Sheridan.' Her voice shook and she rubbed the back of one hand angrily across her eyes, wiping away her tears. 'You. . .you must be loyal to him and work hard and you will continue to be safe here.'

'All of Winterbourne will be safe with me,' a voice said softly behind her.

Henrietta wheeled round angrily to confront him, stumbling on the tussocky grass. 'Leave me alone; surely you have enough to do without persecuting me!'

Matthew cocked an eyebrow. 'Am I persecuting you? I came to see all was right with you.'

'Why should you care how I am, sir? I am not your responsibility!' How could he stand there, so composed and watchful and ask if all was right?

'But you are. Or don't you believe what you have just told the bees? I am master here now.'

'You are neither my father nor my brother nor my husband. You bear no responsibility for me, nor do I claim it.' Henrietta knew her cheeks were burning unbecomingly, but at least she hadn't disgraced herself with tears.

'Walk with me, cousin.' He held out one hand to her.

Bitter words sprang to her lips, then the years of Aunt Susan's rigorous training asserted themselves. She was a lady, schooled to restrain her emotions, behave with an elegant deference to the men in authority over her. 'If you wish, sir.' She ignored his hand and turned to pick her way through the rough orchard grass to the bank of the old moat where a weeping willow overhung a small pond.

'I am sorry this has come as such a shock to you. I too was unaware I had kin in Hertfordshire until Lawyer Stone sought me out.' It seemed to her he was attempting to be conciliatory, but Henrietta moved through the orchard contriving to keep her face averted from him. 'Your father left him sealed instructions should anything befall your brothers. The rift between our grandfathers was so great—a matter of religious conscience at root— that each never spoke of the other again. My grandfather's change of name made even an accidental meeting a remote possibility.'

His concern hurt her pride, brought her near to tears. 'I need neither your apologies, nor your explanations, sir.' Henrietta ducked beneath a low bough of the willow, putting its gnarled width between them before she turned to face him at last. He made no attempt to follow her, leaning instead against the trunk, his eyes on the startled gyrations of a pair of coots on the pond.

She needed to be alone, come to terms with what was happening. And what would happen to her now Winterbourne was no longer her home? She could not think with Matthew Sheridan there. Why was he haunting her footsteps? Now he had what he'd come for, why couldn't he leave her in peace?

'No doubt you will wish to look over the estate after dinner. I will send Robert Weldon, the steward, to you. Aunt Clifford will show you the house whenever you wish.' Why wouldn't he look at her? She turned her their good fortune. You'll enjoy society in the county town, and visit London often, I'll be bound. Why did I never guess how Lawyer Stone cared for you? I saw it so clearly this morning.'

'He knew I would never leave you, my love.' She could not resist the opportunity to point up the moral. 'You see, virtue and attention to duty bring their reward in time!'

I need no lectures about duty, Henrietta thought ruefully as she followed her aunt to the top of the stairs. And what is it going to get me? Not the mature love and companionship her aunt and Lawyer Stone would share, nor the passion and devotion Alice and Robert had found — which perhaps Matthew had shared with his first wife. The satisfaction of being a good housekeeper and devoted mother would have to fill the void where affection should be. And yet, only this morning, that satisfaction was all she had asked for. What had changed? Why was it no longer enough?

'Drat the girl!' Susan had halted at the sight of a large bowl of pot-pourri that had been left on a table in the corridor. 'She has a mind like an empty jar! I distinctly told Letty to place this in the master bedchamber. It smelt musty this afternoon and I would not have Master Sheridan think us bad housekeepers for anything. Take it in, my dear; supper will be a few minutes yet.'

Henrietta obeyed reluctantly, balancing the shallow bowl filled with rose petals, bay leaves, lavender and orris root between her palms. The door was ajar; she breathed a sigh of relief. He must already have gone down.

A nightingale had begun its bubbling song in the hawthorn bushes beside the moat. Henrietta paused by the open casement to listen to the beauty of the clear notes before putting the bowl down on the linen chest.

The melancholy song tugged at her heart. She had heard it often before but it had never seemed so sad and beautiful as here in this room her parents had shared, where she and her brothers had been born and where her mother had died giving birth to Francis.

She ran one hand down the heavy folds of the bed-hangings. They needed taking down and beating; she would see to that in the morning when Matthew had gone. . .Her heart jumped, remembering she had to tell him she had changed her mind, would be his wife. Her fingers clenched on the brocade as she looked down at the wide bed. And in due time this would be *her* marriage bed. . .

'Henrietta, you have come to me,' Matthew's voice said from the doorway. The latch clicked as he pushed it shut behind him and crossed the room to stand before her.

'No. . .' Henrietta backed away from the bed, aghast at what he must think. 'I came to bring some pot-pourri, and to tell you supper awaits you.' In the wall-glass behind him she could see her wide eyes and the agitated rise and fall of her breast reflected clearly.

Matthew's mouth tightened at her reply. 'I had hoped you had come to me with an answer.'

She scanned his lean face, seeing only the harsh lines of impatience, imagining only the urgency of a lawyer wanting to conclude a bargain. Could he not say something soft, make some move to woo her? No, she could not do it; whatever the consequences she could not give herself in marriage without some measure of affection. She could not take her mother's place as mistress of Winterbourne beside this man who wanted only a house-keeper, a mother for his children, who offered no sympathy, no meeting of minds.

'Alice!' She heard Robert's voice calling from the foot of the staircase. 'Do you have the keys to the cellar?'

It was enough to recall her to her duty. 'I have your answer, sir. I. . . I am content to be your wife.' There; it was done and there was no going back.

'Madam, the warmth of your acceptance overwhelms me.' He lifted one unresponsive hand to his lips and kissed it fleetingly. 'This morning I put your rejection down to shock at the suddenness of the news of my existence. Perhaps when we have become better acquainted you will tell me what it is about me that repels you so.' His voice was hard and flat, his hand guiding her towards the door impersonal. 'Come, let us go down and tell the others our *happy* news.'

CHAPTER THREE

AUNT SUSAN and Lawyer Stone looked up together expectantly as Matthew and Henrietta came through the screens separating the staircase from the great hall. They had obviously had their heads together talking, and not only about their own marriage plans, thought Henrietta with irritation.

Her acceptance of Matthew, his coldness at her reluctance were too raw to allow her any composure. She could get through this evening somehow, but not if the others insisted on discussing betrothals and wedding plans.

Aunt Susan looked at her niece's flushed face, the determined set of her mouth, and whispered something to Lawyer Stone. Henrietta caught the phrase, 'Maidenly nerves. . .' and her flush deepened. She curtsied politely to Matthew, removed her hand from his arm and sat down on a settle in a shadowy corner.

Mistress Clifford had directed the maids to lay a small table for supper instead of the long oak trestle. With only four to sup conversation would have been impossible down its length. Now both women regretted the choice: Aunt Susan because she longed to make a fine show for the new master, Henrietta because of the enforced intimacy of a cosy supper.

Despite the warmth of the evening the fire burned brightly in the grate, sending the shadows dancing, animating the embroidered figures on the wall-hung tapestries. Letty was lighting the candles in the wall sconces, standing on tip toe to reach them with her wax taper.

Henrietta watched her aunt re-position the candles on the table to set off the Venetian glass to its best advantage. Pewter gleamed with a dull sheen, reflecting colour

44

Looking up to see the small figure bristling with disapproval, Matthew regained his feet with unhurried ease. 'Madam, I perceive you are about to rebuke me.'

It was precisely what she *was* about to do — Henrietta knew her aunt so well — but his disarming charm took the wind from her sails. 'Sir, you are mistaken.' Henrietta realised incredulously that her aunt was simpering. Any other man caught kissing her niece's wrist in a shadowy corner would have received a sharp reprimand at the very least. 'You are master of the house and must do as you wish — I merely came to tell you supper is served. Will you take your place at the head of the table?'

Matthew offered Henrietta his hand to help her rise and for the first time she noticed the ring on his left hand as the light catching it ignited deep purple fires in its centre. 'What a beautiful ring.' And how unexpected in a man with such severe taste in dress.

'An amethyst, said to be a sure remedy against intoxication.' His eyes on her face were warm, appreciative as he led her towards the table.

'Surely, sir, you do not need such protection? You are not given to strong drink?' Henrietta asked demurely over her shoulder as he pushed in her chair for her. Some of the tension seemed to have left her; perhaps it was the wine warming her blood.

'There is more than one way to become intoxicated, cousin. There is the intoxication of the senses. . .'

Henrietta blushed, but was saved from reply by Aunt Susan. 'Indeed yes! The feel of a fine velvet, the scent of roses on a warm June day — why, they're enough to turn one's head!'

'The smell of a good venison pasty, more like,' Lawyer Stone riposted robustly. 'I could eat an ox!'

'Then carve the leg of lamb, Lawrence; I'm sure we are all ready for our supper. Sir Matthew, may I help you to the fricassee of chicken, or some carp perhaps?'

'Thank you, madam, the chicken would be admirable and I am sure some lamb would be excellent to follow.'

As he leaned across the table to fill her aunt's wine glass Henrietta noticed how relaxed he too had become, as though a spring had been released in that taut frame. The morning must have been an ordeal for him too; the thought was strangely reassuring.

'Is it to your taste, sir?' Aunt Susan was watching him anxiously as he savoured the rich sauce.

'Excellent, Mistress Clifford; you keep a fine cook at Winterbourne.'

'I cannot claim the credit, sir. Henrietta supervises the kitchen as she does all the household. I believe the chicken is a French receipt, with tarragon — is that not so, my dear?'

'Yes, Lady Willoughby told me of it.' Henrietta was well aware of what her aunt was doing — praising her housewifely skills as if to point out to Matthew what an excellent wife she would make. 'My aunt is too modest.' She met Matthew's eyes challengingly. 'On the death of my poor mother ten years ago she came to look after me. If I am a good housewife it is entirely due to her kind and loving tutelage.' And if I stay, she stays, her firm gaze told him.

'You are obviously a mainstay of the household, madam——' he raised his glass to Aunt Susan '— and this will remain your home for as long as you wish to make it so.' Lawyer Stone cleared his throat significantly and Mistress Clifford blushed rosily.

The meal progressed well; the chicken and carp were removed to be replaced with pies and jellies. Henrietta was content to sit quietly, listening to the talk flowing across the table as her aunt questioned the two men about the latest news and gossip from London. Inevitably the talk turned to politics and recent legislation and Henrietta collected her wandering attention and listened with rising indignation.

'. . .but are there no voices raised in Parliament against such radical measures?' Lawyer Stone asked after a while. 'What of my Lord Hargraves? Has he not in the past spoken out for moderation and sense?'

'I do not know his present thinking,' Matthew responded carefully. 'But come, Stone, we are boring the ladies. . .' But it was not fear of boring them, Henrietta could tell.

'But your connection with him—is it now broken?'

'Not broken, no.' The conversation was obviously not to Matthew's liking. His body was tense, a frown-line between his dark brows. 'But the future is more important to me now than remembering the past.'

His tone was brusque and the older man's expression reflected the snub. An uneasy silence fell across the table. Henrietta glanced at the shuttered faces of the men and sought for a way to turn the conversation, but her aunt was before her.

'And the latest fashions? Lady Willoughby tells me necklines are becoming rounder and sleeves fuller. I must be sure my wed—er—new gown is in the mode.'

'I don't notice such frivolous trifles, madam!' Lawyer Stone's besotted smile belied his testy words, his irritation at Matthew forgotten. 'A handsome woman such as yourself has no need to fuss and titivate. You look splendid whatever you are wearing—and it's no good looking to Sheridan; he's too busy a man for such nonsense.'

'On the contrary, I believe I can help you, Mistress Clifford.' Matthew had pushed back his chair and sat at ease once more at the table-head, rolling the stem of his wine glass between his fingers. 'From my observations, the French influence is on the wane. The rounder neckline you speak of is, I believe, a Dutch notion, but the style you wear now is still much in favour. As for sleeves, and the cut of necklines, I believe one can detect a new plainness and modesty.'

Lawyer Stone's jaw dropped at the revelation that his companion in law should exhibit such a frivolous streak, but Henrietta sat simmering. The hypocrisy of the man! To talk of plainness and modesty with such approval while all evening his eyes had rested on her low-cut neckline, her fine lace. . .why, only an hour before his lips had been tracing lines of fire along the inside of her bare arm!

'The Puritan influence, no doubt!' she snapped, surprised to find herself so suddenly out of temper.

'No, madam!' Matthew's eyebrows rose in surprise at her tone. 'Merely a diminuation of the extremes of French style which prevailed at the late court. And whatever your political views may be you would surely not deny the beneficial influence of General Cromwell on the moral tone of the country. Drunkenness and debauchery have much declined in the streets of London; it is safer by far for virtuous women——'

Henrietta cut angrily across his words, 'I will not have that usurper's name uttered at my table!'

'May I remind you, madam, that this is both *my* table and *my* house and I will not tolerate expressions of disloyalty to the Government here!' Matthew was sitting upright, both hands clenched on the table, no amusement in his eyes now.

'Your table it may be,' Henrietta flared back, 'but if it were not for my father and my brother dying for their loyalty to their rightful King you would not set one foot within these walls! Do not lecture *me* on loyalty and disloyalty! We have paid the price here for our faithfulness and others' perfidy!'

They were both on their feet, facing each other across the remnants of the meal. 'Have a care what you say, madam.' His voice was coldly measured, sending a shiver down her spine. 'Your words verge on treason. I do not demand that you change your colours, but you will hold your tongue, keep your opinions to yourself. Beside any other consideration you bring danger to this household with your foolishness.'

'It has been a long and surprising day, and everyone is tired.' Aunt Susan got to her feet with a sublime disregard for the crackling hostility that surrounded her. 'We would all be better for a little music. Come, Henrietta. Gentlemen, will you join us in the parlour?'

Lawyer Stone joined her with an agility that belied his

size. He being a pragmatic man, Henrietta knew he thoroughly disliked confrontation, being a firm believer in keeping his thoughts to himself and his head, and those of his clients, firmly attached to his shoulders.

Stiff-backed, she swept out of the room in her aunt's wake. The last thing she wanted was to sit and entertain the man who had so humiliated her. If this was what he was like now, heaven help her when they were married! If he still wanted her after this evening. . .

'Sit in the window-seat, Henrietta,' Aunt Susan suggested. 'I always think you look so pretty sitting there with your lute.' As she handed her niece the pear-shaped instrument she added under her breath, 'And curb your tongue, show a maidenly demeanour. You sound like a foolish boy, not a well-bred young woman!'

Biting her lip, Henrietta stepped up on to the low platform in the window embrasure and settled herself on the cushioned seat. 'I will need the low stool for my foot, Aunt, if you would,' she said, still pettish.

'Allow me.' Matthew, sounding as if nothing amiss had occurred, was kneeling to place the low stool so that she could support the lute. As he did so it rattled hollowly on the bare boards. 'This is loose,' he remarked, his fingers running over a knot-hole. 'I must get the carpenter to attend to it.'

He stood and returned to his seat, not noticing the blood leach from Henrietta's face. How could she have forgotten? How could something as important have slipped below the surface of her mind only to be recalled by the hollow echo beneath her feet? She ran her fingers over the strings at random, pretending to tune the instrument while she strove to calm her thoughts.

Automatically her fingers took over, plucking out the wistful air of a traditional country tune she'd known since childhood, while her mind conjured up vivid recollections of that night three years ago. The listeners construed her absent expression as concentration as the music filled the intimate chamber but her eyes saw only her brother James kneeling where Matthew had just knelt, his fingers hooking into the knot-hole to lift the loose boards and reveal the priest's hole below.

'Hush,' he'd whispered as the long-case clock struck two in the silent house. 'You need know nothing about this package until a messenger comes for it. It's safer for you to be ignorant, sister, but you must know its whereabouts in case anything happens to me.' She'd clutched his arm in denial of the thought that he might not return, incurious about the contents of the casket he'd placed on a ledge below the boards. 'Swear you will reveal this to no one but the messenger sent to fetch it.'

Henrietta had sworn, one hand clasped on the plain gold cross at her throat, before she'd tiptoed back to her room through the sleeping house. The next day James had gone, never to return.

Since then she'd hardly spared a thought for the casket or its hiding-place. She'd supposed, in time, someone would come for it but no one had and James's death and the responsibilities it thrust upon her left no room for speculation, save to guess that it was undoubtedly something to do with the King's cause.

Henrietta struck a discordant note, jerking herself from her reverie. This was neither the time nor the place for such thoughts, especially after what had passed over supper. Matthew Sheridan was no crop-headed Puritan, but he was a Parliamentarian—and master of Winterbourne now.

She must speak to Alice tonight, send word to Robert to fix the board before Matthew had the carpenter lifting half the floor! Robert was her father's man; even if he was ignorant of the casket and its contents, as a sworn Royalist he would know the best thing to do.

'Sing for us, my love,' her aunt urged, conscious of Henrietta's wandering attention. 'That pretty air you sang for me the other evening.'

'Excuse me, Aunt, but I am quite out of voice tonight. If the gentlemen will forgive me——' she laid the lute on the window-seat beside her and stood up '—I will retire.'

Both men rose, Matthew crossing to take her hand to conduct her to the door. His eyes as he looked down at her were grave and assessing; once again she was aware of the intelligence in their green depths. No fool, Matthew Sheridan; she would have to tread very carefully indeed in her dealings with him.

'Goodnight, cousin.' He raised her fingers to his lips, brushing them with the briefest kiss.

'Goodnight.' She hesitated, then added sweetly, 'Cousin.' It was the first time she had acknowledged their relationship.

If she thought her meek acceptance of it would lull him she was mistaken. Suspicion flared briefly in his eyes, and his voice when he spoke was a sibilant whisper unheard by the other two. 'Do not play games with me, Henrietta. I do not know what you are about but I warn you, I am not easily bested.'

'You mistake. . .cousin. I do not seek to play games; it is merely that this day has been eventful—and my head aches so.' Henrietta let a plaintive note quiver in her voice and noticed the suspicion clear from his face. So, that tactic worked even with men as astute as this one. It hadn't occurred to her before to use on Matthew the wiles she employed to keep other suitors at bay; perhaps even the most intelligent man could be hoodwinked. She must keep her pride and her intelligence in check; only let him underestimate her and she might scrape through this unscathed.

As soon as the door had closed behind him she hurried upstairs to her chamber, knowing Alice would be there already, lighting the candles and turning down the bed.

'Alice! Where's Robert? I must speak with him!'

'At this hour?' Alice's homely face was scandalised. 'In your chamber?'

'No, you silly wench! Is he at the farm? Come, girl, don't gape so—answer me!'

'He's gone to Farmer Johnson's to see if that jobbing carpenter's still there. That young idiot Daniel fell off the roof of the Long Barn this afternoon, broke his leg and now they'll not get the work finished unless he finds another carpenter. . .'

'But that's half a day's ride away!' Henrietta wailed.

'Mistress, are you ill?' Alice stood twisting her hands in her apron, unable to fathom Henrietta's behaviour.

'Well, there's one mercy.' Henrietta pulled herself together and thought rapidly. 'At least there's no carpenter about to mend that board. . .'

'You're overwrought; lie down,' Alice pleaded. 'Let me call your aunt, and fetch you a soothing draught. Does your head still ache? Pray heaven it's not a brain fever!'

'Alice, sit down and listen. I am perfectly all right, but I must have Robert's help—and quickly. I will tell you all, but you must give me your word never to say anything except to Robert.'

Wide-eyed Alice scooped up her skirts and perched on the end of the bed. 'Go on! I promise. . .'

'You remember the morning James left for the last time?' Alice nodded. 'Well, in the night he roused me from my sleep, took me to the front parlour and showed me a priest's hole.'

'The one under the window-seat,' said Alice intelligently.

'You know? How do you know? I didn't until that night—who else knows?' This was dreadful news; she could imagine one of the more garrulous old servants telling Matthew of Winterbourne's curiosities.

'Only me. James hid in it once when we were children and jumped out to scare me. He made me promise to tell no one else, but I thought you must know.'

'He put a casket in it, but he wouldn't tell me what its contents were. His only instruction was to wait until a messenger came for it. Now Matthew has noticed the loose board and will order it repaired. And Alice—if any messenger does come, he will ask to speak to the master of the house, not knowing he is a sympathiser with Parliament.' She dropped her head, now aching in truth, into her hands. 'I can trust no one except you and

Robert. My aunt must know nothing of this; she would be worried to no purpose. And, besides, I am probably breaking my oath telling you and Robert of this.'

'I don't *think* we need worry.' Alice swung her legs off the bed and sat, brow furrowed in thought. 'You can tell Sir Matthew there is no skilled man for indoor work until Robert returns. Robert will undertake the work himself, then we will remove the casket, secrete it elsewhere until he can make contact with someone who will know what to do.'

Henrietta felt relief flood through her; how much less threatening it sounded in Alice's common-sense voice. 'Will Robert know the right person to speak to?'

'He will,' Alice said grimly. 'Although the link is broken now the fighting's over he has comrades still in Oxford. They will know what to do. Take heart, mistress; no one has been for it in three years — why should they come now? Perhaps they never will.' She swung round, eyes shining with conspiratorial delight. 'Why do we not creep down tonight and remove the box ourselves? We could open it, judge its importance. . .'

'No!' Henrietta was vehement. 'How could we tell? If it is letters in cypher we will be no further forward. And besides——' an unwelcome thought struck her '—I do not want to be in a position where I must lie to my husband. I gave James my word to protect that casket, but I have other duties, however bitter they may be.'

There was a heavy silence, then Alice, with her usual happy knack of seeing the bright side, remarked, 'You will have him, then? It is all agreed?'

'I suppose so,' Henrietta said ungraciously.

Alice looked at her sideways, judging her mood. 'I think you protest too much, mistress! It is not Lawyer Stone you are promised to marry — it's a fine, virile man who'll make you a fine marriage bed. All the servants are agreed. . .'

'They've not got to marry him! I have my duty to do.'

Alice twinkled wickedly. 'Shall you get undressed now mistress?'

Henrietta sank down at the dressing-table with a resigned sigh. The less she said, the less Alice would tease her. The girl unthreaded the pearls from Henrietta's nut-brown hair and began to unpin and brush out its length. 'He's been married before, they say,' she remarked, 'which will be the better for you.'

'Will it?' Henrietta asked bitterly, remembering the pain on his face when he'd spoken of his wife in the orchard.

'Oh, yes.' Alice began to unlace the whaleboned bodice. 'You know the saying—"A man once wed is warmer abed."'

'I do not know the saying, I'm thankful to say!' Henrietta replied haughtily. The less she thought about Matthew Sheridan and bed, the easier it was to contemplate marriage with him somehow. 'Fetch that book of sermons and read to me.'

'Your aunt has it,' Alice said without a trace of regret, helping her out of her dress and shaking out the folds before placing it carefully in the oak press. 'There's that book of poetry—I could read from that.'

'No, thank you.' Henrietta pulled her cambric nightgown over her head and tied the strings. 'My aunt is right—we should turn our thoughts to higher things: I am quite resolved to read no more poetry of the lighter kind.'

'Very well, mistress,' Alice said demurely, laying the book down on the window-seat again and going to plump up the pillows. 'Will you get into bed now?'

'Not yet. Snuff the candles and draw back the curtains and I will sit and think in the moonlight a while.' Henrietta caught the sharpness of her own tone and was ashamed. None of this was Alice's fault. 'Alice.' The girl turned in the doorway. 'I am sorry if I have been out of temper today. Thank you for your loyalty; I shall not worry so much now.'

As the door closed behind the maidservant Henrietta curled up on the window-seat, rested her head on one of the mullions and let the cool night air flow over her face.

Below she could hear the buzz of conversation from the parlour, distinguish her aunt's laugh and Lawyer Stone's low rumble.

She looked up sharply as a barn owl shrieked and saw the ghostly white bird glide like a snowflake across the orchard. From the field beyond a vixen barked and Henrietta spared a thought for the chickens at the Home Farm——

All the familiar night sounds of Winterbourne that she'd taken for granted for eighteen years, and so nearly lost. To keep this place all she had to do was marry Matthew, an easy enough choice to make when she thought of some of her suitors, men she'd have been prepared to marry to keep her beloved home.

At one point she'd even thought of accepting Marcus Willoughby's ardent proposal. But Marcus, a lad she'd known all her life, was no threat to her heart or her mind. In a bare twelve hours Matthew Sheridan was threatening both.

A sharp rattle of curtain-rings echoed across the court. In the window opposite hers, the window of the master bedroom, a candle flickered then steadied. Instinctively Henrietta drew back, then realised she could not be seen in the darkness. Silhouetted by the warm glow of candle-light, Matthew stood in the window, unlacing his shirt and staring out over the moonlit orchard.

The light danced on white linen, underlighting his face, transforming the lean features into an enigmatic mask over the darkness where his shirt was open at his chest. Henrietta felt her heart quicken. What was he thinking about, this complicated man? Was he thinking about her, her defiance, her troublesome political opinions? Or had he dismissed her—a mere woman who was part of Winterbourne? Useful, no doubt, pleasurable, when it pleased *him*, but of no real consequence. Was he surveying his new domain before he went to sleep, relishing this new wealth and power that had fallen like a ripe fruit into his hands?

Matthew touched his fingers to his tongue then snuffed

the candle, the brief sizzling coming plainly to her ears
in the stillness. The amethyst on his hand seemed to
hold the light for a moment longer then all she could see
was the white of his shirt.

He had spoken of the intoxication of the senses and
she'd known he was not talking of the caress of fine
fabric or the scent of flowers. She was a countrywoman,
she knew well enough what happened between a man
and a woman, but there was more, some mystery which
Alice had hinted at, that showed in the glow in her eyes.
Something Henrietta had glimpsed briefly when
Matthew's lips had lingered on the sensitive skin at her
wrist, when his arms had tightened round her in the
orchard.

His face was shadowed, but suddenly she knew she
was looking into his eyes, and he into hers. If in the
moonlight she could discern his white shirt, then equally
he could see her nightshift. Even as she thought it the
figure opposite melted back into the darkness of the
room, breaking the spell.

By mid-morning the next day there was still no sign of
Robert. The thought of the hidden casket was like a sore
tooth, nagging at Henrietta however hard she tried to
divert her mind with a basket of mending. She told
herself the loose board was of little consequence to
Matthew, that there was no danger he would investigate
it further. With her own guilty knowledge she'd been
very conscious of the hollowness when her heel had
struck the board, but there was no reason to believe the
others had even noticed.

Where was Robert? In her agitation her needle slipped
and a tiny bead of blood fell on to the fine lace collar she
was darning. With an exasperated sigh Henrietta tossed
the work into her sewing basket and left the small parlour
she and her aunt used as their retreat. She'd hidden
herself away to avoid seeing Matthew; so heavily did the
worry about the priest's hole weigh on her that she was

convinced he'd be able to read the guilty secret in her face.

As she crossed the hall on her way to the kitchens the thought struck home that she *was* feeling guilty. But that was ridiculous; she was acting as a loyal servant of the King, obeying her brother's last request to her — a sacred trust. But everything was complicated now, things that had once seemed clear-cut were blurred. Matthew was master of Winterbourne and her husband-to-be; on both counts she owed him her loyalty.

She stopped in the middle of the great empty room as an idea came suddenly to her mind. Her brother was dead, the King was in exile. No one had come for the papers in three years — why not take them up now to her chamber and burn them? It would be so easy. She'd have nothing to hide from Matthew, no secret to take to her marriage. He'd said he didn't care what she thought so long as she kept her views to herself. It would be the best plan, safest for Robert and Alice too. . .

Kneeling in the window embrasure, she cradled the casket in her hands for a long moment before opening it, wrestling with her conscience. James hadn't made her promise not to look, she told herself. How could she judge if it was safe to burn the contents? The lid creaked back, revealing a mass of folded parchment; in the dim light she could see it comprised a long list of names.

Hurriedly she dropped the lid. She must not read it. To do so would give her knowledge she might unwittingly betray. And to burn it would be cowardly and a betrayal of everything her father, James — even Francis — had died for. Her conscience was no matter compared to this. If she had to begin her marriage with a lie, was that not a small thing compared to the sacrifices the others had made?

She thrust the casket back on to its ledge in the dark hole, sparing a shudder of sympathy for the hunted priests who had crouched in its musty depths all those years ago. The board dropped back with a thud and she pulled the edge of the rug back to cover the knot-hole, smoothing the fringe down carefully with hands that shook.

Henrietta unlocked the parlour door and walked quickly to the door leading on to the kitchen passage. She would find Alice, see if there was any news of Robert.

The kitchen was in its normal state of bustle with preparations for the noonday meal well under way. Henrietta stopped in the doorway out of long habit and critically surveyed the scene.

At the sight of her mistress Letty put down her paring knife and burst into vociferous complaint. 'That useless boy's been gone this past hour! And Cook's calling for the carp, blaming me that he's so long away. I'll tan his hide for him when he gets back, off birds-nesting, I'll be bound — idle little good-for-nothing——'

'Well, send young David after him,' suggested Henrietta to stem the flow. 'He's only sweeping out the bakehouse.'

'What? And have two boys away off, up to no good? You know what they say, mistress — if you want a job done, a boy's worth half a man, but two boys is worth half a boy!'

'Tell Cook to do without the carp, then, and see Sim gets a beating when he returns; I have no time to trouble with this now. Where is Alice?'

Letty looked truculent and muttered something about 'gossiping in the yard'. Stepping out on to the arcade which ran the length of the kitchen side of the yard, Henrietta saw Alice standing close to Robert in the gateway. They were deep in low-voiced talk and Henrietta guessed from Robert's grave expression that Alice was giving him the message about the casket.

She stood and watched them, oblivious to the noise from the hot kitchen at her back. When Alice stopped talking Robert looked thoughtful, then reached to stroke the girl's cheek with a tenderness that brought a lump to Henrietta's throat. There was no doubting he was deeply in love with her, nor she with him. With growing concern Henrietta noticed the gentle swell beneath Alice's apron; they must be wed, and soon, before malicious gossip started.

There was a clatter of iron-shod feet on the cobbles and Sim scuttled through the gateway, three fat carp swinging from a stick in his hand, his stockings and breeches mud-splattered. Alice had obviously heard that the delinquent was late for she cuffed him as he passed.

'And mind you get those fish to Cook this minute!' she turned and called after him as the skinny urchin ducked past Henrietta and into the kitchen. 'Mistress! Robert's back as you see. I've told him about that little job wants doing inside.'

Henrietta walked across the cobbles to meet them at the pump in the centre of the yard, a safe distance from eavesdroppers in the kitchen or dairy.

'Don't worry about that board, mistress,' Robert said soothingly. 'I'll have that fixed down so it won't trouble anyone, and as for that other matter —' his sharp grey eyes scanned the yard behind her '— no doubt there are those in Oxford who will know what's to be done.'

'I was thinking perhaps we should move the casket, destroy it maybe.' Henrietta looked at him anxiously.

'No!' Robert was vehement. 'We don't know what it may contain. This is dangerous, mistress. Something's afoot; there are whisperings abroad, wild rumours about His Majesty. I dare say no more. . .' He looked up quickly and called out over Henrietta's shoulder, 'Good morning, sir!'

Henrietta spun round to find Matthew approaching across the yard. She was certain some hint of what they'd been saying must show on her face and hid her confusion by dropping a slight curtsy. 'Good morning, cousin. I trust you slept well?'

'Eventually.' His voice was as warm as the sun on the cobbles and Henrietta felt her cheeks burn with embarrassment. So he *had* seen her at the window. She had promised to marry this man, share his bed. What that meant was only just dawning on her. Alice was looking at her with speculation in her wide blue eyes; Henrietta shot her a warning glance before turning back to Matthew.

'Have you met my. . .your steward, Robert Weldon, cousin?'

'Sir.' Robert gave Matthew a stiff bow. 'I must apologise for being away when you arrived.'

'Master Weldon.' Matthew was equally punctilious, acknowledging the steward's status in the household. 'No need to apologise for doing your duty—a matter of a careless carpenter, I understand.'

So that was what Matthew had been doing this morning—investigating the estate, the Home Farm. Henrietta took a steadying breath; it was going to be hard hiding anything from the new master.

'Yes, sir. It will delay the barn roof repairs, but I've found a good man to finish the work who can start tomorrow. I'll get him to fix that creaking board Mistress Wynter tells me of first.'

'Creaking board?' Matthew looked puzzled, then his brow cleared. 'Ah, yes, the parlour floor. A small matter—the barn roof is of greater import, Master Weldon. Perhaps you can spare me some time after dinner to go over the affairs of the estate.' He made it an invitation, but both men knew it was a command and that Robert would spare as much time as the new master demanded.

'I am at your disposal, sir.' Robert bowed. 'I will attend you this afternoon if you would care to come to the estate-room.'

Henrietta watched Alice and Robert disappear through the back door with a sinking heart. She cast round for an excuse to leave and, finding none, was forced to comply when Matthew offered her his arm and said, 'Walk with me, cousin. Can we get to the gardens through this gate?'

'If you don't mind crossing the drying lawns.' Henrietta rested her fingertips on his sleeve and allowed him to lead her out of the yard and across the close-clipped

all but the most strait-laced Puritan it was no shame to anticipate the wedding night.

And that, she had no doubt, was precisely what Matthew was about with these soft words. He didn't love her, of course, but he did desire her — that was plain.

He had no need to marry her to get Winterbourne: it was already firmly in his hands. He didn't even need to marry her to protect her position: he could give her enough money to join her aunt and uncle in the Low Countries and everyone would consider he had discharged his duty. But he was a man with a man's needs and marriage to her was an uncomplicated way of fulfilling his desires for a wife in his bed and a son to inherit Winterbourne.

He would put up with her Royalist sympathies because he desired her, not because he wanted to please her, or even cared what she thought. And she had already tasted his cold displeasure when she'd tried to stand up to him.

'Very well, sir. We will be betrothed tonight as you wish. But I must tell you —— ' she swallowed hard and managed to formulate the words with as much dignity as she could ' — I do not consider myself promised in anything but name until the marriage ceremony is performed.'

Matthew looked down at her heated face and let his hands drop from her shoulders. 'As you desire, madam.' There was more in his face than displeasure at her coldness; there was a measure of suspicion too. She felt his scrutiny on her stiff back as she returned to the house across the sunny garden. Henrietta knew instinctively that few people succeeded in keeping secrets from Matthew Sheridan for long.

CHAPTER FOUR

'THERE you are! Henrietta, where have you been, child? Dinner is almost on the table and we have much to do before this evening.'

Henrietta blinked, accustoming her eyes to the cool gloom of the hall after the brilliant morning sunshine outside. Her aunt paused just inside the hall screens, her buxom figure positively quivering with excited impatience.

'This evening?' What could Aunt Clifford mean and why was she in such a ferment? She and Matthew had scarcely agreed between them that the betrothal would take place that evening. . .

'The betrothal, you silly child! Surely Sir Matthew has spoken to you this morning? Do not tell me you have been avoiding him after that foolish dispute last night— indeed, you put me out of all patience with you, provoking him so!'

'Aunt, I have just left my cousin in the garden, where we have been talking this half-hour past and we *have* agreed to be betrothed this evening. But——' She broke off in confusion at the sight of a small group of house-maids waiting behind her aunt and unashamedly eavesdropping. 'How could you know of it so soon when we have only this moment parted company?'

'A moment, my love—there are too many idle hands and long ears here.' Aunt Susan turned to the gaggle of girls behind her. 'Mary, Mathilda, away to the long gallery and sweep it thoroughly. Jane, go to the still-room and collect fresh strewing herbs—Letty will give you the key—and don't gossip; I will be up directly. Go on, go on. . .' She flapped her hands at the giggling group and turned back to her niece. 'Sir Matthew told me last night that it was to be this evening. He is all impatience; it is so flattering to you. I have been up since five making preparations and Lawrence Stone is even now finishing drafting the papers with Sir Matthew's clerk.'

So, her agreement — her submission — had been taken for granted, the whole matter neatly arranged in Lawyer Stone's chambers before he left Hertford with Matthew. It had probably never occurred to the two men that she might refuse.

Those few intimate moments in the knot garden when she'd thought Matthew was asking her to make a free choice had all been part of his tactics to ensure her acquiescence. No doubt a halfway willing wife would be less trouble to him than a reluctant one.

'I suppose I should be grateful he even bothered to inform me of this evening's events in advance!' Her annoyance was giving way to something close to panic: she was but a cypher in Matthew Sheridan's plans for Winterbourne with no more say in events and decisions than a portrait on a wall. In every way, legally, physically, he was stronger than she. 'I seem to have no choice in this matter but to comply with everything he wishes,' she said bitterly.

Aunt Clifford patted her cheek, tidying a wayward curl back behind Henrietta's ear. 'I understand your natural fears, my love, but you must not allow your apprehensions of the wedding night to make you seem shrewish. I am sure if you think calmly you will see that is all that lies behind your uncertainty. Now, wipe that frown from your face — such marks of discontent are most unbecoming to the complexion and will not endear you to your husband.'

'Aunt, he said something just now about his late wife. . .'

'Sarah? Yes, Lawrence has been speaking of her too. They married young, apparently, and, according to Lawrence, were a byword for married devotion. Doesn't that speak well of Matthew as a husband? He was quite stricken when she died, and then of course the war. . .now——' she became brisk again '—run and find Sir Matthew and Mr Stone; tell them dinner will be on the table directly.'

No one understood, Henrietta thought despairingly as she walked slowly in her aunt's wake through the screens to the foot of the stairs. How could they, when she didn't understand herself? What more could she ask of Matthew than that he make her his wife, be a good master to Winterbourne? I am fortunate, *fortunate*, she chided herself. If he had come courting me I would not have believed my luck. In every way he is so perfect for me. In every way, save that he was not her free choice. She was marrying him for duty.

Where would the men be? She heard the murmur of voices from the door to her left and pushed it open. In the centre of the chamber Matthew and Lawyer Stone bent over a drift of papers on the wide library table.

'I am more than satisfied with the provision you are making for Henrietta. Indeed, it is most generous,' the older man was saying. 'Now we must consider the matter of the children, who God willing, will be many and healthy.'

'God willing indeed.' The set of Matthew's mouth was as hard as his tone. He glanced up towards the door and saw her hesitating on the threshold. Immediately his expression changed and softened. 'Were you looking for me, cousin?'

Henrietta found herself smiling back into his green eyes. 'I was looking for both of you. My aunt sent me to say dinner will be served in the hall shortly, if you are ready?'

Lawrence Stone pushed back his chair with alacrity. 'Excellent! Your aunt promised me a baked carp, and after this morning's work I intend to do full justice to it!'

'From what I saw this morning the price of your carp was a well-tanned kitchen lad.' Matthew's eyes glinted with amusement. Henrietta bit her lip; if he had seen Sim return late with the fish he *must* have been in the

yard when she and Robert had been discussing the loose
board and the priest's hole beneath it. Had they looked
suspicious whispering with their heads together? Her
heart lurched; what if he had caught something of what
had been said? His was a keen intelligence; he could put
two and two together.

'Wait.' He laid a restraining hand on her arm as she
made to follow the hungry lawyer. 'A moment, cousin.'

She felt herself go white to the lips; so he had heard
something.

'Henrietta. . .' He drew her close, his voice gentle.
'You must not be afraid of me. It is right that you should
be apprehensive — I would expect nothing else from a
maiden — but it is a husband's duty — and pleasure — to
soothe those fears. . .'

Hot colour flooded back into her cheeks. So he didn't
know; he had heard nothing of her guilty secret. She was
too relieved to feel embarrassment at what he was saying.

Matthew's warm, sure hands cradled her face. 'Let me
show you how it can be.' Before she could protest his
lips were on hers, capturing, stifling her instinctive
denial with a gentle insistence which became a demand
as his hands dropped to her shoulders, pulling her close.

Her own hands came up to his chest to push him
away, but she found they would not obey her. Instead of
pushing her fingers spread, tentatively exploring the
breadth of his chest, the warmth of his body through the
fine linen.

No man had ever taken her in his arms like this; no
man had ever kissed her mouth. Her whole being was
concentrated on this man, alive to his body where it
touched hers, to his mouth moving on her own. The
male scent of him filled her nostrils, beneath her now
questing fingers the muscles were taut and hard, and
when his lips left hers to explore the soft angle between
neck and shoulder she was conscious of the slight
roughness of his clean-shaven cheek.

'Matthew.' It was meant to be a protest but it came
out like a supplication. At any moment someone might

come in. . .this was all wrong, they were not even
betrothed — but every touch of his body on hers sapped
her will. Matthew's hands encircled her waist while his
mouth grazed slowly down the white slope of her bare
shoulder revealed by the low-cut gown.

His heightened breathing found an answering echo in
her own; she felt her eyes closing, her legs weakening
with her will. If he were only to take her up in his arms,
carry her to the big bed above them she would be his
now, at this moment, betrothal or no. And it was wrong,
all wrong; she scarcely knew him.

'Henrietta,' he said gently, still holding her trembling
body against his. 'We are anticipating what can be ours
tonight. Your beauty and your innocence lead me astray,
and the others will be wondering what has become of
us.'

Matthew's lips briefly brushed her heated forehead,
before he released her. Shakily Henrietta preceded him
through the library door. As she paused at the foot of
the stairs to smooth the tumbled lace at her neck Letty
scurried through from the servant's quarters with a dish
of sallets; through the gap in the screens she could see
the others standing by the dining table in the hall and
heard her aunt say clearly, 'We must allow for her youth
and innocence, Lawrence; perhaps I have been too
impatient with her.'

Matthew turned to look for her and with a sinking
heart she realised that to have reached the library from
the knot garden he would have passed through this way
while she and her aunt were talking. He must have heard
Susan speak of her fears of the wedding night and set
out to rouse desire in her before she could take fright
and deny the betrothal.

How well he had succeeded! She could still feel the
heat of his kisses on her throat, her heart knocking
against her ribs. How easy he must think she was to
bend to his will, in this as in everything else.

* * *

The shadows were lengthening in the orchard and a group of villagers were making their weary way home past the gatehouse in the wake of a lumbering farm wagon, their labour finished for the day. Henrietta scarcely saw them as she gazed distractedly from her chamber window, her copy of the marriage settlement Lawyer Stone had spent the last hour explaining to her clutched in her hand.

'Mistress? Which petticoat?' It was obvious from Alice's tone that it was not the first time she'd enquired.

'Oh, any—whatever comes to hand. Do not fuss so; there is no urgency.'

'Well, the master has been dressed and left his chamber half an hour since.'

'Alice! Have you been staring into his room? What will he think of us?'

'That we are interested in him,' Alice replied with some asperity. 'As indeed you should be. In a half-hour you will be betrothed to him. . .'

'Which reminds me, miss,' Henrietta riposted crisply, glad to turn attention from her own affairs. 'He has noticed your condition. I had to tell him you and Robert were already betrothed, so I suggest you do not make me a liar, but swiftly name a day.'

'Robert intends to speak to the master this evening after the ceremony,' Alice announced demurely.

'*Will* you stop calling him the master?'

'But he is, mistress.' Alice looked pained. 'What would you have me call him?'

'Oh, fetch me the petticoat with the French lace, girl; you'll make me late with this nonsense!'

Alice looked as though she was about to say something but instead bent over the large oak press and shook out the fine cambric petticoat.

Henrietta tossed her robe on to the bed and stood still for Alice to drop the underskirt over her head. Why was she the only one who found Matthew's sudden possession of Winterbourne difficult to accept? Everyone else behaved as if he'd been master here for years, instead of a scant two days. They had been without a master for three years, since the death of James at the Battle of Preston; she'd believed she had filled his place, but it seemed she was mistaken if the household welcomed her cousin so warmly. Or perhaps it was simply because he was a man. Henrietta sighed at the injustice of it.

'That's right, breathe in, mistress.' Alice pulled then knotted the laces, fastening the full amethyst silk of the overskirt before helping Henrietta into the whaleboned bodice.

'Ouch! That pinches!' Henrietta protested at the tight lacing. She had a shrewd idea her maid was paying her back for her sharpness earlier.

'But you want him to admire the grace of your figure,' Alice replied slyly, giving an extra tug to the lacing at Henrietta's waist.

'Well, that is tight enough—I don't want to faint in the midst of the ceremony. Find me my mother's best lace collar and cuffs while I put up my hair.'

Alice's deft fingers settled the heavy cream lace collar and pinned it in place. 'I think you need a little powder on your neck, just here. . .' She lightly touched the place where Matthew's lips had kissed. 'You must tell him to be more careful how he shaves, mistress.'

Two pairs of eyes met in the looking-glass. Alice's blue ones alive with teasing laughter, Henrietta's dark with embarrassment. 'Alice. . .is it usual. . .?' She faltered, unsure of how best to phrase her question. 'He kissed me, and I felt. . .on fire. In that moment I wanted nothing more than to be in his arms, in his bed. And we are not yet betrothed. I do not know even if I truly wish to marry him. . .what is *happening* to me? Marcus Willoughby never made me feel like this!'

'Ha!' Alice didn't attempt to hide her scorn. 'Marcus Willoughby is a spotty boy; it will be years before he'll make a woman's pulses race. Now, the master, he's a real man—you only have to look at him! Every maid in the house is hot for him—and green as grass with envy for you.'

'Alice! I should be turning my thoughts to being a dutiful wife and mother to his children, not to being. . ."hot" for him.'

'And how should your children be got?' The maid dropped her voice still lower as she bent to dust the powdered orris root on the flushed skin. 'They do say conceiving comes easier if the pleasure is shared. That's what the goodwife told me when I asked her why I'd fallen so quickly. And I do believe it to be true.' She smoothed the apron over her stomach with pride.

Henrietta sighed as Alice fastened her cuffs in place. Her maid might have convinced her that what she was feeling was entirely natural, even to be desired, but it didn't make it any less dangerous. If she gave her heart to this man who only wanted a dutiful housekeeper then heartbreak would surely follow. She would wait in vain for signs of an affection he could never give her. And if he discovered the secret she was hiding from him — that she was still dealing with the Royalist faction — he would never forgive her. Not he, who spoke so vehemently for Parliament and called her opinions disloyalty.

Aunt Susan's hurried entry cut across her confused thoughts. 'Henrietta, are you nearly ready? The others are gathering in the long gallery.'

'How well that blue becomes you, Mistress Clifford,' Alice remarked as she put the last pin into Henrietta's topknot.

'Thank you, my dear.' The older woman stooped to prink in the mirror. 'It is my second-best gown. . .but never mind about me. Henrietta, let me look at you.' She took her niece's hand and raised her from the low stool before stepping back to regard her maternally. 'Lovely! That amethyst colour strikes just the right note. We must not forget your poor little brother, or leave off our mourning just yet — yet we cannot be doleful at your betrothal. Oh, how long have I dreamed of this day.

'Oh, I nearly forgot why I came in. Your father's ring. . .fetch it from the casket, Alice.'

'What for?' Henrietta took the heavy plain gold band

that had so recently been returned to her with Francis's effects from the Low Countries.

'To exchange with your betrothed, of course.'

'Aunt. . .am I truly doing the right thing?' Rings and contracts were giving a frightening reality to the proceedings. 'Could it be I am betraying Winterbourne, my people? Would my father and James approve? He has no knowledge of our country ways, of how to govern an estate like this.'

'Yes, but he is a man of affairs, of experience and learning. Lawrence tells me he is well regarded, with friends in high places.' She paused to look at her niece with affectionate exasperation. 'Henrietta, my dear, I do not know what your head is full of today, but your thoughts are certainly distracted!'

Alice giggled softly behind her hand. Henrietta glared at the girl; she wouldn't put it past her to blurt out exactly what Henrietta's thoughts *were* full of. . .

'Come, Alice, I think we are ready,' she said with dignity, gathering up her skirts with care to reveal the heavily embroidered underskirt beneath.

The three made their way in silent procession along the passage from Henrietta's room to the long gallery. At the door Henrietta and Alice paused, allowing Mistress Clifford to enter the room first. It was very quiet; Henrietta could hear the sparrows squabbling in the eaves outside, the crackle of logs in the grate, the rustle as someone shifted his or her feet among the split lavender stems that strewed the polished oak floor.

She took a deep breath and stepped inside, her eyes swiftly surveying the room. At the far end the household servants stood in a silent group in their best clothes, the youngest girls nudging each other at the first sight of their mistress in her finery. Robert stood next to Lawyer Stone, wearing his best blue linen doublet, one empty sleeve pinned up. Next to the fireplace, on the other side of the great table, Matthew was flanked by his clerk Nathaniel, his aspect more crabbed and dour than ever.

The branches of beeswax candles guttered in the

draught as Alice closed the door with care behind her. Only then did Matthew turn and look at her as she came slowly to the end of the table to face him down the length of the richly patterned table-carpet. As he stood there under the portraits of her father and grandfather she saw the family resemblance for the first time in the straight nose, the firm chin, the uncompromising green gaze.

But his colouring was darker than that of the Wynters, his hair, curling on the fine white collar of his green doublet, was almost black, as were his brows. His features were set, his eyes assessing as he regarded her without speaking.

Why can't he smile at me? Give me some sign that he really wants this, wants *me*, not just any wife, she thought helplessly, then ventured a tremulous smile at him. She was instantly rewarded; his face was transformed by a smile that curved his lips and warmed his eyes like sun on the sea. The breath caught in her throat; desire mingled with a deep fear that he could make her feel like this, so defenceless and vulnerable.

Matthew saw the sudden colour suffuse her cheeks, saw her lips part in an inaudible gasp and moved forward to take her hands in his. 'You are in lustrous beauty, madam.'

Henrietta sank down in a deep curtsy. 'You are gallant, sir.'

'If you could both approach the table, Sir Matthew,' the old lawyer began, his hands busy among the papers.

Lawyer Stone fixed his eye-glasses firmly on his nose, cleared his throat and began. 'Henrietta Lucy, do you accept this man, Sir Matthew Nicholas Sheridan, as your future husband to love and obey in all things? Do you accept the terms of the marriage settlement here before you?'

'I do accept both Sir Matthew and the settlement.' Her voice was strong and clear in the high-ceilinged room.

'Matthew Nicholas, do you accept this woman, Henrietta Lucy Wynter, as your future wife to love and cherish in all things? Do you accept the terms of the marriage settlement here before you?'

'I do accept both Henrietta Lucy and the settlement.'

'If you would now both sign the document, Steward Weldon and I will witness it.' The lawyer dipped a quill in the standish, handing it first to Matthew. Henrietta watched his steady hand as he signed with bold strokes of the pen, then took the quill and signed below his name. Nathaniel stepped forward to sand the wet ink, the expression of disapproval still fixed on his face, then stood aside for the other witnesses to sign in their turn.

Matthew drew the amethyst from his finger and took her hand in his. 'Henrietta, I plight thee my troth, accept this token of my promise to be your husband.' As she felt the warm metal circling her finger her heart sank within her. How could she promise to be governed by him in everything, to be his true and faithful wife when she would begin their life together burdened with the secret James had entrusted to her?

She had sworn an oath to her dead brother; how could she balance these conflicting loyalties? She had to speak out now, before she sinned irretrievably. . .

She opened her mouth and heard herself say calmly, 'Matthew, I plight thee my troth, accept this token of my promise to be your wife.' As she spoke she slipped on to his finger her father's plain gold ring.

'In this company and before witnesses you have plighted your troth, either to other, and have declared the same by the giving and receiving of rings. I therefore call on you to name the day when this marriage shall be solemnised.'

'The second Wednesday in July if you should agree, madam?' Matthew raised a dark brow.

'That is acceptable to me.'

'Don't just stand there, Sheridan,' the old lawyer hissed. 'Kiss the girl, then we can get on and drink your health.'

Henrietta raised her face compliantly, expecting a chaste token, trying not to remember the last — the first — time Matthew had kissed her. He took her firmly in his arms, bent his dark head, and claimed her lips with an intensity and passion that left her breathless and dizzy. When he finally released her, her heart was beating against the tight lacing like a bird in a net and there was an audible sigh from the assembled maid-servants.

'Hurrumph!' Lawyer Stone cleared his throat and polished his eye-glasses on his kerchief. 'I think we could all do with a glass of Canary after that!'

'Lawrence!' Aunt Clifford whispered. 'I do think that might have been more delicately put.' She raised her voice commandingly. 'Mary, see the household is given ale and cider in the hall. Alice, pour the wine here, if you please.'

Matthew still held her left hand in his. 'Sir, my hand. . .' she protested.

'Mine now.' He smiled down into her eyes, keeping her fingers trapped in his.

Alice brought two Venetian glass goblets, bobbing a curtsy as she offered them. As she turned away from Henrietta her eye almost closed in a wink.

Henrietta tried to calm her fluttering nerves by sipping the sweet wine, but all she was conscious of was the imprint of his lips on hers and the warmth of his fingers interlaced with her own.

'. . .and the consequences of the Bill set before Parliament last week will be far-reaching, I'm sure you will agree, Sheridan. Those of us who live outside Town will need early intelligence to advise our clients to their best advantage.'

Matthew nodded seriously, guiding Lawyer Stone to the window embrasure to continue the conversation.

'Well, my dear,' Susan said drily, watching their retreating backs, 'I suspect we are both about to discover there are penalties attached to marriage with a lawyer!'

'Business certainly claims their attention at the least opportunity,' Henrietta responded, nettled.

'Men are all the same, Henrietta, whatever their calling or station. I recall the afternoon you were born; your father was pacing the floor in this gallery when word came from Lord Willoughby that he had received some news or other from Court. Your father was off like a greyhound after a hare — and not back home till near midnight, two hours after you were safe delivered.'

'Poor mother.'

'In truth, she told me it was a relief to be left in peace and know he wasn't fussing — men are little help and much hindrance on these occasions. But I cannot stand here reminiscing; there is supper to be got, and those giddy girls will be flightier than ever after this evening's excitement.'

Left alone, Henrietta glanced across to where the two men still stood in earnest conversation, dark head against grizzled. Matthew seemed to be winning some point, driving it home with emphatic movements of his long hands.

Once again she was struck by the quality of his intelligence. How was she to keep the secret of the hidden casket from him? She wasn't used to dissembling; in all her life she'd had no need of anything but the truth. But now she had made promises to Matthew that conflicted with the oath she had made to James.

Matthew caught her eye and smiled, a fleeting caress across the room, then turned back to his argument. Henrietta swallowed hard. How could he look at her like that yet continue exchanging dry legal anecdotes with Lawyer Stone? Now he had her would he trouble to woo her at all? He desired her — that much was plain in his eyes, his kisses, the touch of his fingers. She wanted to get to know him, to have him understand her and Winterbourne. Her parents had shared a deep friendship as well as a marriage; would she and Matthew be able to lay the foundations of that before the wedding day?

But however close they did become she must not allow that to blind her to the truth or her duty. She was a loyal servant of His Majesty, he a follower of the usurper

Cromwell. The longer that casket lay hidden in the priest's hole, the greater the danger that she would unwittingly betray its existence. No one knew how much damage could be done if the contents of the casket were revealed.

Suddenly decisive, Henrietta turned in a silken swirl of skirts and left the room. Neither man acknowledged her going. The staircase and hall were empty of servants and she gained the parlour unseen, snatching a branch of candles as she went.

The empty room was shrouded in shadows flickering in the candle-light. She closed the door quietly behind her and leaned against the panels, collecting her thoughts. What to do with the casket once she'd removed it from its hiding-place? She couldn't give it to Robert — that would be to put her burden of responsibility on his shoulders. Nor dared she risk burning the thing — there were too many people in the house, too many questions might be asked about a fire lit on a warm summer's evening.

Then the answer came to her with the memory of Sim and his mud-splattered breeches that morning; she would throw it in the carp pond. The farm workers always claimed the mud in the depths of it was bottom-less, and frightened impressionable kitchenmaids with tales of what lurked in its murky deeps.

She had pushed back the carpet and hooked her little finger into the knot-hole to lift the board when she heard a firm step outside the door. Swiftly she tossed back the covering, then tugged off one pearl drop from her ear. When Matthew entered he found her on her knees seemingly searching under the window-seat.

'Henrietta?'

'Oh, Matthew. . .' Despite her swift deception she was flustered. 'My earring. . .'

'You would do better to have light on the matter,' he said drily. 'Come, get up, you will mark your gown. Where did it fall? On the carpet here?'

'No! I thought I heard it roll under the window-seat.'

But I dare not look there.' She cast down her eyes. 'Alice saw a mouse in here yesterday and I have great fear of them.'

'A very fierce mouse to cause you such emotion.' She saw him take in her flushed cheeks, the rise and fall of her agitated breast framed by the heavy fall of lace in one comprehensive green glance, then he dropped to his knees, a candle in one hand.

So, once more, the feminine wiles she had employed on Marcus Willoughby and his like deceived this man too. But even as she employed them she despised herself for doing so.

'Here.' He held out the nacreous teardrop on his palm. 'Sit on the window-seat and I will restore it to its rightful place.' His fingers were warm and dry on the sensitive flesh of her lobe. They lingered and she shivered, conscious of his closeness. 'I claim a kiss for valour against man-eating mice,' he said, his breath fanning her throat.

'I do not believe there was a mouse under there at all!' Henrietta shifted away from him along the seat, heart beating wildly against the tight lacing of her bodice.

'Not a whisker of a mouse,' he admitted. 'But I was not to know that when I undertook the endeavour — there could have been an army of mice. Come, Henrietta.' The laughter died out of his voice. 'You must not be afraid of me.' He drew her gently to him, tipping up her chin, compelling her to meet his eyes.

'You are mistaken; I am not afraid,' she managed to say. She despised herself for the sensations he was evoking in her — surely a well-bred young lady should be more in control?

'Then what is it? Why have you run away to this parlour to avoid me? That you are not adverse to me I know from your kisses. Is it my political beliefs?'

That was too close to the mark for Henrietta's raw conscience. 'You know my feelings, sir.' Her voice shook and she got to her feet to put distance between them.

'Sacrifices such as my family have made cannot lightly be set aside. My father, my brothers. . .'

'I am one of your family, cousin,' he reminded her gently.

'And you think that makes your treachery any easier to tolerate?' she bit out, incited by the stirrings of her own conscience, of her vow to James and how easily she had almost broken it, shrugged off the responsibility he'd laid upon her shoulders.

'*Treachery*!' he was on his feet too, the angry colour high in his cheeks. 'We stood for King *and* Parliament until the King betrayed us and our liberties. He would be King now if he had not sought to rule absolutely, as a tyrant without Parliament.'

'And so you murdered him?' Henrietta gathered up her skirt and swept out, closing the door carefully behind her, but not before she saw the anger drain from his face, leaving it cold, implacable and unreadable.

'Which nightgown, mistress?' Alice fussed around the bedchamber, twitching the hangings, stirring the fragrant pot-pourri.

'Why, the cambric as usual; what's the matter with you, girl?' An uncomfortable evening of stilted conversation and over-rich food had left Henrietta's already frayed nerves in tatters. After a few minutes Matthew had rejoined her in the long gallery and neither had spoken of her last, unforgivable words. He had not looked at her again, but her eyes had followed him all evening and the scene refused to leave her tired brain.

'I thought the new French lawn might be more to your liking this evening.' Alice shook out the diaphanous garment, a present from Lady Willoughby that Henrietta strongly suspected had been smuggled from France to evade the duty.

'Why?' Henrietta was in no mood to acknowledge her maid's veiled hints. After the way she'd parted from Matthew in the parlour he was the last person she expected to find on her threshold that evening. It was a wonder, she reflected, that he had not repudiated the betrothal.

'Mistress! The master will come to you tonight for sure. He's hot for you — after that kiss at your betrothal, how can you doubt it? Don't you *want* him to come to you?' Her voice was frankly incredulous now.

'We are not yet wed.' Henrietta climbed into bed, ignoring the flimsy nightgown and pulling the concealing cambric over her head. It felt safer.

'But it is the custom! No one would think any the less of you now you are betrothed. . .'

'I can assure you, miss, he will not come to my chamber tonight, nor would I admit him if he did.' Even as the words were spoken there was a light scratching at the door. 'That will be my aunt; let her in.'

The tall figure in the doorway was unmistakably male. With a triumphant glance over her shoulder at her mistress Alice slipped past him into the darkness of the corridor.

'Alice! Come back!' It was too late. Matthew closed the door behind him, turned the key in the lock and pocketed it.

'Now, madam, no one will disturb us.'

Henrietta clutched tight the neck of the plain cambric nightdress, her eyes wide as Matthew approached the bed. 'No!'

'Oh, yes, Henrietta. Oh, yes.'

CHAPTER FIVE

'I NEITHER know nor care what licentious habits prevail in London, sir, but I told you in the garden this morning — do not presume on our betrothal; you are not my husband yet!' Despite her fighting words Henrietta was cornered, her back against the bulbous carving of the bedpost. Her heart was beating wildly; in spite of all Alice's hints she had not truly expected him to come and now he was here she was totally unprepared.

'On the contrary, far from being licentious, the Puritan influence grows daily in London. The frolics taking place in your kitchen at this moment would not be tolerated there.' Matthew stopped a few feet from her, the candle-light shining on the whiteness of his shirt-sleeves, casting a shadow at his throat where he'd discarded his lace and pulled open the drawstrings.

'How dare you come to my chamber uninvited and half-dressed?' He stood before her in shirt and breeches, disturbingly male, disturbingly close. She wondered what would happen if she screamed. 'And if the servants are misbehaving, why do you not discipline them? They are your household now.'

He quirked a dark brow. 'You are even more undressed than I, madam. And as for the servants, why should I spoil their fun? I did not say I disapproved. There is no need for the whole household to be miserable because their mistress is out of temper.' It was he who was out of temper, Henrietta could see plainly. There was colour on his taut cheekbones and no humour in his eyes as he watched her. In the candle-light, his hair disarranged on his shoulders, he seemed saturnine, dangerous. Henrietta remembered his remark about stirring the beehive and knew she had gone too far in provoking him that evening.

'Indeed, you surprise me.' Attack seemed the only defence. 'I would have thought their innocent pleasures would offend your Puritan sensibilities.' Henrietta scrambled out of bed and edged round the post, realising too late that she'd trapped herself between the four-poster and the wall.

'I do not think innocent is the word I would apply.' Matthew sat on the edge of the bed, his back against the carved post and regarded her levelly. 'Tell me, Henrietta, why do you persist in calling me a Puritan?'

'Because you are one!'

'You have an imperfect understanding of the word. Do you assume all supporters of Parliament to be Puritans? I can assure you that is far from the truth. Every shade of opinion other than rabid Royalists are with us. Or is it because I do not dress like a popinjay as your young suitor Willoughby does? I am a lawyer, I dress to suit my profession, although my preference for fine cloth and lace earns me no admiration from my stricter colleagues.'

Henrietta perched cautiously on the opposite corner, holding a pillow defensively against her thinly clad body. If she could keep him talking of politics and religion she might yet succeed in distracting him from his purpose, which was certainly not conversation.

'But you make no secret of your support for Parliament.' Her chin came up as she challenged him, 'How far did that support go in the late war?'

'The past is behind us, Henrietta. Raking over cold ashes will not help us rebuild for the future.'

'You are evasive, sir. Why? Are you ashamed of your actions?'

'You are attempting to anger me, Henrietta,' he said levelly. 'But you will not deflect me from my purpose in coming here so easily. We were discussing religion, I believe.'

'If that is what you prefer. Your clerk is a Puritan; do you tell me you do not share his religious beliefs?'

'Nathaniel is a loyal servant, an old family retainer. I make no claim to direct his conscience, or his life.'

'In that case, sir, may I assume you will afford me the same courtesy?'

'Do you mean I should consider my wife as an equal to my servant?' He raised a quizzical eyebrow.

'That is not what I meant! You are playing games with my words.' Henrietta began to relax; this was altogether safer ground, and he seemed almost to be enjoying bandying words with her. 'I meant I am an Anglican, and nothing you might do or say will stop me worshipping God according to my conscience.'

Matthew sprang off the bed, wrenched open the hangings at the foot and regarded her with cold anger, his eyes glittering. 'Do you never listen to what is said to you? These last ten minutes I have been telling you I am not a Puritan. What do you think I am? An Anabaptist? A Roman Catholic? I am an Anglican like yourself; our religious views are in accord.'

He raked his fingers through his dark hair. 'What would you have of me, madam?' Henrietta shook her head dumbly, her pulse so loud in her ears that she was sure he would hear it too. 'I am giving you my protection, the chance to remain in your home, the chance to bring up your children in safety. Does none of this weigh against your dislike of me?'

Dislike? Surely he knew the effect he had on her? If only he'd offered her sweet words instead of talk of security and religious tolerance he would be beside her on the big bed now. . .

She was so tired of anger and mistrust. Why could he not woo her, be gentle with her in her inexperience and confusion? She felt her lips tremble and suddenly his anger seemed to evaporate. Slowly he skirted the end of the bed andsseated himself once more, just out of arm's reach.

'You must learn to give up this heavy burden you've been carrying. It was thrust upon you by fortune but you can relinquish it. I am here now.'

She would gladly give him the burden of the estate — he would be a good master; she sensed that now. No, the weight around her neck was impossible to renounce; her vow to her brother made that certain. Until she had passed on those papers to the right hands she could not be open and frank with Matthew, as her marriage vows would demand, and as more and more she wished to be.

He reached out his left hand and touched her bare foot, exposed by the hem of her nightgown. Henrietta gasped and quivered at the intimacy of the caress as his warm palm stroked the blue-veined skin, but her treacherous body would not move to escape him.

He seemed to take her stillness for consent and moved closer to her on the big bed, taking her gently by the shoulders. Henrietta's breath constricted in her throat, her eyes riveted on his, bright with desire, all the anger gone.

'You are grieving still for your little brother, but I will give you children of your own to take his place in your heart,' he murmured.

How could she have been so weak as to soften to him like that? The shame burned in Henrietta's veins, driving out every vestige of desire. His words touched the raw nerve of her grief for her family, of everything she had lost. And he thought once he had her with child nothing else would be important to her!

'How little you know of me if you think your children would be enough to replace my brothers in my affection,' she flared at him, jerking free from his embrace. 'You have the legal right to Winterbourne; of that there is no dispute. But do not think I will accept you in my heart in place of my brothers and my father. . . I am not so complaisant!'

She had underestimated the force of his anger. There was a sudden flurry of movement and she found herself pinned against the pillows, his fingers hard through the thin stuff of the gown, his hard eyes fixing her own with the strength of his will.

'And I am not such a fool, Henrietta, as to believe you

will give me anything which is not legally binding on you. Yes, you acknowledge me master of this estate, yes, you will marry me. But that is duty. For some reason you dislike and mistrust me and that overrides any other emotion you may feel towards me.'

'I don't dislike you!' His anger frightened her but his words hurt her more than the grip of his fingers on her shoulders. His closeness disturbed yet excited her and despite her inexperience she could tell his mood was still not all anger. 'But how can I give you all you ask when. . .?'

'When you are already in love?' he demanded, voicing his suspicions at last. 'Deny it, Henrietta; let me hear it from your lips.'

'I-in love?' she stammered, trembling in his arms.

'Do you think I am blind? I know you for a passionate woman; you cannot hide that from me. Why should you shrink from me, unless your love is already given to another?'

She could only shake her head dumbly in denial, her mass of unbound hair tangling on the heaped pillows behind her.

'At least tell me it's not that puppy Willoughby!' he ground out.

'Marcus? No, of course not! Matthew, please listen to me. . .' Of all the accusations he could have thrown at her this was the most unexpected but the most difficult to deny. Her protestations of innocence died on her lips. What can I tell him? That there is no other man? But he knows I am hiding something from him. . .Henrietta bit her lip as she searched for the right words, wary of plunging even further into a web of deceit yet realising her silence looked like guilt.

'No, lady, you listen to me.' And he stopped her protests and explanations with his mouth.

Pinned into the yielding goose-feather mattress by his implacable weight, Henrietta struggled to free her lips, her confusion overtaken by a sudden flame of anger. Why should he demand love from her when he wouldn't — couldn't — show any in exchange, just desire for her body? But he was too strong for her; her fists beat impotently on his broad back but it made not a whit of difference.

His mouth was warm and pliant on hers, his tongue a sweet invasion, and suddenly she was no longer angry, her hands no longer beating on his back but spreading, compelling him closer. She desired this man; that was suddenly inescapably obvious to her. If he wouldn't believe her when she told him there was no other she would convince him with her body.

Matthew's hands no longer gripped her shoulders; one was buried in the scented mass of her hair, the other stroked the soft hollow at the base of her throat where the strings of her nightgown had come undone.

Henrietta let her hands travel, guided by instinct to the hem of his shirt, slipping trembling fingers under the soft cloth until they discovered and stroked the burning flesh of his hard-muscled back. Matthew's lips moved across her temple, into her hair, his breathing almost a moan, a demand.

'No, kiss me again!' she demanded fiercely in her turn and he did as he was bidden, his mouth hard and urgent. His hand moved over the soft stuff of her gown to outline, mould the swell of her breast. This was sensation beyond her knowledge, her expectation and her dreams. . .

So, this was the mystery Alice had hinted at, the pleasure between two lovers. There was no longer any holding back, no shame at being with him like this. He was her betrothed, would be her husband in a few short weeks.

'Matthew!' His weight shifted, his mouth and hands left her and she waited, eyes closed, trembling with expectation for what must surely follow. Nothing happened. 'Matthew?' Her eyes flew open in disbelief.

Matthew Sheridan sat calmly, his back against the far bedpost, regarding her enigmatically. Only his ragged breathing was not controlled. 'Now, madam, when next

couple's open affection, the emotion that was banishing the years, making her aunt young again.

'Matthew, where is your clerk?' Henrietta looked around her, then saw Cobham's sharp features lurking in the shadows of the hall.

'I am leaving him here to assist Weldon and to keep an eye on my interests while I am away.' It was not the estate he was referring to and Henrietta knew it.

'My thanks, sir!' Henrietta dropped a deep curtsy, knowing she should curb her tongue but unable to do so confronted by fresh proof of Matthew's distrust. 'Knowing how indispensable he is to you; I am overwhelmed by your thoughtfulness.'

'You will be in safe hands with Nathaniel; he will watch over you. And do not fear I will feel our separation too deeply—he writes to me daily.'

There was nothing veiled in the threat this time; Cobham had been left beind to spy on her. It was a complication she had not expected, and a deeply distasteful thought that Matthew was right not to give her his trust.

'A safe journey, Sir Matthew,' she said formally, schooling her expression, conscious of Cobham's chilly gaze on her back.

'And a safe return to you both,' Aunt Susan called as the coach wheeled ponderously around on creaking axles and lumbered down the drive, followed by Matthew reining the grey back into a controlled trot. The older woman took Henrietta by the arm as they entered the house. 'My dear, I have had such an illuminating conversation with Lawrence about your betrothed. It seems he was a most devoted husband to Sarah, his first wife. . .'

'The master would want me to look at the rent books.' Cobham materialised from the shadows at the head of the stairs, startling Henrietta so that she grasped the carved newel post for support.

She had contained her impatience to talk to Robert

until after the midday meal, then, believing the clerk to
be in his chamber, had walked openly up the main
staircase as if going to her room, intending to slip down
the back stairs and out through the yard to the Home
Farm.

'The rent books?' Henrietta struggled to hide her
dislike of the dusty little man with the sharp black eyes.
Her immediate instinct was to allow him anything he
asked which would occupy him in the house while she
and Robert planned what to do with the casket.

'Yes, and the list of tenants if you please, Mistress
Wynter.' His very civility was patronising. Henrietta
realised that here was a man who believed all women
were foolish weak vessels and that was a card she could
play to her advantage.

'Oh! I don't know. . . I'm not sure. Are you certain
you need them now? Could it not wait?' She widened
her eyes and let one hand flutter at her bosom, the very
picture of an alarmed and empty-headed woman.
'Wouldn't you rather see the Home Farm this afternoon?' She paused as though seeking a convincing
excuse, seeing the dawning suspicion in his face. 'It's
such a lovely afternoon, and the walk is very pleasant.
You'll understand the books much better for seeing the
farm. . .'

'Thank you, Mistress Wynter, but I think not. I
would not wish to waste the master's time
in. . .excursions. The books are in the steward's room, I
assume?'

'I expect so, but Robert will know for sure.' Henrietta
toyed with the idea of fluttering her eyelashes helplessly
at him, then thought better of it. 'He's at the Home
Farm — why don't you ask him?'

There was a thin triumphant smile touching the clerk's
lips now. 'I will remain here. I will speak to Master
Weldon after I have seen the books.'

'As you wish.' Henrietta hoped she was successfully
concealing her own triumph behind downcast lids. 'Perhaps if you see my aunt you will give her a message? Tell

her I have gone to the Home Farm to see how the injured carpenter goes on.'

That should set him to work on the books with a will; he would assume she had gone to fetch Robert to conceal whatever secrets he imagined the books held.

With a sketchy bow the clerk hurried downstairs. Free to leave openly now, Henrietta changed her silk gown for a plain, fine wool one and her house shoes for a sturdy pair of buckled leather, threw a light cloak around her shoulders and took the back stairs.

As she passed the sewing-room she gestured to Alice, one finger on her lips, and led the maid further along the passage, nearer to where the steward's room door stood ajar.

'I'm just going to the Home Farm with a poultice for Jack's leg. Look after Master Cobham—take him refreshment, see if he would like to see the cellars. . .'

It was a good thing Cobham could not have seen the look of almost comic astonishment on the maid's face or he would have had real grounds for suspicion. Henrietta permitted herself an unladylike wink, took a few jars at random from the stillroom shelves and walked into the warmth and bustle of the yard.

Sim, the kitchen boy, was listlessly working the pump handle to fill a row of buckets for Cook, who was vociferously supervising the scrubbing of the kitchen floor. Letty emerged from the laundry-room with an armful of clean linen and aimed an automatic cuff at the boy as she passed; he speeded up his pumping until her back was turned then resumed his previous rhythm.

Satisfied everyone was fully occupied—including Master Cobham—Henrietta left the yard, crossed the bridge over the dry moat and walked down the sunken green lane leading to the Home Farm a quarter of a mile away across the park.

Now the carpenters had repaired the damaged roof trusses on the long barn the thatchers had started work. Henrietta stood in the farmyard, shading her eyes against the glare of the sun, watching for a few minutes while the bundles of straw were secured with bent pins of split willow and hammered home hard.

Robert emerged from the central double doors brushing straw from his jerkin. 'Mistress! I had not expected you today.'

'I have come to see how Jack's leg is mending.' Henrietta gestured towards the basket at her feet and Robert picked it up, leading the way towards the low, sprawling farmhouse.

Inside, away from curious eyes, he put the basket on the table and looked at her keenly. 'It is good of you to come — the lad's in the back-room, but Widow Perrott's been looking after him. He's young; he'll mend well.'

Henrietta glanced towards the far door and the steward pulled it to, guiding Henrietta to stand beside the fireplace. 'We won't be overheard here. What is it, mistress — the matter of the papers?' He sounded uneasy.

'Yes. Sir Matthew has gone but left his clerk here as spy. The man is all eyes and ears — I managed to shake him off just now by pretending I didn't want him to look at the rent books. No doubt you'll be in for an inquisition about those, but we may not get another chance to speak privately.'

'I sent Dick to Oxford yesterday after we spoke.'

'On what pretext?' Despite the closed doors they spoke low-voiced.

'To purchase a new book of husbandry Sir Matthew recommended to me; it was the only excuse I could think of readily. I tell you plainly, mistress, I'd hoped we were quit of this plotting!'

'How fortuitous you had a ready-made excuse. Try not to worry, Robert; once we are clear of this we will get on with our lives safely again.' Despite her firm words Henrietta felt apprehensive. 'How will he find the right man? Does Dick know of the casket?'

'Like myself, Dick is loyal to the King, knows where to find our old comrades in Oxford. But for his own safety I have sent a message in cypher and told him it is about funds to help those old soldiers who are suffering now.'

'Good.' Henrietta heaved a sigh of relief. Dick was a sober lad; he'd come straight home, not be seduced by the taverns of Oxford. 'Whom has he gone to see?'

'Better you don't know, mistress. I'll tell Alice the moment he returns.'

Henrietta removed the stoneware medicine jars from the basket. 'I'd best leave these as they were my excuse for coming. Widow Perrott will no doubt use them as she sees fit. I'll just look in on Jack before I go.'

Robert was already outside when she emerged from the sick-room. 'There's another matter I wanted to ask you about, mistress.'

'Alice?' Henrietta arched a quizzical brow at him as she picked her way among the chickens to the garden gate.

Robert's weather-beaten face reddened. 'You know, then?'

'I'd have to be blind, Robert, not to! I told Alice the other day, you have my blessing—and the sooner the better. I know Alice has stayed unwed out of loyalty to me, but there's no need now. And, in any case, living with you here, she'll still be close by.'

'Sir Matthew has given his permission.' Robert pulled his broad-brimmed hat over his eyes and turned to look in the direction of the church. 'He expressed a wish to be here for the ceremony, but as he's away for a month. . .'

'You'd better get the banns called this Sunday,' Henrietta finished for him. 'Then you'll be married the week before us. I'll talk to Alice at once about what she needs.'

'Goodbye, mistress.' Robert doffed his hat. 'And don't worry about that other matter.'

'Goodbye, and thank you, Robert.' She hesitated then added low-voiced, 'And watch that clerk—he's a clever man, and already suspicious of us.'

Henrietta's mind was buzzing with all she had to do

over the next few weeks: two weddings to arrange, a new lady's maid to train—and Cobham's suspicions to appease. She paused on the bridge to watch a gaggle of maids spreading out sheets on the camomile of the drying lawn, wondering which would be the best substitute for Alice who had been her maid—and companion—for so long.

Letty seemed the obvious choice—not that Alice would approve. But then she would be jealous of anyone attempting to take her place after all these years.

Sighing at the thought of losing Alice, Henrietta turned and found herself facing Nathaniel Cobham who had just emerged from the lane to the Home Farm.

'Cobham! Were you looking for me?'

'No, Mistress Wynter. I decided to heed your advice and take the air, look at the Home Farm.' The little man looked even dustier in the bright sunshine.

'I didn't see you,' Henrietta said coldly, picking up her skirts and leading the way into the yard.

'You were inside the farmhouse, in conversation with Master Weldon.'

'I was visiting our injured carpenter.' As soon as she had said it Henrietta realised she had fallen into the trap of justifying herself. The knowledge he had been spying on her frightened her. 'And of course making plans for Master Weldon's wedding,' she added with more assurance. But she was uneasy; could be have overheard anything that had passed between Robert and herself? No, Robert had closed the farmhouse door, and they had kept their voices low; Cobham couldn't have overheard anything.

They were safe this time, but the clerk's almost supernatural capacity for silent appearances spelt danger. She would have to keep her wits well about her.

Alice dumped an armful of shifts and petticoats on the bed and pushed her hair back under her cap. 'I still think Martha would be steadier. She's younger than Letty, but she's got a good head on her shoulders.'

'But my aunt speaks highly of Letty.' Henrietta looked up from her dressing-table where she was making a list of wedding guests who would be staying overnight and which room should be made ready for each. 'And I really must make up my mind today. You are to be married next Wednesday. . .'

'I'm not going away. I can still look after you,' Alice said mulishly.

'Your first loyalty now is to Robert and your child,' Henrietta chided gently, realising her maid was jealous of Letty's supplanting her, instinctively preferring the meeker Martha. Alice sat back on her heels, rubbing the small of her back.

For the first time Henrietta noticed smudges of tiredness under her maid's eyes. 'You must rest; you're doing too much in your condition.'

'There's much to do,' Alice retorted briskly, although she accepted Henrietta's hand to help her to her feet.

'Letty will be my new maid——' Henrietta took her by the shoulders and shook her gently '—but no one could replace you in my heart. We've been friends all our lives, Alice; we can be closer friends still.'

The tip of Alice's nose went pink with suppressed emotion, but all she said was, 'Well, I suppose I'd better begin teaching the silly wench her duties.'

'Before you go, I've got something for you.' Henrietta led Alice to the oak clothes-press. 'I want you to have these gowns.' She spread the grey silk and the blue wool on the bed and added two sets of lace collars and cuffs.

Alice's eyes widened with joy and disbelief. 'Mistress! You've already given me a gown. . .'

'I want you to look your best for the wedding, and afterwards. You will have a position to support as Robert's wife. Now take them and ask Martha to help you with the adjustments; she's the nimblest with a needle. I won't need you for the rest of the day. Send Letty to me; she can start learning at once!'

Alice gathered up the fine fabrics, her eyes sparkling with excitement, and hurried out without a word of protest. Henrietta laughed and closed the door behind her.

As she sat down she felt the smile fade from her face. Everything was going well, preparations were in hand for both weddings and the household buzzed with happy excitement like a summer beehive.

Alice and Robert radiated a quiet happiness, Letty was full of excited pride with the expectation of her new position and Aunt Susan, delighted that her niece was so well settled, spent every spare moment mooning over letters from Lawyer Stone.

The only fly in the ointment was the lack of news from Oxford. Dick had returned after five anxious days to report he'd been unable to speak to the man he'd sought. Finally he'd entrusted the message to another confederate but since then nothing had happened.

Robert maintained stoutly that all would be well — the man Dick had seen was reliable. But Henrietta could not be reassured. Matthew was due to return in less than two weeks — time was running out fast.

CHAPTER SIX

'IF MY Aunt asks for me, Letty, tell her I shall be in the orchard.' Henrietta hesitated on the front step, unsure she could trust Letty to remember to say where she was if anything important occurred. Training an unlettered village girl to take the place of Alice was proving more difficult than she had expected.

'Shall I go and tell her now, mistress?' the girl asked.

'No, Letty.' Henrietta took a deep breath and told herself to be patient. Letty was pathetically eager to please, but she wasn't Alice, who had been Mistress Weldon the past week and was now assisting Aunt Susan in preparations for Henrietta's wedding. 'There is no need to tell anyone where I am unless it's important; do you understand? I want a little time to myself in peace and quiet.'

'Yes, mistress.' As Henrietta crossed the gravel towards the fruit trees she head the plaintive question, 'How do I know if it's important?'

She fervently hoped Letty would never find the answer to her own question. What with the preparations for the wedding, the presence of three maiden cousins of her father's from Aylesbury who never stopped chattering and now the arrival of Lady Willoughby, come to add matronly support to Aunt Susan, her head was aching and she longed to be alone to think.

The wedding was only a day away; Matthew would arrive early tomorrow morning, so Cobham informed her. Letters had come by messenger for Cobham from his master two or three times each week, but he rarely passed on news to Henrietta, and she was too proud to ask. Matthew had not addressed a line to her.

His silence left a small, empty ache in her heart; however coldly they had parted she'd expected at least a formal note to acknowledge that they were betrothed and soon to be married. Aunt Susan had noted the omission and commented on it, despite the excuses Henrietta found herself making for her betrothed.

'I do not understand it. Why should he be so silent? He seemed so fond. It is beyond my comprehension,' she kept saying until it was almost a litany and grating on Henrietta's nerves. 'Manners have declined of late, but I cannot believe he has not sent you a gift at least — some gloves perhaps, the latest book of verse from the London booksellers. . .'

'I'm sure he is busy, Aunt,' Henrietta kept protesting. 'He has to leave his affairs in such order that he can stay at Winterbourne a while. He cannot leave his legal clerks for weeks on end without guidance, and his practice is large with many important clients.'

'Well, I repeat I cannot understand it; you are to be married shortly. . .' It was at this point after dinner that Henrietta made her excuses to Lady Willoughby and fled the parlour.

The sky was leaden with the threat of thunder and the air filled with swarms of irritating small flies. Under the low-growing trees the atmosphere was stifling and oppressive; Henrietta wanted nothing more than to ride her horse to the top of Beacon Hill, breathe the fresh breeze, escape the whole hot, heaving household, forget marriage and duty, casket and secrets.

But it would be extremely discourteous to abandon her guests for such a length of time, and, besides, all the grooms were occupied in clearing out the long barn before setting up the long trestles for the servants' wedding feast. And however rebellious she was feeling it was unthinkable for a well-bred young woman to ride out unescorted.

Casting round for escape, Henrietta saw the bulk of the old Tudor gatehouse rising above the trees, a clear forty feet above the dusty ground, the flag on top flapping gently from its pole. A gentle push sent the door creaking open and without hesitation she gathered up her skirts and whisked up the cobwebby spiral staircase to the roof.

Halfway up the stairs she heard the sound of hoofbeats under the arch but took no notice; servants had been coming and going all week with food, presents and messages, and they were expecting no more guests today.

She reached the leads breathless, a fine perspiration sheening her brow, but it was worth it; the air was immediately fresher and the slight breeze that stirred the family banner over her head lifted the hair at her temples.

A figure, unmistakably Aunt Susan, a voluminous white apron pinned over her gown, came out of the front door, a shallow trug on her arm. She would be bound for the herb garden, Henrietta surmised, guiltily remembering she should have gathered fresh supplies that morning when the dew had dried. The large company of guests had depleted the stillroom supplies of cooking herbs, nor were there more than two bunches of strewing lavender left.

Surely her aunt would not begrudge her an hour's peace on the eve of her wedding? Resolved to make up for her neglect later by helping with preparations for the evening meal, Henrietta remained in her eyrie.

Dabbing her damp throat with a lace kerchief, she turned her back on the house and leaned her elbows on the crenellated parapet. Like a tapestry the rolling park and fields spread out their quilt of green and gold squares before her, punctuated by the darker green of coverts. A ribbon of trees grew thickly along the sinuous course of the Bourne that gave the house its name. Here and there single figures or small groups worked in the fields or moved along the headlands, unaware that they were being watched by their mistress.

To her left the land rose steeply into sheep-cropped pasture land, to her right as she leaned out over the parapet she could just discern the thatched roofs of the village beyond the knapped flint tower of St Swithen's church where tomorrow she would be married.

Everything would change when she became Lady Sheridan, yet how much would her life remain the same? Winterbourne would still be her home, its people would still be around her. At least their future was assured by this alliance. Henrietta bit her lip in speculation. The more she came to know of Matthew, the more she realised he would never have carried out his threat to dispossess her workers if she had refused to marry him.

By this time tomorrow she would be his wife, but yet a maiden. She shivered with a delicious apprehension at the thought of being in his arms later, of understanding the mystery people hinted of but would never talk of openly. Even Alice, when she ventured a tentative question, would only smile and say, 'Wait and see.'

A dust cloud hanging heavy in the air marked the approach of another horse. Henrietta welcomed the diversion for her thoughts, leaning out almost dangerously to see whose servant was riding so hard on this hot day.

As he drew nearer Henrietta recognised the rider as Marcus Willoughby by the florid plumes in his hat. She drew back, dislodging a fragment of mortar from the crumbling crenellations. Marcus looked up in surprise, saw her and reined in at the foot of the tower.

'Mistress Wynter — Henrietta! What are you doing up there?' He swept off his hat in an extravagant bow, marred only by the uncooperative cavorting of his horse which nearly unseated him.

'Marcus, do be quiet! Stop shouting,' she urged. 'I don't want anybody to know I'm up here. I just want to be by myself for half an hour.'

'Can't I come up too?' He was already kicking his feet from the stirrups.

Henrietta sighed, then shrugged. 'All right, I suppose so.' Marcus's conversation could hardly be more wearing than that of Cousins Katherine and Deborah and their endless prattlings. And now she was betrothed, about to be married, Marcus would surely revert to the easy childhood friendship they had enjoyed before he'd become such a determined suitor. At least she could rely on him not to prate on about domestic matters. He might even have some news from London, which would make a pleasant change.

Marcus's progress up the spiral staircase was marked by the sound of his spurs clinking on the stone and the bang of the heavy wooden doors on each landing. He emerged into the sunshine with traces of whitewash on his doublet where his elbows had brushed the walls and a cobweb in his blond curls, looking absurdly young.

'This is a good place! With a brace of cannon we could have held out against the Parliamentarian dogs for weeks.' He began enthusiastically pacing across the leads from side to side, training imaginary firearms with sweeping gestures.

'Really, Marcus, do stop that—I came up here for a little peace and quiet, not to talk about sieges and guns. And Winterbourne was never in any danger of being attacked, as you well know.' But despite her repressive words she couldn't help smiling at him; at times like this it was only too obvious Marcus was but a boy of seventeen. For all that she was just one year older he made her feel a grown woman by comparison.

'It might come to it yet,' he said darkly, fingering the hilt of the dress sword that hung by his side. 'If the King returns. . .they say he will—my father came back from Aylesbury yesterday and I heard him telling my mother that the coastal levies are arming—— ' He broke off, eyes shining, 'But that isn't why I wanted to speak to you, Henrietta.'

'Hmm?' Henrietta had stopped listening some minutes since and was once again looking out over the soothing, familiar landscape.

'Henrietta! Madam! You must not despair; I will not let that Puritan take you. I have come to tell you it is not too late—marry me!' He had fallen to one knee at her side and seized her hand, carrying it ardently to his lips. 'You only have to fly with me; I will save you from that

Puritan usurper. I cannot give you Winterbourne, but I will give you everything in my power.'

'Marcus! Have you taken leave of your senses? Are you in a fever with the heat?' Despite his words she still couldn't take him seriously or be alarmed at his extravagant words. In her eyes he would always be the boy she'd played hide-and-seek with as a child. 'Stop this play-acting and stand up.' She tugged at his hand and he sprang to his feet, throwing his arms around her.

'No, I love you, Henrietta!' He kissed her passionately, clumsily on the mouth, catching the lace at her shoulder in his eagerness, crushing her against the stonework.

Henrietta, acutely aware of the spectacle they would present to anyone passing by the tower, tried to get her mouth free but to no avail.

Seconds later Marcus was seized from behind and sent spinning across the leads to sprawl ignominiously in a dusty gutter. Matthew's voice cut through the overheated atmosphere like a sword through silk. 'You insolent puppy! Save your clumsy pawing for some kitchenmaid!' He turned his back contemptuously on the shaken boy and addressed Henrietta with icy politeness.

'I warned you, madam, what would happen if I found you with another man. I suggest you leave us; what must follow now is not for the eyes of a. . .lady.' The heavy irony of the last word cut like a whip. 'Go to your chamber; I will speak to you later.' With one long, withering glance he raked her flushed cheeks, the torn lace at the bosom, her tousled hair, and turned back to the youth who was scrambling to his feet. 'I see you are armed as a gentleman, sir; can you fight as one?'

Courting Henrietta had been a delightful game, half serious, half make-believe. There was no make-believe now, only death in the cold green eyes fixing him so contemptuously. Marcus was white with fear under the smears of dirt on his face, but he found the courage to respond with dignity. 'To the death, sir, in defence of the lady I love.'

There was a rasping whisper as two swords were swept from their scabbards and the scuffle of booted feet on the leads as the two assumed a duelling stance, then Henrietta found both her voice and the use of her legs.

'Stop this nonsense!' She stood between the two of them, facing Matthew, bosom heaving, chin up. 'Are you mad? Do you believe for one minute I was about to give myself to this boy? He's young and impetuous, his head stuffed full of foolish notions of chivalry and love. Would you kill him for that? It would be murder!'

Matthew slammed his sword back into the scabbard, his mouth a thin line of disgust. 'No, I'll not kill him, but I'll give him the beating he so richly deserves for his impertinence—and as for you, madam. . .'

'You shall not speak to her like that!' Marcus was hopping from foot to foot behind her, trying to get past and use his sword.

'Oh, I lose all patience with you!' Henrietta turned on him in a swirl of plum-coloured silk. 'Put up that rapier and get up to the house at once. I ought to let Sir Matthew beat you as you deserve for your foolishness, but your mother is both my guest and my dear friend, and I would not have her hurt with the knowledge of your folly for the world—now *go*!' She turned to Matthew as the youth disappeared down the stairs. 'How could you suspect me of taking him as a lover? Just look at him! Yet he has courage enough to fight you! He is just a boy,' she added softly, almost pleading.

All she could see of Matthew was his rigid back, the leather riding jerkin taut across his shoulders as he stood, hands braced on the parapet.

'Matthew?' Henrietta touched his shoulder, then dropped her hand as he spurned her touch with a quick movement. 'What are you doing here today! I had not expected you until tomorrow.'

'That much is obvious.' He turned slowly to face her, his features set, his eyes adamantine.

'Oh, give me patience!' Henrietta stamped her foot with exasperation, raising a little puff of dust. 'You're no better than Marcus — in truth you are worse, for you are nearly twice his age and should know better! Or have you forgotten how stupid youths are? Marcus Willoughby is nothing to me but a childhood friend. You are my betrothed. . .' She saw his eyes narrow and abandoned that argument. 'And if I did wish to dally with him give me credit for the sense not to do it in broad daylight, on top of this tower with his horse at the door!'

To her utter astonishment Matthew burst out laughing, his dark head thrown back. When the laughter died away the smile was still in his eyes, and something else, as he said, '*My* horse is in the stables.'

Henrietta felt herself turn pink as his meaning struck her. 'Matthew. . .you are not suggesting that we. . .? We cannot. . .'

'Cannot what?' He moved closer, his expression disingenuous. 'What is it we cannot do?'

'I — er — whatever you were suggesting. We ought to go in. . .'

He stopped just in front of her, so close that she could smell the Spanish leather of his jerkin, the warmth of his skin. The teasing smile played around his lips as he raised one hand and gently traced the line of her jaw. 'Why? No one knows we are here, the parapet is high, the air warm.' He gestured at the dusty leads. 'I can spread my cloak for you.' His voice caressed her, as insidious as the warmth of the sunshine on her bare shoulders. 'You have aroused my jealousy, madam; now you must assuage it.'

To lie with him here, under the open sky, to learn his body in the sunlight with the larks spiralling above them — the thought was as seductive as it was sinful.

'Matthew. . .' Her voice was almost a whisper, she was drowning in his gaze, then she saw the spark of devilment and her voice changed to indignation. 'Matthew! You are *teasing* me!'

'Did you think me humourless?' The long fingers continued to caress her face, mapping every contour. 'A dry, dusty, *Puritan* lawyer?'

Henrietta's heart was thudding, her lips parted, her brain a whirl with emotions, sensations. She struggled to cope with his verbal fencing while all the time the nearness of him was driving every rational thought from her head.

'You said you were jealous,' she managed to say, breathless against the lacing of her bodice which suddenly seemed constricting, over-tight. This was a dangerous, delicious game.

'Jealous?' he queried, stooping to brush his lips over her damp throat. 'Of that puppy? He made me angry for a moment, that is all.' His breath was stirring the fine hair behind her ear as his lips traced upwards. 'But you, Henrietta, you have roused my blood.'

Henrietta stood quivering, transfixed as he caressed her with his mouth, anticipating with every nerve the clasp of his hands on her shoulders, the kiss that would follow.

Matthew was in no hurry and his very gentleness began to unnerve her. She wanted him to sweep her with him on a tide of passion so she didn't have to think, only feel. Inside she felt her desire, her attraction to him now touched by another feeling, a growing apprehension, a *frisson* of fear she couldn't understand.

Matthew was no longer nuzzling her neck, but looking at her, brows drawn together in the beginning of a frown. 'Henrietta? What is it? There's no need to be afraid of me, or is it marriage that frightens you? I know you are a maiden, that you must fear our wedding night. But I understand. . . Sarah——' a fleeting shadow touched his eyes ' — Sarah was as young, as innocent as you when I took her to wife. . .'

That name, the name of his dead wife that had hung unspoken between them every time they had met, was the charm breaking the spell that kept her fixed to the spot. How could he think a description of his first wedding night could be anything but painful to her? Unless he needed to talk of it, relive it because he could not bear to let it go, to let the precious memory of that first time with Sarah be blurred by his lovemaking with her.

But she was not Sarah. With a sob Henrietta gathered up her skirts and ran pell-mell down the winding stairs, away from him, away from the woman she couldn't hope to replace in his heart.

She didn't know whether he tried to follow her or whether he watched her flight from the tower. All Henrietta wanted was the sanctuary of her room. Heedless of decorum, she fled up the driveway, skirts tangling in her legs, her hair coming loose from its pins.

'Henrietta!' Her aunt's scandalised voice caught her as she dodged round a knot of serving-maids to reach the stairs. 'Child, come back this minute. . .' One glance at Henrietta's smudged, tear stained face turned to her beseechingly and she pushed the pile of linen in her hands into Martha's arms and hurried to her niece.

'Come, my love. Up to your room.' Aunt Susan took her arm and bustled her, unresisting, upstairs and along the cool, dark corridor. 'Now, what's all this about?' She shut the bedroom door and regarded Henrietta's disarray with alarm. 'Your lace is torn, your hair come down, and your face —— ' Without waiting for a reply she tipped water into the basin from the ewer and dipped in a corner of linen cloth. 'Let me clean this dust off. Where have you been, child, to get so begrimed? And why these tears?'

'Up the old tower.' Henrietta sat quietly while her aunt gently wiped away the fine dust and tear-tracks.

'Up the tower! Whatever possessed you? No one goes there now; I am sure it is not safe. What if you had fallen on those stairs? We would never have thought to look for you there. Foolish child!' She scolded on, still dabbing gently. 'Matthew was looking for you; what a miracle he did not find you looking like this.'

'He found me — and Marcus Willoughby.'

'Marcus Willoughby? What have you done?' her aunt wailed, the cloth dropping unheeded to the floor. 'You foolish, foolish girl!' She took a pace towards the window, wringing her hands in her skirts. 'Whatever possessed you? Where did I fail that you should behave so? Sir Matthew will never marry you now. . .we'll all end up in the Low Countries——'

'I wasn't doing anything!' Indignation dried Henrietta's tears as sympathy never would. 'I was up there alone, looking for peace to think in, and Marcus saw me. He tried to kiss me and Matthew found us— but he could tell I was unwilling. He sent Marcus off with a flea in his ear, no more.'

'Then he has not broken the betrothal?' Her aunt was urgent. 'Tell me it is all right.'

'No, he has not broken it,' said Henrietta with a sigh. 'Quite the opposite.'

A knowing smile touched the older woman's lips as she took in the torn lace at her niece's bosom, the tangle of disarrayed hair. 'Ah, so jealousy made him passionate and that scared you?'

Henrietta turned wide brown eyes on her, searching for reassurance. 'Yes.'

'Well, well.' Susan settled on the bed in a comfortable rustle of skirts. 'I had meant to talk to you tonight, but I see we must come to it sooner. Sit by me.'

Henrietta sat down as she was bidden, twisting the ends of her girdle between her fingers.

'Now, you know what passes between a man and a woman?'

Scarlet-cheeked, Henrietta nodded.

'What happened when he came to your room the night before he left?'

'You knew he was here?' Henrietta was startled; her aunt had given no indication that she was aware of Matthew's visit.

'Of course I knew. You do not think a man could go to my niece's room alone, at night, without my cognisance?'

'And you permitted it?' Henrietta discovered she was shocked.

'You were betrothed. . .it is accepted.' Susan hesitated, obviously finding this difficult. 'And I thought the waiting was preying on your fears.'

'He didn't. . .we didn't do anything.' She wasn't going to tell her aunt about that kiss.

'I know he did not lie with you; Alice told me. But did you not at least talk of your future together?'

'We quarrelled. And again just now.' Perhaps she could tell her aunt, explain how he still loved his first wife and how that pained her. Susan had so much more experience of life; she would tell her what to do.

'What ails you, girl? Not only is he a good man but he has been married before; he will understand and guide you. By all accounts his devotion to Sarah was admirable. . .'

Henrietta jumped up from the bed in annoyance. 'Speak not to me of Sarah! I am weary of hearing her name on every lip! Sarah was so perfect, the devoted wife. . .'

'Niece, you shock me! She is dead—how can you speak so of her? It is sinful and unworthy of you. Look to your conduct, miss, or your jealousy and shrewishness will drive him away. I have nothing more to say to you on this matter. I believed it was your innocence causing these problems; now I can see it is your wilfulness.' Henrietta felt a wave of shame sweep through her and dropped her eyes in the face of her aunt's anger. 'Be meek and obedient to your husband, be guided by him and all will be well. As for your wedding night, put away your frowns, at least pretend to welcome his embraces. Any right-thinking girl would rejoice at the thought of such a well set-up husband.' She frowned at Henrietta, her cheeks mottled with annoyance. 'Now I have much to do. *I* have no time to spend on vapours and silliness!' She swept out of the room, banging the door behind her, leaving Henrietta speechless and aggrieved.

'Mistress?' Letty sounded puzzled, and Henrietta,

pulling herself together with a jerk, realised the girl must have been standing in the doorway for some minutes.

'What is it, Letty? I did not call for you.' She glanced down at her skirts as she spoke, realising for the first time how dishevelled she was. 'Never mind; now you are here you can help me change. The brown linen will do.'

Henrietta sat down at her dressing-table and began to brush out then re-pin her hair. 'Hurry up, girl, there is much to be done.' Perhaps by throwing herself into the preparations for the wedding she could regain some sort of composure.

'But. . . I've got a message.' Letty still found it difficult to do more than one thing at a time.

'Well, tell me. Your tongue will work while your hands are busy, won't it?' Letty looked pained and Henrietta reminded herself yet again of the need for patience.

'Master Weldon says,' Letty began, the tip of her tongue stuck out in the effort of remembrance, 'I was to give you his compliments and could he please speak with you as soon as possible?'

Henrietta's heart leapt in her chest, her fingers clenching round the hairbrush. It must be the messenger from Oxford at last—and Matthew was in the house. Did Robert know the master was returned? She must act very carefully but speedily if the papers were to be safe away before she walked down the aisle with Matthew.

'Thank you, Letty.' She controlled her breathing and finished pinning her hair. Too much haste would arouse suspicion.

As she passed her aunt on the stairs she dropped a slight, repentant curtsy. 'I am sorry, Aunt. You are right, and I am ashamed for what I said. Now I must see Robert, then I will come and help you. I know you have much to do and I have been neglecting my household duties.' Despite her words Henrietta was guiltily aware of a little worm of jealousy still gnawing at her.

'There's my good girl. We will forget all that foolishness.' Mistress Clifford patted her cheek in passing. 'Just

show a pleasant face and all will be well. These megrims
are natural at such a time. When you have seen Robert,
please oversee the girls in the stillroom — they are finding
rosewater for the bedlinen.' She bustled off importantly
with Mary in tow and Henrietta hurried down to the
steward's room.

Robert was sitting at his desk, pen in hand, but he
dropped it in the pewter standish, shook sand over the
wet ink of the document and rose at her entrance.

'Mistress.' He cast a swift glance over her shoulder,
then pulled the door to behind her.

'Where's Cobham?' Henrietta moved to the window
and glanced out, but the garden beyond was empty.

'Summoned by his master. Did you know Sir Matthew
was returned?'

Henrietta nodded, sitting on the long settle against the
wall. 'A day early. Is there news from Oxford yet? Is
that why you asked to see me?'

'No. That is what concerns me. I would send another
messenger, but how to explain his absence at this time?'
He was right; everyone in the household and Home
Farm from steward to potboy was fully occupied in
preparations for the wedding of their master and
mistress.

'But why the delay?' Henrietta demanded fretfully. 'I
was so sure you were going to say you had word. What
if a messenger comes now?'

'The next few days are perhaps the safest,' said Robert
thoughtfully. 'The house is so full of people, some of
them from outlying farms — one strange face will not
look amiss.'

'Yes, you are right. And so many messengers are
coming with letters and gifts from our neighbours. . .there's still tomorrow.' If only the messenger
would come, take those papers, relieve her of her vow to
her brother before she had to make her vows to
Matthew — pledges of obedience and loyalty she would
break as soon as she made them.

'Let me know directly there is any news, Robert,' she

was saying as she opened the door and came face to face with Matthew and Cobham, just emerging from the head of the cellar stairs. 'That mare had such difficulties last time she foaled,' she added quickly to account for her words.

Matthew's nod of acknowledgement was coolly distant and he continued talking to his clerk. 'There's enough ale and cider in the cellars to intoxicate the entire village twice over.'

'They should drink small beer like God-fearing, sober persons,' Cobham said with a sour sniff.

'Even the Apostles drank wine, Nathaniel,' Matthew answered his clerk's grumbling with a clap on the shoulder. 'Speaking of which, see if we have wine enough — Master Weldon should know.'

Robert joined them in the corridor. 'I sent the wagon to Aylesbury yesterday, sir; it should return this afternoon.'

Henrietta left the men and slipped quietly down the passage to her right. The stillroom was empty, a row of rosewater jars on one broad slate ledge proof that the girls had obeyed Aunt Susan's instructions to scent the linen before making up the guests' beds.

The light filtered dim through cheesecloth draped across the latticed windows to protect the delicate herbs and spices from the sun. The room was cool and still, redolent with smells, an exotic mingling of flowers and spices with an underlying astringency of medicines and potions.

Henrietta gathered a bunch of long-stemmed lavender, then searched through a basket on the work-table for a piece of ribbon to tie it. It was quiet and peaceful, the only sound in the room the steady drip, drip of an infusion straining through a muslin bag.

She would make lavender bunches for herself and Aunt Susan to hang among the folds of their best dresses to scent them for the wedding-day. It was a task she should have finished the day before, but at least she was doing something useful, not just running away.

Her fingers worked dextrously among the stiff stems, weaving the ribbon into a lattice pattern to hold the bundle firm. It was a skilful art her aunt had taught her young, one she was trying to instil into Letty along with countless others that a lady's maid needed to master.

The door opened behind her and, without turning, her mind on the girl, she said, 'Letty, take these and hang them in the skirts of my yellow gown; throw away the old bunches — their savour will be quite gone after all this time. Then come back; I will have finished the bunches for my aunt.'

There was no reply. She turned enquiringly, expecting to find the girl hesitating on the threshold, but it was not Letty.

Matthew was watching her across the wide stone flags. Even in the gloom she saw the watchfulness in his eyes. The blood rose hectically to her cheeks and she made an instinctive backward movement away from him. Whatever he had been about to say died on his lips and they stood in silence for a long moment.

'What do you want?'

'Only to say that I shall endeavour to keep apart from you until our wedding-day as you seem to find my presence so. . .upsetting. After tomorrow morning I am afraid as my wife you will have to resign yourself to my company.'

Before she could deny that was what she desired, before she could move across the shadowed room to touch him, read his face, he was gone.

CHAPTER SEVEN

LAWRENCE STONE stood in the church porch. 'Come along, my dear Henrietta, your bridegroom awaits you impatiently.'

Henrietta looked up and met the kindly smile of the old lawyer. He patted her cold hand as it lay on his forearm with his own gnarled paw and waited while Letty and Alice fussed around, smoothing Henrietta's primrose silk skirts, dusting the faint traces of their slow procession from the house from the silver embroidered petticoat revealed at the front.

'Ready?'

Henrietta took a deep breath and nodded against the weight of unbound hair cascading down her back from a circlet of palest yellow roses.

The interior of the church was shadowed and after the brilliant sunlight and warmth outside the air struck chill, despite the throng of people lining the side-aisles and filling the pews. On Lawyer Stone's arm she walked slowly towards the altar, conscious she was the focus of attention, of faces turned to watch her as she passed.

The smiling faces were all familiar, all friends from her childhood, members of her household, villagers she had known all her life. Yet at that moment she could not have put a name to a single one of them, her entire attention focused on the tall dark figure whose garnet-red jacket glowed like a beacon at the altar steps.

Snatches of overheard words reached her ears but meant nothing; the old building was full of sound, the rustle of best clothes, the whimpering of small children, coughing and clearing of throats—all of it could have been a hundred miles away as Matthew turned to face her.

She was close enough to see his expression change

119

from sombre calm to warm welcome and knew then that
all the hours of preparation that morning had not been
in vain. She could not doubt he found her beautiful and
desirable.

The lingering warmth in his eyes in the moment before
he turned back dutifully to the altar and the waiting
vicar unfroze her numbness and she became conscious
of sensation again. Beneath her fingers the rich stuff of
Lawyer Stone's best coat, through the thin soles of her
embroidered slippers the cold of the stone floor, the
tickling caress of her hair on her bare shoulders—all this
and the buzz of voices in the church hit her as if she had
just opened a door.

And she knew also, as clearly as if someone had
opened a door in her mind, that she was falling in love
with Matthew.

They reached the altar steps at last and she glanced
shyly up at her bridegroom, convinced that her dawning
love for him must show on her face.

Matthew had grudged no effort for his wedding day.
Newly trimmed, his hair curled thickly on the heavy lace
of his collar, the deep red velvet of his coat moulded his
lean, well-muscled body, the darker breeches empha-
sised the length of his legs, clad to the knee in burnished
black leather boots.

He put out a hand to receive her from Lawyer Stone
and Henrietta saw that the only adornment on his long
fingers was the ring she had given him at their betrothal.

She glanced up at his face again, but his attention was
on Mr Halsey as he opened his address to the congregation. Dutifully Henrietta followed the words, trying not
to let the disturbing presence at her side distract her
from the seriousness of what she was about to enter into.

If the old vicar, Mr Hale, had still been alive she
might have gone to him and told him of her divided
loyalties to James and to Matthew, sought his counsel.
But she knew little of Mr Halsey beyond his willingness
to obey every directive of Parliament concerning the
running of the church. The vivid wall-paintings depict-

ing death and redemption that had survived the purges
of Edward's reign had been whitewashed in the past
year, leaving the church plain and unadorned. No doubt
he would be as eager to obey the rumoured directives to
make all things in the church as plain. No, this was not
a man to trust with a Royalist secret.

As she rose from her knees beside Matthew Henrietta
could see the tombs of past Wynters in what had once
been the Lady Chapel. Knights and their ladies lay in
effigy, lapdogs or lions at their feet forever frozen in
stone. On the wall a new tablet stood out from the rest,
the writing sharply chiselled, as yet unworn by time.
Her parents' names and that of James were clear from
where she stood; the mason would be coming from
Oxford soon to add the short record of Francis's life.

Matthew's fingers tightened on hers and she realised
he had followed her eyes. 'They would have told you
this is the right thing, Henrietta.' His whisper was so
low that she was not sure he had voiced the words, but
she pressed his fingers in return, grateful for his unexpected understanding.

The vicar began on the vows and Henrietta listened
with a full heart to Matthew's clear, firm voice repeating
the words. She watched his face and saw the fleeting
touch of pain as he spoke the final phrase, '. . .'til Death
us do part.'

He was thinking about his first wife, about Sarah
whom he had loved and lost, and true to his vow was
loving even now beyond death. It might be a sin to be
jealous but how could she ever rival the perfect memory
of the other woman when she was only human and
imperfect?

'Henrietta?' The vicar was prompting her and she
gathered her painfully wandering thoughts. Whatever
Matthew's feelings for her she had her duty to do, and
that duty began with the vows she was about to take.

She spoke clearly and calmly, her voice audible in
every part of the packed church as she swore to love,
honour and obey the man beside her. The first was

becoming a fact, the last two were more difficult; they would only be attained when she had got rid of the casket according to her conscience. She made a silent vow to herself to fulfil those promises as swiftly as possible.

The congregation launched into a psalm and Henrietta found herself isolated in the sea of sound beside Matthew, her husband. At the end of the first ragged chorus the vicar led them to the vestry to sign the register. The old book held the record of her parents' marriage, her birth, the burials of her father and James. She took the pen from Matthew's hand and signed her old name for the last time, the last Wynter ever to sign in that book.

'You may kiss the bride.' Mr Halsey appeared to regard this as a necessary but distasteful part of the ceremony. Blushing, Henrietta lifted her face to Matthew who took her lips in a warm, gentle kiss.

Aunt Susan, who was signing the register as a witness along with Lawyer Stone, Alice and Robert, looked up and sighed sentimentally. 'How overjoyed your dear mother would have been to see you so happily married. I feel I have fulfilled my promise to her today.'

'Now, now, my love, don't weep.' Lawrence Stone hurriedly produced a large kerchief and dabbed her cheeks for her. 'It will be our turn next, and I wish it with all my heart.'

'Oh, Lawrence. . .' Susan began to weep in earnest until Matthew bent to kiss her cheek.

'I'll not have tears at my wedding, my dear aunt — if I may call you so — even though they are of joy.'

'Are you not going to kiss Alice too?' Henrietta asked slyly, knowing her friend's soft spot for her handsome bridegroom.

'Willingly.' He clasped Alice's rounded figure and gave her a smacking kiss under Robert's tolerant eye, leaving her flushed and giggling. 'And now, Lady Sheridan, if you are ready. . .'

Matthew offered her his left arm and she rested her

turf where two laundry-maids were spreading out sheets in the warm sunshine. The girls straightened up, bobbing curtsys, giggling and blushing at their first sight of the new master.

'A cheerful collection of servants you have, cousin,' Matthew remarked drily as he opened the wicket gate into the knot garden. 'Everywhere I go I'm greeted with smiles and blushes.'

'They are a pack of silly wenches who will giggle at any personable man, whatever his station,' Henrietta retorted without thinking.

'So you consider me personable? I thank you, cousin, for that compliment at least.'

'You have a mirror, I presume, sir? You do not need me to flatter you.'

Matthew's lips twitched but he didn't rise to the bait, bending instead to pick a clove-scented pink. 'On the subject of servants, cousin, is Weldon betrothed to that maidservant of yours? Because, if not, the sooner they are, the better.'

Henrietta stared at him blankly. How could he know about Alice and Robert?

He misinterpreted her puzzlement. 'I assume the child she is carrying is his?'

'How did you know?'

'My wife had the same look about her when she was carrying our son.'

'But you said you had no children——' Henrietta blurted out, then stopped at the sight of his face. 'Matthew. . .forgive me, that was clumsy. Did he. . .did he die too?'

'She died bearing him. He lived a scant two days longer.' His face showed no emotion, but his clipped voice, the vicious jerk with which he threw the crushed pink from him told her everything she needed to know. 'I should have spent more time with her at our home in Highgate Village, but I was too concerned with business matters in Town; I did not see how much she needed me.'

'I am so sorry.' It seemed a woefully inadequate thing to say. 'You too have had your losses——'

'It is in the past.' He cut off her stumbling sympathy but his very abruptness underlined the pain in his eyes.

'They are betrothed.' Henrietta retreated to the safer ground of someone else's marriage. 'But Alice would not leave me before I was married.'

'There would be no need for her to leave you; I have no intention of supplanting Weldon as steward. The man is obviously able—the affairs of the estate are in good order. I suggest you make arrangements for the wedding as soon as maybe.'

'Yes, cousin, I will do so. It will be a weight off my mind. Does this mean you have reconsidered your threat to dismiss all my people?' She had to make certain.

'Do you believe I would have done that? You were living a fantasy, thinking you could go to the Low Countries—I had to focus your mind, that is all. You called me Matthew just now,' he added. Henrietta couldn't tell from his tone if he was teasing or reproving.

'I am sorry; it was forward of me——' she began stiffly, swallowing her resentment that he had tricked her but knowing he was right, then broke off as he took her gently by the shoulders.

'I liked it, Henrietta. Why are we wasting our time discussing other people's betrothals when we can think about our own?'

Henrietta felt the world go still and silent around her, conscious only of the warmth of his palms cupping her shoulders, the nearness of his body, the promise in those deep green eyes.

'Tonight Lawyer Stone shall draw up the papers and witness our promise. And then, my dear Henrietta, we will be bound by an indissoluble vow. . .'

Listening to his voice, suddenly husky, feeling the tension in his body, Henrietta was aware of her own instinctive response to him. She knew many couples regarded betrothal as tantamount to marriage and that to from the bowl of apples set in the centre of the table, the last few from the autumn store.

The big room had shrunk to a rich, glowing circle around the table. It should have been the perfect setting for two pairs of lovers, Henrietta thought. As she sat there the candle-light smoothed the lines of strain from her young face and struck copper flames in her hair. So absorbed was she in her thoughts that she was unaware of Matthew watching her until he offered her a glass of wine.

Henrietta glanced up, startled. In her agitation in the bedroom she hadn't noticed he had changed out of his riding clothes. He was still in black, but the light gleamed on the richness of silk and the severe white bands had been replaced by a linen collar bordered deeply with fine lace.

The light was kind to his face, she thought, softening the angular cheekbone, sensually shadowing the firm lips. Her heart thudded uncomfortably as she looked at him, a half-smile trembling on her lips. In any other circumstances the thought of marriage with a man like this would have seemed the answer to her dreams, the lover that the poets spoke of. Then she remembered; Matthew wanted a sensible housekeeper, a good mother for his children. If he'd wanted her affection he would have spoken of love. The shade of his first wife, that unknown woman, seemed to fall between them, and Henrietta realised her feeling must have shown on her face as she saw his expression alter too.

'A glass of wine might cheer you,' he said coolly, handing it to her and remaining standing before her.

'Thank you, sir.' Henrietta gave herself a little shake. Common courtesy demanded she behave better than this; he would think her a sulky child. If only she could explain to him the tangle of emotions that tied a knot around her heart. In just one day she had lost her home and regained both it and a husband; been shaken by her own unwelcome response to this stranger who was yet a relative. . .

'You are in great beauty tonight, Henrietta.' His voice was low, unheard by the others. 'Come, cousin, we can deal better together than this.'

Henrietta swallowed hard, her pulses fluttering. Matthew pulled up a low stool and sat in front of her, foiling her modestly lowered eyes by confronting her. He picked up the hand that was not holding the glass, turned it over and began tracing the fine blue veins in her wrist with surprising delicacy for so big a man.

'You're not scared of me, are you?' His voice was husky, his gaze compelling her to respond.

'No. . .' But she was. He was only being kind, trying to soothe her fears, but if he seduced her now with these soft words, gentle caresses, she would be so vulnerable to him. And what she was doing was for duty only; to believe anything else was possible was pure folly.

Matthew bent his head over her hand. His lips were warm on her wrist where the blood beat, tracing lingeringly over the translucent skin. The wine slopped in the glass and she put it down quickly on the settle beside her, her breath tight in her chest. His hair curled crisply at the nape, inviting her touch; more than anything she wanted to taste the texture of it with her fingertips. Hesitantly she reached out her hand then snatched it back as his lips reached the sensitive crook of her elbow under the rich fall of lace.

'Sir!'

'Cousin?' His eyes glinted dangerously in the muted delight. 'What's amiss?'

As if he didn't know exactly what he was doing to her! 'You are too hasty, sir!'

'On the contrary, I am a very patient man. Especially as I suspect you do not find me as unacceptable as I first feared — or as you would have me believe.'

Henrietta was saved from rebutting this dangerous assertion by the sudden appearance of Aunt Susan. The table finally set to her satisfaction, she must have realised that her niece was enjoying an intimate and unchaperoned conversation.

fingertips lightly on the soft pile of the velvet doublet, feeling the hardness of muscle beneath.

Her heart was beating faster than the measured steps they were taking down the length of the aisle. The bright sunlight streamed through the stained-glass windows, casting pools of colour on the grey stone flags as they walked past the rows of beaming faces, the knots of flowers Alice and the girls had tied to the pew-ends, and out into the brilliant sunshine.

The villagers had turned out in force, forming in chattering groups along the church path, enjoying the spectacle and their rare holiday. Behind their parents' backs children played tag among the gravestones, dodging in and out of the lichened tablets until the sudden peal of bells brought them running to gape with the rest.

A party of village maidens were giggling in their Sunday best, baskets of rose petals and rosemary on their arms. As the wedding party emerged they began to strew them on the path before them to be crushed sweetly underfoot.

As they passed under the lych-gate two small children, a boy and a girl, were pushed forward by their curtsying mothers to present tight nosegays of hedgerow flowers for both Henrietta and Matthew.

'Your people are loyal,' Matthew remarked as they turned to walk slowly up the hard-packed chalk road towards the house.

'*Our* people now.' Henrietta smiled up at him through a mist of happiness. No matter what happened in the future she would always have this in her memory as a perfect moment: her husband, tall and handsome at her side, the joyful faces surrounding them, the bells pealing out over a countryside at peace at last after eight years of civil strife and uncertainty.

'I am glad we have married this year,' Matthew said quietly. He saw her puzzled look and added, 'Of course, you would not know, but there is much talk now of ending the ceremony we have just gone through and replacing it with a civil one.'

'And you would not have welcomed that?'

'No!' His voice was suddenly vehement. 'We have been married in the sight of God.' Then almost to himself he added, 'Sometimes I fear this fervour for reform has gone too far.'

The last cottage on the outskirts of the village was Widow Perrott's. The wisewoman was waiting for them, a small sheaf of ripe corn plaited into a dolly in her hands.

'A blessing on you, mistress.' She curtsied before them, pressing the brittle stems into Henrietta's hands.

'Thank you, goodwife.' Henrietta blushed as she took the traditional offering and met Matthew's quizzical gaze. 'It is a token of fertility; each village has its own design,' she whispered to him. 'Do you not know the custom?'

'I have never been to a country wedding, although I appreciate the offer of assistance.' There was laughter in his voice and Henrietta's blush deepened. 'But I cannot but feel it is a matter you and I must discuss alone tonight.'

'*Matthew*!' But she was too full of this unexpected happiness to protest too hard.

The slow procession continued down the dusty road towards the big house. Behind them rose the babble of happy conversation from the party on foot, the creak of wheels from the coach carrying Lady Willoughby and the older guests. In front, village boys skipped and hollered, revelling in the unaccustomed licence, mimicking the stately progress of their betters secure in the knowledge that this was one day they could get away with such mischief without a beating.

The gatehouse had been hung with swags of evergreen and myrtle; the stable boys who had been set the task were still on their vantage-point waving makeshift banners in honour of their newly united master and mistress. Henrietta could make out Sim, freckles shining on a face unaccustomedly clean and pink.

'I hope none of them falls,' she worried.

'A coin for you if you will come down for it!' Matthew tilted back his head and called up to the youths above. The heads disappeared as if my magic; seconds later the lads piled out of the gatehouse door, palms ready for the largesse.

The driveway was freshly raked, among the apple trees white ribbons fluttered like flags from the bee-skips and as the procession neared the house the household staff emerged, Letty at their head, to line the steps and strew more herbs under their feet.

Aunt Susan had attired them all in new caps and aprons over their Sunday dresses and before leaving for the church Henrietta had given each girl a knot of ribbon for her hair.

Henrietta had one foot on the bottom step when she was swept up into Matthew's arms, held hard against the broad strength of his chest. 'This is one custom that holds good for both town and country weddings.' For a moment he stood looking down into her face, his green eyes bright with desire. 'If I had my way I'd take you up to my chamber now, throw away the key and leave your aunt to entertain this throng.' His voice was a husky whisper for her alone and for one breath-stopping moment Henrietta thought he would do it.

He carried her over the threshold and set her on her feet in the hall to the cheers of their guests waiting to file through the door with their good wishes and gifts. Henrietta schooled her face to composure but her heart beat wildly and her fingers tightened on Matthew's sleeve. With a shock of self-discovery she realised that she would have gladly gone with him, abandoned their guests, scandalised convention to be in his arms alone.

Surely it was immodest to think like this even though he was her husband now? Henrietta cast a quick, upward glance at his face and was scorched by the heat of his answering look. All the anger and mistrust of the day before had left him and the message in his eyes was unmistakable. Then she turned back to her guests and gradually the trembling subsided.

A late dinner would be served in an hour, at five o'clock, then the servants would retire for their own celebrations, leaving the wedding party to dance in the long gallery. As Henrietta kissed her guests, opened and exclaimed over gifts of scented gloves, gilded ginger-bread, embroidered kerchiefs and several pairs of scissors for good luck, she was aware of the smooth organisation around her.

She took advantage of a moment's lull to seek out Mistress Clifford. 'Aunt!' She hugged her fiercely, regardless of crushed silks and lace. 'Thank you so much for today — and for all the past years when you've been a mother to me. My own dear mother could have wished no better, nor more loving for me.'

'And I could have wished for no better daughter, lacking children of my own.' Sentimental tears were standing in her aunt's grey eyes. 'And soon, God willing, you'll be giving me grandnephews and nieces to love.'

'Lady Sheridan, forgive our lateness.' One of their more distant neighbours was waiting at her elbow, and Henrietta turned from her aunt, realising with a thrill of surprise that *she* was Lady Sheridan, no longer Henrietta Wynter. Everything was changing; she was no longer the unmarried keeper of her dead brothers' patrimony, but the wife and helpmeet of the master of Winterbourne.

The wedding feast was set out down the burnished length of the oak table. Aunt Susan had ordered the best silver retrieved from its hiding-place behind the casks in the cellars where it had spent the long, uncertain years of war. Now, polished and gleaming, it caught the late afternoon light, illuminating the big chamber, reflecting off the jewels and silver lace of the guests.

Matthew took Henrietta's hand and escorted her with due ceremony to the mistress's place at the foot of the table before assuming his own at the head. There was a moment's silence while Mr Halsey said grace then the wedding party sat down and fell to with a will.

There was a rich variety of pies and pasties, baked and roast meat and fish, sallets served warm, possets and main guest chamber. 'They be in long gallery dancing, surely?'

'They are awaiting us in the yard,' Henrietta hissed, slipping from his arms and smoothing down her hair. 'We cannot just. . .disappear, leave all our guests.'

'I can.' Matthew pulled her to him again, his lips in her hair. 'These country weddings go on too long for my liking.'

'Come *on*.' She tugged him by the hand while her resolve was still strong. 'Our guests have come from afar to be with us; we owe them hospitality. It's not like a town wedding, where your neighbours are all to hand. And,' she added, seriously, 'you are master here now; you must learn our ways.'

Matthew dropped a kiss on her forehead. 'We both have a lot to learn, a lot to teach each other.'

They were greeted with a rousing cheer as they entered the yard hand in hand. Shadows were lengthening across the cobbles, but the enclosed space was warm with the heat of the day and the press of bodies. Flights of swifts still swooped overhead, their high, piping calls piercing the laughter and joking below.

Kitchenmaids were constantly on the move fetching flagons of ale from the dairy where it had been cooling on wet stone slabs to quench thirsts raised by the fine spread now completely demolished.

'A health to the master and mistress!' John, the head groom, stood on the bench and raised his wooden flagon high. 'Here's to long life and many fine sons for Winterbourne!'

The party surged to its feet, mugs and flagons clanking, their voices echoing the toast. Only Sim, the worse for cider, slumped off the end of the bench and slid, snoring gently, beneath the trestles.

Matthew climbed the stone steps of the mounting-block, holding up a hand for silence. Gradually they subsided, shushing the unruly, nudging each other while they waited for him to speak.

'Friends, for I feel I may address you so, so welcome

you have made me in the short time I have been at
Winterbourne, my wife, your mistress, and I thank you
for your good wishes and hard work this day. Now we
are all together I pledge you that I will protect Winterbourne and its people, so long as you repay me with your
loyalty. . .'

As Matthew spoke Henrietta watched the rapt faces,
attentive to the speech. He was imposing, his long, lean
authoritative figure dominating the yard, the garnet-red
of his clothes glowing in the dying light, his trained
lawyer's voice reaching every corner without effort. This
was her husband; it was a strange new sensation to be
watching him, proud of him—and proud too of her
people.

'Mistress.' Robert was at her elbow, low-voiced. 'A
package has come for you by messenger.'

'Put it with the others.' Henrietta paid him scant
notice.

'From Oxford.' The quiet words brought him all her
attention.

'From *Oxford*? From. . .our friend in Oxford?'

'Yes.'

'Where is the man? No one must see him.'

'Gone; do not fear, mistress,' Robert soothed her
agitation. 'If anyone saw him they would think him just
another servant with a gift.'

'Where is the message? Is it safe?'

'I have it here.' Robert handed her a limp package. 'It
feels like a pair of gloves.'

Her fingers closed round it as Matthew jumped down
from the block and joined them. 'Another gift,
Henrietta?'

'Er—yes. I was just asking Robert if he had made the
messenger welcome, but he tells me the man has already
left.'

'Will you not open it? See who sent it?'

'I shan't trouble now, I want to get back to the
dancing.' Henrietta wove her way back through the

throng of servants, stopping here and there to receive congratulations or to admire a new gown.

'No, let us see who has sent you this kind gift.' The bantering tone held the faintest edge of suspicion at her haste and Henrietta shrugged carelessly, ripping open the unstamped sealing wax with sinking heart.

Inside, as Robert had predicted, was a pair of kid gloves, the cuffs heavily embroidered with bullion. 'Very fine,' Matthew commented. 'Is there a message?'

There was—Henrietta could feel it through the thickness of the left-hand glove, a page, not a brief note of greeting. 'How strange; the card must have fallen off.' She drew on the right-hand glove, turning her wrist for Matthew to admire the workmanship, hoping to distract him from the missing greeting. 'They are a good fit, perfect for riding.'

Suddenly she shivered. 'Can we go in now? It is cool here in the shadows.' The goose-flesh crept on her arms, but the fine hairs were rising through nerves, not chill.

Matthew put his arms around her shoulders, drawing her against the warmth of his body. 'Come inside, have a glass of Canary wine and warm yourself with a dance.'

Passing the cloak chest at the foot of the stairs, Henrietta sat down abruptly, one hand at her ankle. 'Ouch! I have a pebble in my shoe. Go up to our guests, Matthew; I will follow directly I have shaken it out.'

As soon as he had disappeared round the half-landing she was on her feet, her heart in her mouth, the message pulled from the glove. Quickly she scanned it; someone would come as soon as maybe, but the message was so oblique that no one who did not know of the casket's existence would understand it.

Hurriedly she lifted the lid of the chest. With a swift glance round she bent and tucked the gloves under the topmost winter cloak. No one would touch the contents of the chest until the autumn; the message was quite safe until she chose to retrieve it. Now she must get back to Matthew before his vague suspicions hardened and he came to seek her out.

The party in the long gallery had become boisterous while they had been away. The consort of viols were refreshing themselves with a well-earned tankard of ale but one young man among the guests had appropriated a fiddle and was scraping out a tune for his less inhibited friends in a corner.

Aunt Susan, pink-cheeked, was head to head with Lawyer Stone, obviously deep in her own wedding plans, and a group of the older guests were dissecting the gossip from London over several bottles of Canary.

Henrietta stood just inside the door, unnoticed, surveying the scene. She jumped as Matthew came up behind her, girdling her waist with his hands, each warm finger tangible through the thin silk. 'You see, no one missed us. We could have gone to our chamber after all.'

The hairs on the back of her neck rose in a sensual *frisson* at his plain speaking, the promise in his voice. Matthew's hands moved slowly upwards until they just cupped the lower swell of her breasts. He stepped backwards, pulling her gently towards the door. She melted back against him; perhaps after all this was best, to slip away quietly before anyone noticed them. . .

'Ah! There they are!' Too late — or just in time — Aunt Susan had been them. 'Time is getting on. Come, Henrietta, ladies.' She beckoned to the female guests. 'Leave Sir Matthew to the menfolk; we have our own matters to attend to.'

Blushing furiously, Henrietta was swept on a giggling tide of femininity to the master bedchamber, pursued by the masculine laughter of the groomsmen bearing a protesting Matthew off to the Spanish chamber.

Aunt Susan shut the door firmly on the gawping maids, leaving Henrietta closeted with Alice, Letty, herself and the female guests. The maiden cousins from Aylesbury, flushed with wine and vicarious excitement, bustled forward with silver scissors to snip off the knots of ribbon sewn around the hem of Henrietta's wedding gown. As each was freed she handed it with a kiss to one of the unmarried guests as a token to be sewn on their own wedding gowns. The girls took them with much teasing, giggling and speculation as to which of them would be next at the altar.

Then Alice and Letty began to undress her, unlacing the primrose silk, lifting the heavy skirt over her head, leaving her standing in a flurry of silver embroidered petticoats.

'Time for the stocking-throwing!' Alice declared gleefully.

Laughing, Henrietta pulled up her skirts and untied her ribbon garters, rolling each silk stocking down her leg and over her foot. Alice, as most recently married, picked them up, turned her back on the assembled women and tossed the stockings over her shoulders.

Shouts of muffled laughter from the chamber beyond showed that the men were following the same ritual.

Shrieking and scrambling, the unmarried women pounced on the stockings; Aunt Susan emerged victorious with one, to cries of 'Unfair! Unfair!' and Serena Willoughby, Marcus's younger sister, captured the other.

'Who is he, Serena?' 'Own up! It's William Latham, isn't it?' 'Oh! You flirt!' Poor Serena blushed scarlet under the teasing onslaught, but no amount of cajoling could persuade her to admit her young man's name.

Henrietta stood in her petticoats among the laughing, teasing friends and found herself smiling with pure happiness. She had been dreading this ritual, but now she was caught up in the infectious joy of it.

'Robe the bride!' Alice and Letty removed the rest of her wedding garments, then slipped the new, fragile lawn nightshift over her head. Henrietta caught a glimpse of herself in the glass and gasped involuntarily. 'Aunt! This is not seemly!'

The diaphanous fabric clung where it touched, a mere illusion of covering for her naked body. It pooled round her bare feet, slipped treacherously from her shoulders.

'It is very seemly for a wedding night,' Serena said

daringly. 'I'll vouch Sir Matthew would pronounce it so!'

'Serena!' There was a chorus of automatic disapproval from the married women present, but they laughed none the less.

Alice was patting rosewater on to Henrietta's shoulders, letting the cool liquid trickle between the bride's breasts, touching it to the fluttering pulse-points at her wrists and neck. She and Letty brushed out Henrietta's chestnut hair until it crackled before two of the youngest girls crowned her with a chaplet of white bud roses and silver ribbons.

The giggling and laughter died away into an almost palpable silence as the women stood together regarding their handiwork.

'Ahh. . .' It was Lady Willoughby. 'I declare, my sweet child, you are the most beautiful bride I ever laid eyes on.'

Susan, tears standing in her eyes, dropped a kiss on her niece's scented hair, but her soft words were drowned by a sudden clamour in the passageway outside.

'Open up for the bridegroom!' Lord Willoughby's stentorian tones shook the panelling.

'To bed! To bed!' The knot of women inside the bedchamber broke into a whirlpool of activity, sweeping back the sheets, plumping up the bolsters, installing Henrietta in the centre of the big bed.

The banging on the door grew more insistent as the women smoothed the coverlet back into place. Letty arranged Henrietta's hair, fanning it over the pillows, and at the last moment, as Aunt Susan opened the door, Alice darted forward and tweaked the ribbon loose at the neck of the gown.

Henrietta, her hands flying to her bosom, was overwhelmed as the chamber filled up with jostling, laughing men, Matthew calm and robed at their centre.

'The posset! Bring in the posset!' The aroma of hot spiced wine tinged the air, chasing away the delicate scent of rosewater. The two-handled loving-cup was splashed full and passed to Matthew by Lord Willoughby who exhorted him to drink deep. 'Sweet and strong, that's what you need tonight, my boy!'

In the second before she closed her eyes on a tide of embarrassment Henrietta saw Matthew's mouth twitch sardonically. He might not have been to a country wedding before, but he was certainly in no doubt as to the older man's meaning.

'Thank you, my friends, for your good offices and no doubt excellent advice.' Matthew's voice was dry. 'I shall endeavour to follow all of it.' Henrietta wondered if it was possible for the floor to open up and swallow her and the bed both. 'Now, may I suggest you escort the ladies to the long gallery where you will find a light supper laid out?'

There was loud laughter, and ribald suggestions, then the whole party surged out, leaving an echoing silence behind them.

Cautiously Henrietta opened her eyes. For a moment she thought the big chamber was empty, then she saw Matthew leaning against the panels of the oak door, the key in his hand.

The collar of his nightshirt was very white against the tobacco-brown velvet of the nightrobe tied loosely at the neck. His feet were bare on the oak boards and his green eyes were warm and steady on her face.

For a long moment each regarded the other in silence, Henrietta's breathing so shallow that she could hear his rasping slightly in this throat, the only outward manifestation of his feelings.

Across the courtyard music struck up again as the guests resumed their celebrations, but they could have been a million miles away from the two alone in the candle-lit room. Then Matthew began to walk across the emptiness towards her.

At the foot of the bed he stopped, one hand on the hangings, and looked into her eyes. Henrietta gazed back, drowning in the intensity, afraid yet yearning for what was to come, the touch of his hands, the touch of his lips. . .

'You are beautiful, Henrietta. Your loveliness threatens to unman me.'

Henrietta trembled, her fingers tightening on the ribbon at her neck. She wanted him to come to her so badly, yet she could not find the words to tell him so; her tongue did not yet know the phrases.

He must have mistaken her trembling for apprehension. His face softened and he came to kneel beside the bed, his hand covering hers at her breast.

Henrietta waited, breathless for his kiss, but instead he insinuated his fingers into hers, pulling her hand gently to make her rise. 'Come, wife, there is something I want to show you.'

Eyes wide with surprise, Henrietta allowed herself to be led to the south window, the hems of their robes whispering across the bare boards. Matthew threw back the hangings and sat in the window-seat, pulling her down to sit in front of him on the wide tapestry cushion, his arms coming round to cradle her against his warmth.

'What do you see?' He was whispering into her hair.

'Why, Winterbourne.' She could see in the moonlight out over the orchard, past the gatehouse, across the wide fields where a barn owl glided, soft as a snowflake.

'Yes, Winterbourne. Not the house, but the land and the people. It was here long before our time and it will be here long after we are gone. Here for our great-grandchildren, Henrietta.'

She turned, her cheek on his shoulder, and looked up at the reflective face above hers. 'What are you telling me, Matthew?'

'That you and I are part of the tapestry; we have our own picture to weave that is but part of the greater whole. That now England is at peace we should not war. Let us put aside the past, live in harmony for the sake of our people and our children.'

If he had but spoken of love she would gladly have forgotten everything that divided them: the casket, his

politics, his first wife; but no words of love had passed his lips.

But though she couldn't forget those things they could not stop her loving him, wanting him; she knew that now. And he was so close; his warmth and strength encompassed her. With a little sigh, half-regret, half-desire, she twisted in his embrace, her arms around his neck, and sought his lips.

His mouth on hers, Matthew stood, lifting her bodily and carrying her to the waiting bed. He laid her among the soft goose-feather bolsters and reached to pinch out each candle in turn.

The moonlight was bright in the room, silvering his skin as he shed the nightrobe then the shirt after it. The bed dipped as Matthew joined her, then all Henrietta was aware of was the sensation of his warm fingers as he smoothed back the fragile lawn to brush the fine skin of her breasts.

CHAPTER EIGHT

HOT, bare flesh under her fingers, warm breath fanning her face, an unaccustomed weight next to her dipping the feather mattress. . .

Henrietta blinked and opened her eyes to brilliant sunshine spilling through the uncurtained south window, over the boards, across the foot of the bed to splash a thick golden bar across Matthew's naked back.

He was lying face down, his head cradled in the crook of his arm, still deep in sleep. Cautiously Henrietta lifted her hand from his back and eased herself into a sitting position against the pillows. For the first time in her eighteen years she found herself looking at a man's unclothed body. . .her husband's body. The body of the man with whom she'd just spent the night.

She had never realised a man could be described as beautiful, but he was: the long, taut, finely muscled body; the smooth suppleness of his skin; the satisfying symmetry of shoulder and hip. She stretched out a fingertip to trace the dipping line of his spine then drew it back, afraid to wake him before she had come to terms with this familiar stranger in her bed.

The Matthew who had come to her bed, taken her virginity in the moonlight, he was a different man from this one who would soon wake in broad daylight, look at her with new eyes. Last night he had wooed her with gentleness, caressed her awakening body with infinite patience and skill until he had swept her up in a passion that overrode all shame.

Henrietta's hand stole blindly out to taste his skin again, feel the unexpectedly smooth texture over the hard muscle beneath. Were all men this curious combination of rough and smooth, force and sensitivity? She

could only guess, having nothing in her experience to compare with last night.

Her fingertips just grazed the skin in the small of his back then drew back swiftly as he stirred, muttering something into the bolster. Part of her wanted to watch him wake, become aware of her, but part of her wanted him to sleep on so she could have him all to herself — and think.

A small, cold knot tightened in her chest. She had given him everything her untutored body could offer. He would expect no less of her mind — and that she could not give him until James's secret was no longer hers to guard. And now there was the added complication of the message in the glove. Henrietta told herself there was no need for panic. The chest held only winter cloaks; no one would open it for months.

But the thought was the worm in the bud. It had spoilt her tranquillity, shattered her mood. Suddenly restless, she wondered what she should do now. From the height of the sun it must be at least eight and the household would be long about its business. She was unused to sleeping on this side of the house, close to the main stairs. As she lay listening she could hear the clatter of heels on the treads, the muted voices of the servants as they hurried to and from the guest chambers, shaking out the feather mattresses, hanging bedcoverings to air from the rear windows overlooking the yard.

No doubt the wedding guests would be breaking their fasts below in the hall even now, and the early risers out taking the air in the knot garden or walking up to the Home Farm to see what changes had been made since their last visit. Should she get up, look to her duties as hostess? No, as soon as it was thought she knew they would not expect it, not on the morning after her wedding. Nor, after that boisterous bedding ceremony, did she feel able to look her friends and neighbours in the eye. Not yet at any rate. Aunt Susan would be getting much pleasure from overseeing such a momentous and happy occasion for Winterbourne.

'You are very pensive, Henrietta. What's going on in that dark head?' Matthew had woken and turned over quietly while she sat lost in thought. One long, questing finger stroked a lock of hair back from her bare shoulder, cool against her suddenly heated flesh.

Taken aback to find him awake, Henrietta coloured betrayingly and was rewarded with a lazy, sensual smile that sent shivers down her spine, presaging her body's instinctive response to the promise in that smile.

'Our minds are in accord, I see.' His smile broadened as he reached up to pull her down into his arms, cradling her soft naked skin against his long frame.

'Matthew,' Henrietta whispered half in shocked protest at his boldness, half in delighted anticipation. 'Not again!'

'That's not what you said at dawn, when, as I recollect, I was trying to get some sleep.' His teeth nibbled wickedly along her earlobe, the roughness of his unshaven chin grazing her neck. 'Where has my wanton wife gone? Or are you showing proper consideration at last for my years? There's many an old husband been worn out by a passionate young wife before now.'

'I am not wanton — and you are not old!'

Matthew rolled her on to her back, tickling the soft skin over her ribs to make her giggle. She looked up into his unshadowed, laughing eyes, which held none of the suspicion they so often held before. Surely his suspicion that she might be in love with another man was now well and truly banished. . .

'Not wanton?' he teased. 'Let me be the judge of that. . . I want you to be wanton — with me. There should be no shame between man and wife.'

'I — I know,' Henrietta faltered, her breath catching in her throat at his caresses, the movement of his fingertip tracing maddening circles round and round the tip of her breast. 'But our guests. . .it must be eight of the clock at least. . .' Why was she protesting, fighting her emotions? The very least of her desires was to get up and leave this room.

'Our guests are in good hands and well able to entertain themselves. Besides,' he added, his weight pressing her gently into the yielding goose-feather mattress, 'if they see us at this time in the morning they will conclude I have failed to please you. Perhaps that's true?' He raised an interrogative eyebrow before dropping his dark head, his lips seeking the swell of her breasts.

'No, Matthew!' It began as a denial, then became a protest, but ended in a moan of pure pleasure, her fingers interlacing into the mass of his dark, tumbled hair as desperately as she would have held on to the mane of her horse before a jump.

Warm, pleasured, shameless, Henrietta curled up against the bedhead and watched her husband stroll naked to the foot of the four-poster and pick up his bedrobe. What had she, Henrietta Wynter, done to deserve a husband like Matthew Sheridan? She had had many suitors, resigned herself to the thought she would marry for duty, to ensure the future of Winterbourne and its people. And now, out of the worst possible beginning, she was falling in love—even if she couldn't yet tell him. And perhaps, one day, he would love her in return.

She allowed herself to relish the graceful strength of his back as he bent to pick up the robe, the golden sheen of his skin, the length and straightness of his legs—then caught her breath in horror as she saw the savage slash of the scar running across his ribcage.

'Matthew! How did you come by that terrible wound?' She scrambled from the bed, dragging on her robe anyhow. By his side she touched its beginning below his left nipple with tentative fingers. 'Does it pain you still?' The wound had knitted badly, leaving a raised, reddish welt against the smooth skin. Her own smooth flesh knotted in a spasm of sympathetic pain.

His fingers captured hers, abruptly arresting her exploration. 'It aches now and then when the weather is both wet and cold.' He shrugged on his robe, lacing it loosely, then pulled the bell-rope by the bedhead. His body was suddenly tight, withdrawn from her and their intimacy.

'But how came you by such a terrible wound? You must have been in danger of your very life.' Henrietta was appalled, amazed that even in the darkness her caressing fingers had missed the puckered flesh. With her new awareness of him his face and body should have warned her this was forbidden ground, but she still had much to learn about Matthew Sheridan.

A discreet tap at the door stopped her questions. Matthew turned the key sharply and opened it to reveal Letty standing shyly on the threshold. 'Yes, sir?'

'Breakfast for your mistress and myself, then bring warm water.' Wide-eyed with curiosity at her first sight of the newly married pair, Letty bobbed a hasty curtsy before the door was shut on her.

'Was it very dreadful?' Henrietta would not, could not let the subject drop as he so obviously wanted.

'Yes.' His mouth twisted in a smile that did not reach his eyes. 'Too dreadful to fill your ears with.' Perhaps that would silence her, allow him to push those memories back into the dark recesses of his mind.

Henrietta tugged urgently at his sleeve. 'Matthew, I am your wife; if something has hurt you so grievously I want to know, to share it with you. Do you not trust me?'

Matthew's eyes rested on her face, his expression considering. Then he seemed to reach a decision. 'It was a pike-thrust. It laid my side open to the rib bones; another inch and it would have disembowelled me.' It was as if he were describing something which had happened to someone else; there was no emotion, no colour to the bare words.

'A pike-thrust?' she said slowly, her mind working on the few facts he had given her. 'You were in battle? You *fought* in the Rebellion?'

'I fought with Parliament; it was no rebellion.' There was a warning in his voice but she chose not to heed it.

'Against the King?' Why had she not realised he

would have been a solider? The great Roman-nosed grey
was so obviously a cavalry horse and Matthew was no
thin-blooded clerk to skulk in his chambers while the
country took up arms for a cause he believed in. She had
known in her heart, but she had chosen not to face it,
not to press it when he had evaded her questions earlier.

'Against the King's tyranny, madam.' His eyes were
growing angry now, hard as emerald, the lines of his face
tautening as he fought to control his words.

'I am sorry, Matthew, I did not seek to cross you.'
This was awful, arguing with the man she loved,
moments after he'd left her bed. And he was her
husband; it was her duty to respect his opinions, even if
she couldn't share them. 'But how could you be slashed
by a pikeman if you were in the cavalry? Surely only
foot-soldiers. . .'

'You think gentlemen fight with swords only and get
nice, clean wounds which heal into scars that leave no
effect on the body or the mind?' His voice was harsh, his
bleak face frightened her.

'I know some of the common soldiers suffered badly,
but surely that was not the fate of gentlemen such as
you?' She was pleading with him, willing him to say it
was not so.

'War is no respecter of class or quality, madam,' he
flung at her. 'You have a strangely idealistic view of
slaughter and mutilation.'

Henrietta flinched. 'I know these things happened —
Robert lost his arm. . .'

'And I suppose he came home when it was healed.
Thinner perhaps and paler, with his sleeve pinned up
but otherwise little different on the outside. Do you
think he would tell you or Alice what that battlefield was
really like? The days of agony he endured after the
ministrations of some clumsy surgeon with his saws and
knives? What he — and what I see when we close our
eyes and think of it?'

He took her arm and shook her. 'Well, I'll tell you. At
Newbury it was like a butcher's shambles: men dying in

terror and pain in the mud; cries for help where no help could be given except for a merciful sword-cut across the throat; disembowelled horses, men trapped beneath them, dying or dead; limbs hewn off in pools of blood. . . And always the noise, the clamour of battle, the shouting and screaming and the clash of steel——' He broke off, seeing her sway, the colour leaching from her face. 'What's the matter, Henrietta? Did you not realise what *your* King had unleashed on his suffering people?'

'Newbury?' In that sea of horrors it was the only word her mind could grasp. Her lips were stiff, but she had to ask the question. 'Which battle? The first or the second?'

'What does it matter?' He flung away from her, the robe swirling around his ankles. 'Each battle was as bad as the others for those who fought in it.'

'I must know.' She followed him across the room. 'First or second?'

'Second. The Second Battle of Newbury in the year of Our Lord 1644. What is it to you?'

Henrietta felt the floor shift beneath her feet and caught hold of the bed-hangings for support. 'That was the battle where my father died.' The words came slowly, from between stiff lips. 'I know you think me foolish, innocent, but until this moment I had no idea he died like that. . .in a bloody shambles. How could I know?'

It was his turn to lose his colour. He made as if to reach her but she flinched away angrily. 'Don't touch me! For all I know you were the one who killed him, cut him down to die in the mud.' It was Matthew now who flinched as if the accusation were a knife in her hands.

'Henrietta. . .there were sixteen thousand men on that field. . .'

'And James——' Her voice shook and broke. 'He rode away in his armour and plumes, so young and fine, thinking only of honour and glory. He too must have died like that, like a dog in a ditch.'

The silence between them hung deep and heavy in the

sunlit room. She was willing him to take back the words, tell her he was embroidering the truth through anger.

'I wish I could lie to you, tell you it was not so, but I will not betray those who died on those battlefields. You are not a child now. You are a woman, Henrietta; I made you so last night and there are things you must face.'

All at once the anger had gone from his voice, replaced by a deep sorrow. 'Why do you think I want peace for my country now, for our children? Do you want this senseless slaughter to go on and on? Do you want young Marcus Willoughby butchered on a field somewhere in the middle of England? Because, Henrietta, make no bones about it, if you and your Royalist friends agitate, hope and plot for the return of the King, it will all happen again.'

She realised he had opened his heart to her, spoken of things he'd vowed never to utter. 'I was a fool to think I could alter the strength of your sympathies by telling you the truth. It was too deeply ingrained in your upbringing, reinforced by the sacrifices of your father and brothers. Why should one night with me change that?' Matthew strode to the door, wrenching it open.

'Matthew! Come back!'

'I think you need time for reflection, Henrietta. I find it illuminating that after our wedding night your first thoughts are still for your father and brother — and the King's cause. Let me remind you, Lady Sheridan, from now on my loyalties are yours.'

'Sir!' she flared, all her love and compassion for him consumed in a flame of anger and guilt. 'You cannot command my conscience, not now, nor in the future!'

She felt Matthew's furious gaze rake her figure from her dishevelled hair and flushed cheeks to her bare toes revealed by the disordered nightrobe.

'Think again, madam, before I remind you tonight that I can command everything else.' The door shut behind him with the finality of a hammer-blow.

Henrietta sat on the edge of the bed, staring blankly at the hangings on the opposite wall. The vivid hunting scenes swam in and out of focus as she blinked back her tears. How could all that warmth and tenderness and passion have turned into ugliness, violence, mistrust? And in the midst of all her misery there was a nagging burr of doubt. What if Matthew was right and she and everything she'd been brought up to believe was wrong? What if her father and James had died bloodily, not just in vain, but for the wrong cause?

The door opened slowly. Henrietta was on her feet in an instant, hope surging that he had come back, that all would be well between them, then sank back drearily when Letty's cautious face appeared.

'Here is your breakfast, miss. . .my lady. . .' She sidled in with the tray, placing it on the table by the window without looking at Henrietta. Eyes averted, she began to pick up Matthew's velvet breeches, doublet and linen shirt from the oak chest on which they lay.

'What are you doing, girl?' Henrietta demanded sharply. Surely her husband had not given orders that his things be moved to another chamber! Her cheeks burned with humiliation at what the servants must be thinking — and saying.

'Master told me to bring his clothes to the Spanish chamber.' Letty fumbled with the boots and pricked her finger on the spur. 'Ouch!'

'Take care,' Henrietta scolded her half-heartedly. So it was true; he was so angry with her he couldn't bear to share the same bed. 'Stop sniffing; it's only a scratch! What did the master say?'

'He said he wanted to leave you to break your fast while he went down to see Master Weldon. He's very kind, the master, isn't he, miss — er — my lady?' The maid scurried out, her cheeks burning with her boldness in talking so, almost colliding in the doorway with Aunt Clifford.

'What consideration your dear husband shows,' Susan commented cosily, kissing her niece's flushed cheek without apparently noticing the tears of relief in her eyes or the troubled set of her mouth.

'In what way?' enquired Henrietta with dangerous calm. Her relief that he had not left her was overwhelmed by an emotion she could hardly recognise. Anger, fear, guilt and misery churned inside her so that she could hardly think straight.

'Why, in sparing your blushes and allowing you to make your toilette alone.' Susan heaved a sentimental sigh. 'Ah, so much to ponder on in tranquillity. . .'

'The opportunity would be very welcome——' Henrietta began with uncharacteristic sarcasm, then broke off as Alice tapped on the door. 'Oh, come in, why don't you? Everyone else is here—it's like Aylesbury Midsummer Market!'

Alice and Susan exchanged sharp glances, then the older woman sat and took Henrietta's hand in hers, patting it comfortingly. 'Now, now my dear. I know last night must have been a. . .shock for you. As indeed it would be for any innocent maiden,' she added hastily. 'But I am sure Matthew was considerate, and you will grow accustomed to it, might even grow to welcome your husband's nightly. . .visits.'

Henrietta sat meekly, letting her aunt ramble on through thinly veiled advice and old wives' lore, all the time conscious of Alice's silent gaze. She looked up and met the look, saw her friend take in the total disorder of the bed, her discarded nightgown, her dishevelled appearance. Alice raised one quizzical brow and a knowing smile touched the corner of her mouth. Henrietta felt the blush scald its way up from breast to temple.

Her aunt saw too, but misinterpreted the cause. 'We will talk of this no more, my love, if it distresses you. Believe me, these are but maidenly qualms born of inexperience, and as such very welcome to your husband. Your husband. . .'

Fortunately her words were curtailed by a loud crash from the foot of the stairs. 'Those careless girls! If that was the best pewter. . .' She left the threat unsaid and bustled from the room, leaving Alice and Henrietta regarding each other in silence.

Automatically Alice moved to the end of the bed and began to pour warm water from the ewer into the Delftware basin. She shook out clean towels, then unlaced Henrietta's nightrobe as though she were still her maid.

Driven by habit, Henrietta washed while Alice found clean underlinen in the press. The unnatural silence stretched on while Alice helped her into her lavender-scented holland shift and smoothed down the lace trimmings. It wasn't until Henrietta was seated in front of her glass and Alice was dabbing orris root powder on the delicate skin of her shoulders where Matthew's lips had grazed that she found words.

'Alice, tell me. . .' The other girl nodded encouragingly, sure that Henrietta needed reassurance about her wedding night. 'Does Robert ever speak of the war, of the battles? How he was wounded? What it was like in the heat of the fighting?'

'Never,' Alice replied, surprised into frankness. 'But at night he dreams. Terrible dreams: he screams and shouts and when he wakes he is drenched with sweat. And he shakes. . .But he would never speak of it to me, even when I asked direct. He grew angry with me and said I would not understand.' She picked up the hairbrush and busied herself removing the tangles from Henrietta's curls. 'Does the master dream?' she asked carefully. Perhaps this was at the root of Henrietta's trouble.

Alice had recognised from the start the difficulties in the match, inevitable given their strong feelings for and against the King; but she had seen how they had looked at each other from the first day they'd met and had been certain the wedding night would make them forget all that.

'No. No matter, Alice; it was something I had meant to ask you before. Nothing you have said to me will be spoken of again.'

Alice worked silently, forming each long curl around her finger in turn, knowing her silence would draw

Henrietta out where questions would only make her stubborn. Something was wrong, but she was certain in her heart as a woman and as a friend that it had not been Matthew's lovemaking. There was no mistaking the glow of satisfaction that radiated from Henrietta even through her unhappiness.

So, Matthew had told her true, Henrietta mused, had not been deliberately callous when she was at her most vulnerable to him. If Robert — stolid, dependable, easy-going Robert — had nightmares, snapped at Alice when she tried to speak of them, then that was how it must have been. She drew a determined breath; she would think no more of it now or the horror of it would fill her mind. She had guests and duties — and a husband to find and pacify.

Surely he would forgive her; they were too newly married for quarrels. Last night in his arms he must have sensed *something* of what she felt for him. She would find him quickly, build on those moments of tenderness and intimacy, banish the morning's misunderstandings.

Henrietta caught Alice's eye in the glass, and spoke without thinking. 'Alice, is it proper for me to find such pleasure in my husband's arms? My aunt seems to think I would dislike it, but nothing could be further from the truth.'

'Oh! So that is what worries you!' Alice exclaimed with relief. 'It is just as it should be — and far better for the making of children.'

'As you found out,' Henrietta commented drily, her equilibrium almost restored to normal. 'Remind me, when is your child due?'

'In mid-November, according to Mistress Perrott, and I have never known the wisewoman wrong.' She laid a hand on the swell of her belly and smiled proudly.

'Take care! Do not use that word while Matthew's clerk is in the household. His sort see witchcraft in every country way, and wisewomen and their potions will smack of the Devil to him.' Both girls glanced instinc-

tively at the closed door, then without another word
turned back to the dressing-table.

Gowned once more in the primrose silk, Henrietta
entered the long gallery, unprepared for the reception
she received. Her mind was still filled with confusions
and the tension of her parting with Matthew, but her
training in deportment allowed none of this to show
outwardly as she stepped out of the shadows.

It was mostly the male guests who lingered in the cool
room, talking of politics and county affairs to the new
master of Winterbourne while their wives walked in the
pleasure gardens or gossiped in Aunt Susan's parlour.
Lady Willoughby, however, was as usual where the talk
of politics was, engaged in vigorous disparagement of a
newly appointed local Justice. She broke off when she
saw Henrietta hesitating on the threshold.

Even to the older woman's cynical eye she looked like
a rosebud that had blossomed overnight into a perfect
rose. Lady Willoughby stepped forward to offer her
felicitations then she saw Matthew's face and with rare
tact stayed where she was.

Expecting cool formality at best, Henrietta watched
Matthew stride swiftly across the room to her side,
nothing but warmth in his face. She held out her hand
to him in formal greeting, but he took possession of both
and before she knew it stooped to kiss her full on the
lips.

There was a murmur of approving laughter, and quite
open admiration, but Henrietta was oblivious to it. This
was no formal salute — his kiss was insidious and deep,
intimate and knowing. And her newly tutored body
responded, her hands clenching the linen at his chest,
her eyes closed in languorous surrender.

When he released her lips they were both trembling
and Henrietta coloured as she became aware once more
of their audience.

Matthew smiled down into her face before offering her

his arm and conducting her to stand with him below the great carved fireplace.

'Matthew,' she whispered. 'I'm sorry about this morning.'

'We will not speak of it now,' he replied, low-voiced, and despite the lingering warmth of his kiss she felt a slight chill. He had neither forgotten nor forgiven; he was no boy like Marcus Willoughby to be placated with a pretty apology—or a pretty kiss. She told herself Matthew was a complex man, and his mind and emotions worked on many levels. And on one of those levels he didn't trust her, however much he might admire and desire her. The thought of those papers, of the message still hidden in the glove, was like a canker in the centre of a rose.

'Sir Walter was asking me if we have had as much trouble with foot-rot in the flocks as the rest of the Vale, and I had to tell him I have no idea.'

Henrietta forced all her attention on to her neighbour's enquiries. Sir Walter was a keen if tedious agriculturalist and rapidly exhausted Henrietta's limited knowledge. Eventually she said, 'I really think you need to speak to Robert Weldon, our steward. He should be about somewhere.' She heaved a sigh of relief as Sir Walter set off in pursuit of the unfortunate Robert, but was soon claimed by another guest, this time with more entertaining talk of London.

All the time as she chatted Henrietta was acutely aware of Matthew by her side, of the ease with which he had slipped into the role of master of the estate. That in itself was a relief; she could admit it to herself now. After all, he was a lawyer, not a farmer; he made no pretence to be a countryman, bred to this life, these responsibilities as she was.

She excused herself after a while and crossed the room to Lady Willoughby. The older woman was in full flow, recounting a scandalous piece of gossip about a recently pregnant noblewoman of her acquaintance and Henrietta listened with half an ear while watching Matthew.

He was standing easily, one booted foot on the hearth-stone of the unlit fire, his arm resting on the mantelshelf. Over his head hung the portraits of Henrietta's grand-parents. The resemblance between Matthew and his great-uncle was striking: the same strong features, the arrogant nose and dark brow. One day, perhaps, their children's portraits bearing the same characteristics would hang in this shadowy room.

'My dear child.' Lady Willoughby's penetrating voice cut through these strangely reassuring musings. 'Let me kiss you; you look radiant today — as every bride should, but does not always, the morning after her wedding. Mind you,' she continued in a voice audible in every corner, 'you're a lucky girl to have such a fine figure of a man as your husband. He'll make your duties a pleasure, give you lots of fine sons, ensure the future of Winterbourne. . .'

Henrietta caught Matthew's eye across the room, suppressed a giggle at his expression and turned quickly back, composing her face. He was amused, thank good-ness, not offended by the earthy Lady Willoughby's comments on him, more suited to the stud farm than polite company.

'While on the subject of children, my dear,' Matthew's voice said suddenly beside her, making her jump, 'we must see about getting your likeness taken, to hang here, alongside those of your parents.'

'And you too must be painted,' Henrietta insisted, delighted at the thought.

Matthew waved a dismissive hand. 'Oh, I've had mine done.'

Lawyer Stone broke into the conversation. ''Twas a very fine portrait of Sarah, I always thought; it caught her sweet nature so well, although I never felt Paget had succeeded as well with you.'

Sarah again! Henrietta thought with a fierce, painful stab of jealousy at the thought of the paired portraits of Matthew and his first wife. Where did they hang? she wondered. In the house in Highgate? Or did he keep them closer, in his chambers in London?

'I want us to be painted together, to celebrate our marriage,' she said vehemently.

'I am flattered.' Matthew raised a brow at her fervour. 'But it may be difficult for us both to find time. Perhaps I can have mine done while I am in London, then the artist can travel here afterwards.'

'In London? Matthew. . .'

'Dinner, my friends!' Aunt Susan called from the doorway. 'Your wives have been waiting below these five minutes past, and you must be all sharp set.'

The guests surged in a happy, hungry crowd to the door; many had been up since before seven and it was now midday. Henrietta caught Matthew's sleeve. 'When do you go back to London?' she asked in alarm. Only a few days before her heart had sunk at the thought of his return; now she was devastated at the thought of parting from him.

'Later, my dear. We have our guests to attend to.' He seemed amused, flattered by her clinging, conducting her to her seat at one end of the long table with almost exaggerated ceremony, before taking his at the opposite end. He said grace and the guests fell to with enthusiasm.

Aunt Susan had produced another sumptuous meal, making up in few short days for all the dreary months of mourning and plain fare. There were dishes of chicken with fruits, fat carp that had kept young Sim busy since dawn at the pond, lark pie, fricassee of rabbit with cream, duck with peas. . . The long sideboard groaned under the weight of sweet dishes to follow: pastries and jellies, curds and cream, honey-rich syllabubs and tansies. Lawyer Stone was already eyeing them with a gleam of anticipation in his eyes.

Henrietta turned conscientiously from one guest to another, ensuring that this cup was filled, that plate was passed, that all their guests had the roast or pie or sallet of their choosing. At the other end of the table Matthew did the same. At last the first rush to fill plates was over and the guests fell to.

Catching Martha by the arm as she hurried past, Henrietta reminded her to refill the flagons of cider and ale then turned at last to her own plate. She seemed to have very little appetite, despite leaving almost untouched her breakfast bread and small ale.

She had helped herself to stewed carp and the fragrance of fennel and onions curled up to meet her nostrils temptingly. Henrietta spooned up a morsel, raised it to her lips then put the spoon down with a hand suddenly unsteady. Matthew was watching her down the length of the table, a smile curving his lips, one long-fingered hand toying with a flagon of ale.

A senior colleague of Matthew's was complimenting her on the meal and she turned to answer him politely but Matthew's eyes drew hers again and she turned back like a lodestone to the north.

Around them rose the hubbub of conversation and laughter, the clatter of knives and pewter. The drink passed round and faces grew red with good food and the warmth of the room, despite all the windows and the great door standing open. Matthew's eyes glittered strangely; Henrietta told herself it was the ale, but knew it was not.

She found herself laughing too often, rather too shrilly. Her skin prickled between her breasts, not with the heat but with the intensity of the silent stare Matthew directed at her. She knew now, after last night, why her knees felt weak, why her pulses raced and there was a hollow feeling deep in her stomach.

As the conversation of the guests grew louder the two of them remained still quiet islands in the sea of noise. Henrietta supposed she was responding properly to the questions of her neighbours but it was mechanical. All her consciousness was focused wholly on Matthew. She wanted to be in his arms on that big soft bed, learning his body in even greater detail, exchanging kisses and caresses that burned and tormented until at last they lay custards. Aunt Susan and Lady Willoughby had had their heads together for days, poring over family kitchen books, considering the latest French receipts. Thanks to Robert's good husbandry, wine and ale flowed in abundance and the voices diminished to a conversational buzz while the guests, most of whom had not eaten since they broke their fast, ate and drank heartily.

Matthew looked down the length of the board past thirty-odd flushed and animated faces to where his new wife sat, her eyes modestly cast down, made shy by all the unaccustomed fuss and attention.

Against the primrose and silver of her gown Henrietta's shoulders rose creamily, veiled only by the fall of her chestnut hair. Her face was beautiful but pale and she was picking at her food, her wine untouched in the goblet. What was in her mind? He wished he knew what was going on behind those intelligent brown eyes.

She desired him; he knew that without vanity; her response to his caresses told him that. But some part of her was kept from him, some secret held back; every time he touched her her response was tempered by a reserve he could not explain.

Matthew saw a sudden flush touch her cheeks as a neighbour made a teasing comment. Perhaps he was reading too much into her reticence; after all, she was a virgin, young, sheltered from the world, recently bereaved of the last of her family. Discovering he was the rightful master of Winterbourne must have been a blow, enough perhaps to colour her attitude towards him.

Henrietta looked up and found his pensive gaze on her. Uncertainly she smiled and was rewarded with one of his rare, warm smiles. She felt reassured. All would be well later, when they were alone. He would make it so.

As he swept her a low bow at the end of the third dance Henrietta drew her husband to one side, leaving their guests to form sets while the musicians retuned for a country measure. 'Now would be a good time for us to visit the household; they will be at their feasting and ready to drink our health.'

Alice, swinging by on Robert's arm as the musicians struck up a rumbustious tune, paused to whisper low to her mistress. 'Is all aright? I could wish the master would send that long-faced Puritan out of the room; I expect him to stand up and announce we are all damned at any moment. His face could curdle milk; he quite spoils my pleasure.'

Henrietta followed Alice's nod. Nathaniel Cobham stood by the window, his face as black as thunder as he watched the swirl of dancers. 'Forget him, Alice,' she shrugged. 'He finds as much satisfaction in his disapproval as we in our dancing: he shall not spoil my wedding-day.'

A servant came and whispered low to Robert, who excused himself and followed the man below. One of the local farmers immediately claimed Alice as his partner and Henrietta and Matthew left as she was swept off laughing.

Away from the hubbub of the long gallery Matthew caught her arm. 'We are but a step from our bedchamber; no one will miss us if we slip away now.' He pulled her to him, his breath warm on her neck, his arms holding her hard against the length of him, then his lips claimed hers, possessive and demanding as they had never been before. Henrietta responded immediately, her guests, the servants, everything forgotten in the heat of the moment.

'Henrietta!' It was a groan. Once more he bent and swept her into his arms, starting down the corridor towards the master bedchamber. Henrietta let him carry her, unresisting, her fingers twining in his hair, her lips urgent against his.

A voice echoed up the back stairs, 'Martha? You seen the master and mistress, girl?'

'Not come by me,' a female voice answered from the

fulfilled together. She stifled a sigh; it was a long, long time until nightfall.

Her husband was listening with a very straight face to Serena Willoughby telling a tale which was causing her to blush prettily and cast down her eyes coyly. Henrietta suspected she was asking for advice on her suitors. To all intents and purposes Matthew was following closely, but Henrietta knew his eyes and attention were focused on her. He saw her watching him and one eyelid drooped in a slow wink.

Covered in confusion, her heart fluttering madly, Henrietta cut herself a piece of cheese. He must have forgiven her for this morning; she wanted his forgiveness so much. She loved him, craved his love with a hunger that astonished her. But he didn't love her, not yet. But he would, she vowed. She would replace Sarah in his heart by being the perfect wife, and then perhaps one day he would love her as he'd loved his first wife.

The cheese was sharp on her palate, but she didn't notice. Before she did anything she must quit her promise to James, send those papers on their way — and the message in the glove from Robert's Oxford contact promised help.

The last of the meal had been eaten, the dishes almost cleared. Many of the ladies were already retiring to the cool of Aunt Susan's parlour but Serena Willoughby hung on her mother's arm, begging permission to go and play bowls with the other young people.

Lady Willoughby cast a sharp look round, decided none of the young men presented a threat to an unchaperoned girl, and gave her permission.

'Come with me; I'll find the bowls for you.' Henrietta gathered the laughing group around her and led them through the screens to the large press at the foot of the stairs. She showed the men where the wooden bowls lay and reassured the enthusiasts that the green was newly mowed and rolled. They trooped off, leaving her suddenly alone, her skirts brushing the oak chest containing the glove and its message.

Some of the older men still lingered in the hall talking. She heard Sir Walter and Matthew, still apparently discussing sheep, and realised she had the perfect opportunity to retrieve the message and take it to her room.

It was the work of a moment to lift the lid and extract the package from between the folds of her heavy winter cloak. The scrap of parchment was where she had left it rolled into a cylinder in one finger of the right-hand glove.

A step sounded on the flags behind her. With a guilty start she dropped the heavy lid of the chest, the sound echoing like a thunderclap up the stairwell.

Hands, warm and sure, clasped her shoulders, and Matthew's lips caressed the line of her neck from earlobe to collarbone. 'What are you doing out here alone?' he murmured against her skin, sending the fine hairs on the back of her neck into tingling arousal.

'F-finding the bowls,' she managed to stammer, finding speech more and more difficult as his lips moved down the curve of her shoulder and his hands dropped to girdle her waist. Slowly, deliberately, he turned her to face him and as he did so her full skirts knocked the gloves to the floor.

Matthew stooped, picked them up and examined them. 'These are fine.' He ran an appreciative finger over the bullion embroidery. 'Who gave you them?'

'I'm not sure; there's no card with them. They're the ones that arrived last night while we were in the yard with the servants. I must have left them here when we came in.' All of that was the literal truth; her conscience was bad enough already without adding lying to her sins.

Matthew discarded them without a second glance, pulling her into his arms against his hard, disturbing body. 'It's too hot in here,' he murmured against her lips. 'Come outside.'

Striving to stifle her disappointment that he was not carrying her off to their chamber, Henrietta allowed herself to be led across the orchard. Silently she chided herself for having such immodest thoughts; Matthew would come to her in their chamber at night as was fitting. Wanting anything else would make her the wanton he'd teased her with.

Ducking under the low branches laden with hard, unripe apples, her hand in Matthew's, she thought only of the gloves lying on the chest in the hall. What if a servant or a guest picked them up, felt the message secreted in the finger? Oh, James, she thought despairingly, if only you'd found someone else to bequeath your secret to, how happy I could be now.

But there had been no one else, and there was no one else now to pass the burden to. It was her responsibility to deal with — and quickly.

'Matthew, stop. I must go back to the house, speak with Letty.'

'It can wait.' His voice was smoky with promise, lighting an answering fire in her.

'No.' She wriggled her fingers free of his grasp and managed to look coyly shy. 'It is something for. . .a woman's ears.'

The passion was still in his eyes, but he nodded understandingly and let her go. 'Don't be long. I will be waiting for you at the willow by the pond.'

Her heart was thudding, but not because she was running back to the house. She hated deceiving him, using womanly wiles to cajole him. But the message had to come before everything; there were lives at stake.

The gloves were where she had left them. With a sigh of thankfulness Henrietta lifted the lid and thrust them deep into the folds of her winter cloak, releasing a strong smell of camphor and wormwood from the stored cloth.

Matthew was waiting for her at the pond where he'd first offered her marriage that day when he had arrived so unexpectedly. Now that it was summer the old weeping willow made a canopy of green sweeping almost to the ground. Matthew held apart the branches like opening a curtain and they stepped inside the green coolness. He dropped the branches behind them. 'I found this place the other morning. Did you realise you could conceal yourself here like this?'

'Oh, yes!' Henrietta clapped her hands in joyful recollection, her worries suddenly banished. 'Alice and James and I used to play here when we were children, but I had quite forgotten. It is like being in a room with just a window out on to the pond.'

'And only a coot to watch us.' His voice was suddenly husky, full of longing as he drew her down on to the dry grass.

'Matthew? What are we doing here?' But, joyfully, she knew only too well as his lips travelled down from her temple to the corner of her mouth.

He traced the curve of her lips with the tip of his tongue, tasting, tantalising, sending shafts of fire coursing down her limbs. Expecting him to kiss her full on the mouth, Henrietta closed her eyes and raised parted lips, but his tongue was busy now at her wrist, teasing the pulse-point, his teeth nipping the swell at the base of her thumb.

She opened her mouth to protest but only managed to whisper. 'What if someone were to come?'

'No one will come; they are all occupied. And none will think to seek us today of all days.'

Questing fingers were loosening the laces at her back and Henrietta leaned against his chest to make it easier for him undo her bodice. Part of her mind was stunned by his audacity but the drugging sensuality his knowing fingers was orchestrating in her overrode all her reticence.

The light was green and heavy on her closed lids, the silence absolute save for the murmur of bees and the susurration of blood in her veins.

Matthew laid her back against the cushioning turf and took a deep, ragged breath. 'You are so beautiful,' he said, so low that she hardly caught the words. He slipped the bodice from her shoulders to savour her creamy skin for a long moment.

He lowered his mouth to the swell of her breast

revealed by the slipping bodice, caressing the warm skin with gentleness. 'I cannot believe you are really mine,' he murmured against her skin.

The tenderness in his voice unleashed all the pent-up guilt and her burgeoning love for him. Her throat thickened with tears and a sob she could not repress shook her.

One hot tear splashed on to Matthew's cheek. 'My darling. . .Henrietta, why are you weeping?' He sat up, pulling her into his arms. 'You are overwrought. My passion for you is driving me too fast. . .the wedding. . .last night. Forgive me. Do you want to go back to the house?'

'No!' Henrietta protested with more haste than modesty, her vehemence bringing a smile to his lips. 'I want to be here, alone with you. Only, I thought you would be angry with me after this morning. I am sorry; I should not have pressed you so or said those things about my father and James.' He looked away, not meeting her eyes. 'I know it pains you to speak of it — I will never mention it again.'

Matthew got slowly to his feet and stood staring out through the screen of spear-shaped leaves to the pond beyond. For a moment Henrietta feared she had awoken his anger again until he turned to face her.

'No. We must speak of it. I was a fool to think I could keep it from you; this marriage must be a clean beginning for both of us. Secrets are like droplets of acid, corroding where they touch; there will be no secrets for us.'

Henrietta dropped her eyes, unable to match the sincerity in his green gaze. 'Go on,' she whispered.

'I knew the King was wrong. His demands were ruining the country and had to be resisted. But I thought then, at the beginning, I could not bring myself to fight. . .to fight my fellow countrymen. I was already involved. . .as lawyer to Lord Hargraves, a moderate man whose views were much in accord with my own.'

He shredded a leaf between unconscious fingers, gaze

opaque. Henrietta felt he was looking back at his younger, more idealistic self.

'When he became a colonel with Cromwell's army he asked me to accompany him as an intelligence officer.' Henrietta met his eyes and he spoke sharply as though rebuffing a criticism she had not intended. 'I held the rank of major; I was not a spy skulking around the taverns for scraps of gossip. Hargraves used me to interpret the information and reports that reached him, to handle his correspondence and cyphers.' He smiled ruefully. 'The roads of England must have been thick with couriers carrying concealed messages. It is a wonder any of us can write an open letter in plain English now!'

Henrietta's answering laugh was hollow. 'How came you to fight, then?' She had to turn the conversation from secret messages before her guilt showed on her face.

'As a man of honour I could not avoid it. When the fighting came I found I had no choice; there was no middle path, no party of compromise to join. It was Parliament or the King and to choose either meant to fight and kill.'

Henrietta looked at him with compassion. How difficult it must have been. Her father and James never had a moment's doubt that their cause was right and that to fight and kill for it was right also. But this man, her husband, had thought deeply, made a difficult choice. He had faced the consequences of that choice and his conscience and his scars would never let him forget.

'I understand, Matthew. Please believe me—I admire your honesty and I respect your convictions even though I cannot share them.'

Matthew knelt beside her, his eyes on her face. 'I have opened my heart to you, Henrietta. I have never spoken of my feelings about this to anyone, not even to Sarah. There is nothing else I am keeping from you. I beg you, be as honest with me. Let us not start this marriage with secrets between us. . .'

If only she could. Her heart contracted painfully

within her but her conscience held firm. She had sworn an oath not to reveal James's secret and now he was dead no one could release her from that promise. She was a poor liar and he must have read her unease on her face.

'Nothing you are prepared to tell me even now,' he finished coldly. 'If this is the way you want our marriage to be, madam, then so be it. I shall return to our guests and leave you alone to the contemplation of your secrets. I hope you find them adequate company.'

CHAPTER NINE

THE harvest was early that year, so hot was the August weather. The scything gangs had finished cutting and the wheat stood stooked across the shorn landscape. The village boys were enjoying themselves earning a few pence scaring birds off the drying ears of grain with catapult and pea-shooter.

From her vantage-point on the gatehouse roof Henrietta could see the gleaners stooping to their task in the last field to be cut. The village women and children moved slowly between the stooks gathering the fallen ears of wheat in their kilted-up aprons. Beyond them the occasional gleam of silver marked the course of the Bourne, sadly diminished by the lack of rain since late Spring.

Henrietta's back ached in sympathy with the women who had been working since sunrise. But they would feel the labour worthwhile; the right to glean their lord's fields would keep them in flour the whole winter long. Small children played among the stooks at hide-and-seek and, when they thought themselves unwatched, sliding down the polished slopes of stacked wheat. The older children sat in what shade they could find, minding the babes in arms and watching over the water flasks and baskets of bread and cheese.

The sight reminded her why she had climbed the tower and her momentary happiness evaporated. She had come to look for Matthew, who had left her bed that morning before she woke as he had done every morning of their marriage.

Try as she might, nothing she did or said broke through the unnatural pattern of the last month. Matthew was punctiliously polite to her by day, but no more. There was no conversation, no exchange of news, no discussion of the estate. On the occasions when he went up to London on legal business he told her nothing when he returned.

Her refusal to tell him the secret he sensed she kept had put an unsurmountable barrier between them. Henrietta knew she had hurt him deeply, even though he didn't love her. For a proud and private man to open his heart as he had done and then to be rebuffed was something he could not forgive.

Matthew avoided her company, her touch until they were alone together at night. But in the darkness of their chamber he was passionate, fevered almost, like a man who had thirsted all day but who could now drink his fill. He never spoke to her of his feelings, never asked of hers.

When he fell asleep she wept into the pillow, silently so as not to wake him in case he thought her using her wiles to soften him. She could find nothing to alter his coldness. He had demanded her duty and obedience and she gave both in good measure; the household ran with clockwork precision despite the grumbles of servants used to more easygoing ways. Matthew appeared to accept this as the usual way for Winterbourne. In desperation Henrietta forced standards of deportment and behaviour on herself that had Aunt Susan shaking her head in wonderment and no little concern.

When Lawyer Stone came to visit to advance their wedding plans she confided her worries to him. 'She has lost her joy, Lawrence. I cannot understand it; Matthew is so good to her. He seems the perfect husband.'

'There is no such animal,' the old lawyer grunted. 'They are both trying too hard. The first child will put an end to this striving for perfection. Speaking of which,' he lowered his voice, 'any news in that quarter?'

'She has said nothing to me, but I fear not. Still, it is early days yet and she is a healthy young girl.'

'And Matthew fathered a son on his first wife,' Lawyer Stone reminded her. 'Early days, early days. But to return to our own concerns, when will you allow me to fix a day?'

If anyone had thought to ask her opinion Henrietta would not have said it was early days. Matthew came to her every night, yet only yesterday her hopes that she was with child had been dashed. There was no one in whom she could confide her disappointment. Her aunt and Alice would merely tell her to be patient; she could hardly confide the real reason for her unhappiness to them.

The crunch of wooden-soled shoes on the gravel of the carriageway recalled her to the present. She leaned over the parapet to see Alice's broad-brimmed straw hat as the girl turned out of the gate and took the road towards the downland. Mistress Weldon carried a laden basket on one arm, its contents concealed by a white napkin.

'Alice! Wait for me!' Henrietta clattered down the staircase, careless of the dust and cobwebs, her own straw hat swinging by its ribbons from her fingers.

'Mistress!' Alice took in the dust marks on Henrietta's plain green linen gown, and her bare head. 'You should not hurry so in this heat.'

'And you, Mistress Weldon, should not be carrying that heavy basket in your condition.' Alice, nearly seven months with child, looked flushed and tired despite the coolness of the loose robe she was wearing.

'Give me that basket,' Henrietta ordered, wresting it firmly from Alice's grip. 'Where are you taking it?'

'Mistress,' Alice protested, 'it is not fitting for you to carry it.'

'Alice, you are not my maidservant now, nor have you been this six weeks past. You are Mistress Weldon, Robert's wife as well as my friend as you have always been. Could you not now bring yourself to call me Henrietta?'

'Very well, Henrietta,' Alice agreed gravely, very much the dignified matron. Henrietta concealed a smile behind her hand. Alice had taken to the role of steward's wife like a duck to water. As Mr Halsey was unmarried

Alice's social standing was high in the village, second only to the ladies of the big house. The learning and graces she had acquired as Henrietta's companion from childhood stood her in good stead now and the child she was carrying could one day marry into good yeoman stock.

'Where are you taking this basket?' Henrietta lifted the edge of the napkin and the smell of fresh bread and the tang of cheese rose into the dusty air. A stone bottle nestled in one corner.

'To my husband. He is overseeing the new sheep pens in Lammas Mead and told me not to expect him home for dinner. I worry he will not stop to eat.'

Henrietta looked at her flushed face. 'I'm certain he did not expect you to carry food to him—a good mile, and all uphill on a day as hot as this.'

'I do not like to think of him going hungry. And you know what he's like with Sir Matthew—they become so engrossed in their plans and schemes for the estate.'

Henrietta's heart missed a beat. She moved the basket from one arm to another to cover her emotion. 'Oh, my husband is with him, then?' It was Robert he spent all his time with, it was Robert who heard of his plans for the estate, Robert who shared his thoughts and dreams for the future of Winterbourne.

It was only right he trusted his steward to that extent, but it did not salve the hurt; he could not even bring himself to discuss his day with her in the evening.

'Does Robert talk to you much of his doings when the day is ended?' The track had begun to narrow between high hedges and Henrietta brushed away the dancing flies that bothered them.

'Indeed yes. And he is so happy now, it is like the days when your father was alive. There is so much to do, so much to plan. Everyone is so happy with the new master. . .' She sensed Henrietta's restraint and quickly added, 'I did not mean you were not a good mistress to us, but a man is different.'

Henrietta inwardly acknowledged the truth of this,

knowing how whole-heartedly Matthew had thrown his energies into the running of the estate. She had never been brought up to understand the running of the great estate, although she had done her best when the task had been thrust upon her.

No, Matthew with his legal mind and wide experience was far better fitted to the task, although by his own confession he was no countryman. And this way, of course, he didn't have to spend time with his new wife while he made Winterbourne the perfect place for his son to inherit.

The girls reached a gap in the hedge and stopped, seeing their men standing together across the field. They were deep in conversation, their horses' reins looped over a sheep hurdle. Even at that distance they were easily distinguishable, each from the other, Matthew lean and dark, half a head taller than his sandy-haired steward.

'What are they doing?' Henrietta demanded, opening the gate.

'Do you not know? That book on husbandry young Dick brought back from Oxford has new ideas for sheep pens. Robert has spoken of little else these five days past, his mind is so full of the new ways of farming. Last night I told him if he could talk only of sheep he could go do it in the barn!'

There was so much amused affection in her voice that Henrietta was in no doubt Robert could have talked of sheep in his sleep before his fond wife would have complained. She envied their happiness, the easy friendship between them built on so much mutual love and trust, the pride in Robert's eyes when he looked at his wife.

The two men were still unaware of their wives' approach, 'I confess I am surprised Matthew and Robert work so well together,' Henrietta confided. 'I was concerned their beliefs would make a barrier between them, especially since your husband was so badly hurt in battle.'

'I too. I asked him about it and he said Sir Matthew had told him he did not seek to command his conscience, only his loyalty, that when all's said and done each was working toward the same end—a safe future for their children and the country. Robert says you do not need to share a man's political beliefs to respect and like him.' Alice struggled to explain a difficult abstraction. 'Robert thinks he sees Winterbourne as a symbol for the whole country. If we can work together despite our different beliefs, be honest with each other, all the scars will be healed. Sir Matthew fears the extremists of both sides, I think.'

It was the same compromise Matthew had offered Henrietta on their betrothal. But her refusal to be honest with him had shattered that peace, and she could see no way back. Alice's tripping on a tussock broke into her bitter thoughts. 'Take care!' she scolded, putting out her free hand to steady her friend.

The sharp note of worry in her voice carried on the still air. The two men turned together and walked to meet them. Matthew took the heavy basket from Henrietta and dumped it on the ground.

Her broad-brimmed straw hat had fallen off and was hanging down her back by its ribbons. With surprising gentleness he placed it on her head and tightened the ribbons under her chin. 'You should not be walking in this heat with your head uncovered; we have had one man in a fever already today from a surfeit of the sun.'

The concern in his face was genuine, a fleeting glimpse of the tenderness she hungered for so much. The unexpectedness of it made her clumsy. 'It is Alice, not I, who is with child.'

Henrietta could have bitten off her tongue the moment the words were out. She turned from him and walked over to the pile of wattle hurdles, away from Robert who was settling his wife in the shade of an oak tree and pouring her a cooling drink.

The next thing she knew Matthew's hands were on

her shoulders, compelling her to face him. 'You are disappointed again?'

'We are both disappointed, husband. It seems our disappointment is the only thing on which we agree.'

'There is much on which we agree.' He looked into her hurt, angry eyes and seemed to reach a decision. 'This coldness between us cannot continue, wife. . .'

'It is not I who am cold,' she began bitterly.

'No, it is I. I admit it. Perhaps I was asking too much of you, punishing you for keeping something of yourself back from me.'

'A drink, Sir Matthew? Mistress?' Robert held out a horn cup.

Henrietta accepted quickly, grateful for the interruption. She was so used to Matthew's coldness, his disregard of her, that the warmth in his eyes, his voice threw her into complete confusion. She wanted a reconciliation more than anything, the sort of marriage Alice and Robert had. . .Yet he had still not spoken of love.

The four sat in the shade sharing the simple meal. Henrietta had no appetite but she forced herself to eat a little bread and cheese and swallow some ale. Robert and Alice sat close, laughing softly together, unconscious of the unsettled mood of the other couple.

'Your son kicks, Robert — feel,' Alice took his broad, freckled hand, placing it gently on her swollen stomach.

'It might not be a son.' Robert's face creased in a delighted grin at the child's vigour. 'It might be a daughter as beautiful as her mother.'

Henrietta stood up abruptly, pierced by a sudden jealousy of Alice's pregnancy. 'I must get back to the house.' Perhaps Matthew would come with her. Yet she could not find the words to ask him.

'I too.' Robert jumped to his feet. 'I must not dally here, my love. Now walk back slowly. Leave the basket — Sim can fetch it later.'

'Put Alice up on your horse,' Matthew suggested. 'You can lead her down; it's a long walk back.'

'Thank you both,' Alice said briskly, 'but I am quite

recovered. You have much to do, Robert, and I would
not hinder you. Lady Sheridan and I will walk back to
the house together.'

Henrietta smiled reassurance at Robert. 'I will make
sure she walks slowly; she will come to no harm.'

Robert took some convincing, but finally he and
Matthew rode off to oversee the watering of the cattle in
the few pools left now the Bourne was scarcely flowing.

The two girls walked in silence for a while down the
chalky track. The tall grass was dusty and dry but a few
flowers remained for the chalk blue butterflies that
danced like jewels in the air before them.

'Have you spoken with the wisewoman?' Alice asked,
out of nowhere.

'The wisewoman? Why would I wish to talk to Mistress Perrott?' Henrietta queried cautiously.

'Because you are worrying that you are not yet with
child.' How well Alice knew her.

'My aunt says it is early days yet.' Henrietta tried to
convince both Alice and herself.

'But then, Mistress Clifford never fell for a child.'

'I am sure she knows what she is talking about, Alice,'
Henrietta chided. She did not want Alice to snatch away
the comfort her aunt's words gave her.

'The master does. . . I mean you do—er——' Alice
shuffled her feet in the dust, suddenly at a loss for words.

'Yes, Alice. I have nothing to complain of in his
attention to me.'

That embarrassing question out of the way, Alice
turned back to her original advice with more confidence.
'I doubt anything is seriously amiss. Perhaps Mistress
Perrott could suggest some herbal draught for you.'

'I hope she suggests nothing for my husband, I doubt
he would take it. He has little trust in our country
potions.'

'He has no need of any,' Alice remarked thoughtlessly.
'After all, he has fathered a son. God rest his soul.'

So it is all my fault, Henrietta thought bleakly. Even

her beloved friend thought so. Was that another reason Matthew had been so cold?

'So you believe I am worrying unduly?' Henrietta asked eagerly.

Widow Perrott touched her hand reassuringly with her own work-worn fingers. 'Yes, mistress. You are young, healthy and beautiful. You have a lusty bridegroom.' She ignored Henrietta's telling blush. 'You have not been married long; do not be impatient and nature will take its course. Worry less; anxiety will hinder conception.'

'That is well to say, but difficult advice to follow.' None the less she was relieved by the wisewoman's reassurance.

'You have lost your rosy glow, child.' The older woman peered at her closely in the dim light filtering through the oiled parchment covering the few windows. 'Do you sleep well in this heat? No? Well, I have a remedy for that at least.'

Henrietta sat back on the long settle by the hearth and watched Widow Perrott sort through the array of wooden boxes on a long shelf, muttering to herself as she did so. 'Grated valerian root. . .not too much of that, for it is a powerful sleeping draught; dried mint, camomile. Now where did I put that lavender?' She found a bundle and rubbed a handful of the flowers off the stems on to the other herbs on a linen cloth. She put the tied bundle on Henrietta's lap. 'Now infuse this mixture with boiling water for the usual time and take a small glassful thrice daily.'

'Does it taste bitter?' Henrietta hated taking medicines.

'The taste is not a pleasant one, but you could add honey. It will soothe your nerves, help you to sleep. Now tell me, how is Mistress Weldon going along?'

'Well, but tired in this heat. And she tries to do too much, despite all her husband and I advise.'

'That will be a large child.' The wisewoman shook her

head, 'You must persuade her to rest more, and I will walk up tomorrow to see her. Meanwhile, do not concern yourself for her; I will be with her in November when she comes to term. Here, you could take her this.' She lifted a small phial from the shelf. 'It will strengthen both her and the child.'

'What is it?' Henrietta regarded the oily yellow liquid doubtfully.

'Raspberry leaves, yarrow and lady's mantle. She knows to add honey for taste.'

'I must go; the household will be wondering where I have got to.' Henrietta rose, stooping under the low lintel, and pressed a coin into the woman's palm.

'And your fond husband too, I'll be bound.'

Henrietta smiled uncertainly. 'Yes, he too, of course.' If only he meant what he'd said that afternoon; if only they could regain the companionship they had begun to build. . .

She latched the wicket gate in the fence around Mistress Perrott's small, crowded garden to keep out any wandering livestock and stepped out on to the roadway to Winterbourne. Seconds later she collided with a man; the figure was immediately familiar.

'Your pardon, mistress.' Nathaniel Cobham bowed stiffly and stepped back from her.

'Oh! Cobham. . .it was my fault; I was not attending to where I was going.' Henrietta forced herself to speak amiably, determined not to let the clerk see her distaste for him.

'You mind was on other matters, no doubt.' His eyes flicked to the low thatched cottage behind them, then to the bundle in her hand. 'May I carry that for you?'

He put out a hand and Henrietta drew back instinctively, 'Thank you, you are kind, but it is not heavy—a few herbs only to replenish our stillroom.' She was doing it again, falling into the trap of justifying her actions to this man who was nothing to her, however loyal a servant to Matthew. 'You are a long way from the house, Master Cobham.'

If she had hoped to disconcert him she had failed. 'Yes,' he agreed calmly.

'Your master has sent you on some errand perhaps?' she persisted with a touch of hauteur.

'Sir Matthew gives me wide discretion in the exercise of my duties.' He stood, apparently respectful, but allowing for the first time his dislike of her to colour his tone.

'And just what might those duties be, Cobham?' she asked, nettled.

'I do not discuss my master's business with anyone, madam.' He ignored the angry spots of colour staining Henrietta's cheeks. 'Allow me to escort you home, Lady Sheridan.' He made it quite clear he considered her part of his business and not for the first time Henrietta was convinced he was spying on her.

Stiff-backed, Henrietta stalked up the road. 'Very well. I believe we are both going in the same direction.'

'Mistress Perrott has some small reputation for her healing. . .powers.' He managed to make the suggestion sound sinister.

'Most countrywomen have a familiarity with herbal remedies,' Henrietta said as casually as she could. 'We are far from the nearest surgeon — not that the common people could afford his ministrations. We are in the country here — apothecaries are not two a penny as they are in London Town.'

'It is a dangerous power none the less.'

'There are many families in the village who have cause to be grateful for Mistress Perrott's skills,' Henrietta reproved him sharply. 'She has delivered most of the babies hereabouts, myself and my brothers included.'

'So she is a midwife too.' He turned his sharp black eyes on her face for the first time since they had begun to walk. 'Women have cause to thank the midwife for more than safe deliveries — children are not always welcome.'

Henrietta knew what he was implying. 'How dare you suggest such a thing? She is the God-fearing widow of an honest tenant of ours, a respected member of our congregation. If her sons were to hear your words you would live to regret them.'

'It is not her sons I would fear, but her arts, madam,' the clerk said softly.

Suddenly Henrietta was afraid, her anger banished. He had not spoken the word 'witch' but it was on the tip of his tongue. His religious views were extreme enough for him to make the accusation, and once made it was a charge rarely disproved.

That witches existed she had not doubt, along with other instruments of the Devil. Did not Mr Halsey, and before him Mr Hale, warn against them from the pulpit? But they did not lurk in Winterbourne or its village.

Yet Henrietta knew enough of human nature and its envies and spites to know that if the cry of, 'Witch!' was raised someone would take it up, remember a hard word or black look or a cow sickening inexplicably.

She walked on in shaken silence until they reached the front door. Cobham bowed, wished her farewell, and took himself off round the side of the house.

'Good riddance!' Henrietta shivered, trying to convince herself that her fears were fanciful. Matthew was master here; he would permit no unjust witch hunt.

Even as she thought of it her husband came out of the front door and stood on the steps looking down at her. 'You are troubled? Do you wish to speak of it?'

The doubt in his voice stung her, but she nodded eagerly. 'Yes, Matthew, if you please. I am worried, but what I have to say may anger you.'

His eyebrows lifted in surprise, but he came down the steps and offered her his arm. 'Let us walk in the herb garden.'

In the herb-scented peace of the garden she sat on a bench and handed him the bundle she carried. 'Your clerk believes these are potions obtained from a witch.'

If she had hoped to gain his attention she had succeeded. Matthew flicked open the cloth and sniffed the contents. 'But these are simple herbs. A sleeping remedy if I am not mistaken.'

'Perhaps you will tell Cobham that before he has Mistress Perrott, that good woman, burnt as a witch!'

'Nonsense! He would never do such a thing.'

'Matthew, the man is extreme. He dislikes and distrusts me—indeed I do believe all women are damned in his eyes. He truly believes Mistress Perrott to be an agent of the Devil. You must silence him, counsel him in moderation.'

'The old fool.' Matthew sounded both weary and angry. 'I am so used to him I have failed to see how extreme he has grown. I knew he did not like you as he did Sarah, but he had known her as a child. But believe me, Henrietta, I would not tolerate him showing you disrespect. I will deal with the man. There will be no more talk of witchcraft at Winterbourne.'

'Send him away, Matthew,' she pleaded. 'He has a malign influence on the household.'

'Your dislike of him leads you to exaggerate. I will speak with him, but not harshly. He served my father well, and has been a good servant to me. His life has seen much tragedy; I will not turn him out because he has grown crabbed with age.'

'Thank you.' With that she must be content. At least Matthew was speaking to her now.

He took her hands and pulled her to her feet. 'Come, Lady Sheridan, show me round your domain; the gardens are looking very well despite this dry weather.'

The fine, hot weather persisted into the opening days of September. Consulting the farm log, Robert predicted a record harvest and the village looked forward to a fine autumn and a comfortable winter.

Henrietta set every maidservant who could be spared to harvesting the hedgerows for blackberries, elderberries, sloes and hips. The stillroom was alive with activity as cordials were distilled, jellies and syrups boiled and strained. Work in the cool room was envied by the

kitchen staff who still had to boil in front of the spits
and fires and by the girls boiling coppers in the laundry.

The tenth of September saw the last corn gathered in.
Henrietta, dressed in her oldest gown, went out to the
fields to help with the final wagonloads, part of
Winterbourne's long harvest home tradition.

She waited for Alice, concerned to see that her friend
sat quietly in the shade when they reached the field and
did not tire herself walking among the chattering, laughing harvesters. Matthew and Robert had gone on ahead;
she glimpsed her husband's tall figure, jerkin discarded,
sleeves rolled up as he worked with the others to toss the
heavy stooks on to the wagons. Her heart contracted
with love for him, and hope. Things were still not
perfect, her secret still hung unspoken between them,
yet they had attained some measure of peace and trust.

The older boys were employed on top of the loads,
spreading the corn evenly, treading it down. As the
wagon trundled slowly down the shorn field from stook
to stook a lad occasionally tumbled to the ground to be
hoisted back up again, bruised but laughing.

The sun was high overhead when Robert called them
in for dinner. The womenfolk had spread cloths on the
ground beneath the shade of the high hawthorn hedge
and set out bread, cheese, onions and ale. Baskets of red
apples waited for anyone with room to spare after they
had eaten their fill of the coarse bread.

Some of the women sat a little apart, nursing the
babies the little girls had been minding while their
mothers worked. Henrietta went over to admire the new
son of one of the grooms, sucking lustily at the breast. A
wave of longing hit her at the sight of the small, downy
head nestled against his mother and she reached down to
stroke his cheek before returning to where Alice was
presiding over their open-air meal.

Henrietta was aware of Matthew's eyes keen on her
face as she took her place on the rug beside him,
accepting a cup of ale from him with a murmur of
thanks.

'How does it go, Robert?' He leaned on one elbow, chewing the end of a grass stem. 'I confess this is the first time I have ever been harvesting—will it all be in today?'

'Easily, sir, easily.' Robert swallowed a draught of cider, then shaded his eyes, assessing what remained to be done. 'Two more loads should do it, and we'll have most of that stacked in the rickyards by tomorrow's end.' Alice handed him a thick slice of bread, liberally spread with butter. 'Thank you, my love.'

'I hope you have been marking my prowess with the pitchfork, Henrietta.' She looked up, warmed by the friendly, bantering note in his voice. Matthew was grinning broadly, his teeth very white against his tanned face. Country life suited him; the already muscular body was honed by long hours in the saddle or walking about the estate.

She smiled back hesitantly, her heart missing a beat with love for him. Was he falling in love with her? Or was it simply that he was content and at ease with the whole world, his troublesome wife included?

Emboldened, she took his hands in hers, turning them palm up. 'You were doing very well for a beginner, husband, but I see signs of blisters coming; you are not used to this manual labour. A linseed poultice will stop the blisters swelling.'

'I would rather have the blisters than smell like a horse with saddle-sores!' he teased.

Robert was on his feet again. 'Well, sir, shall I set them on again?'

'Sit down, Master Weldon; it is too hot for speed and you said yourself we have time in hand. Let them rest for an hour.'

'Thank you, sir; the people will be glad of it. They are good workers and it does no harm to acknowledge it now and again.' He strode round the field, waving each group back to take their ease.

'Come walk with me, Henrietta.' Matthew stood and

pulled her to her feet, taking her hand and leading her away from the cornfield into the neighbouring hayfield.

'Matthew, you must not walk on the hay — they will be cutting in a week! Will we ever make a countryman of you? Where are we going?'

'Need we be going anywhere? I want to walk with my wife a while.' His voice was warm and his hand now slid round her waist, drawing her close to his side as he made his way to the banks of the River Bourne.

'You are in great beauty, Henrietta.' They were the words he had used at their betrothal and the colour flooded her face, yet she was still uncertain of his feelings for her. Was it just desire, or the beginnings of something more?

'In this gown?' She gestured shakily at her old linen skirts, stained here and there with fruit juice from bottling.

'You do not need silks and lace to be beautiful. Today you look like a simple village maiden — and very desirable.' He drew her down the shelving bank, out of sight of the cornfield. 'May I claim a kiss?'

'Do you ask that of all the village maidens, sir?' Henrietta asked with mock coyness.

'Only the ones with big brown eyes and straw in their hair.' He picked a piece out of the simple snood into which she had bundled her hair. 'Oh, yes, and they must answer to the name of Henrietta, of course. No one else will do.'

Henrietta found she was leaning against the rough trunk of a poplar. Still uncertain, she glanced up through her lashes at her husband whose face was now so close to her own, his lips seeking hers. 'Very well, sir,' she managed to whisper. 'Take your kiss, and anything else you desire.'

The soft turf under her, the sunlight filtering through the whispering leaves of the poplar on to her closed lids and the weight of Matthew's arm resting across her waist were all she was aware of, all she wanted to know.

She sighed, snuggling contentedly against his bare shoulder, wondering how long he would sleep, what he would say when he woke. There had been something new in his lovemaking, something that went beyond tenderness.

'Sir Matthew! Sir Matthew!' Sim's reedy treble reached them from across the hayfield. 'Where are you, master?'

'Damnation!' Matthew sat up, dragging his shirt over his head. 'What is it now?'

Sim continued to call, but more urgently now. With another curse Matthew got to his feet, tucking his shirt into his breeches and retrieving his jerkin. 'I'm coming!' He raised his voice to a shout, then softened it again. 'I had better go and see what the trouble is. Can you make your own way back, my love?'

Henrietta nodded dumbly, the impact of the endearment hitting her only as she watched him break into a run up the bank and out of her sight.

My love! He had never used those words to her before. Was that the explanation of his sudden tenderness? Could he have discovered that he loved her and therefore would forgive whatever she might have done?

Hastily she scrambled to her feet, filled with delight as she smoothed down her rumpled skirts and bundled her hair back into its confining snood.

In a daze of happiness she wandered back through the hayfield, swinging her sunhat, humming a little tune under her breath. There was no sign of him when she reached the cornfield.

'Where did Matthew go?' she asked Alice, plumping down beside her.

'Back to the house—a messenger had come for him.' Alice looked at her and clicked her tongue chidingly. 'Turn round, Henrietta; let me relace your bodice—it is coming loose.'

'Thank you Alice,' Henrietta responded with a sly smile. It was all very well for Mistress Weldon to look prim, but she had a good idea where Alice's courting had been done.

How tiresome that business from London had intruded on this idyll. The workers were laughing and happy despite the hot sun and their labours, a nursery of babies were asleep under the shady trees while the little girls played cat's-cradle and rhyming games and the boys chased harvest mice among the few remaining stooks.

At last all was gathered in except one lonely stook in the middle of the field. 'Mistress! This one's for you,' they called and, smiling, Henrietta kilted up her skirts and took the proffered pitchfork. Old Tom gave her a hand and the last sheaf was safe delivered onto the wagon.

Strong arms lifted her up on to the tail-gate and voices called for silence. 'You have all done well. Robert tells me this is the best harvest Winterbourne has ever known. You have worked hard this summer, and now it is time to play: harvest supper awaits us in the yard as soon as this load is home.'

There were loud cheers and the cart creaked off to the accompaniment of robust singing. Henrietta sat down on the tail-gate with an undignified thump as Alice was handed up beside her. The labourers straggled along in front and behind and one of the older boys tapped Henrietta on the shoulder. 'I've made you a corn dolly, mistress. Didn't think you needed one, Alice,' he added cheekily.

'You mind your manners, Cousin Harry. It's Mistress Weldon to you.' But she was grinning all the same. 'Pin it to your dress,' she whispered to Henrietta. 'I know it's heathen superstition, but they do say it helps with the getting of a child.'

Henrietta did as she was bidden. She was feeling so happy and contented that she was quite willing to believe in Alice's white magic.

The ricks cast long shadows as the happy procession wound its way into the yard. The women left their menfolk and walked off chattering towards the house to help the kitchen servants set out the harvest supper of cold meats and cool ale — the best meal of the whole year.

The heavy horses were unhitched and led off. The last wagon would be left loaded until the morrow when the stacks would be finished and thatched. Willing hands lifted Henrietta and Alice down, all formality forgotten as she mingled with her people in her patched old gown.

'I must see where the master is,' she said laughingly to Alice. 'Make him put aside whatever tiresome legal business has been brought to him from London and join our celebration. He must not miss his first harvest supper at Winterbourne.'

The quickest way back to the house was through the stableyard. As she stepped under the archway she saw to her amazement the big grey horse, Matthew in the saddle, his cloak strapped behind. He was dressed for travel, booted and spurred with his long sword hanging by his side.

'Matthew!' Henrietta started forward as a groom carrying saddle-bags and leading a second horse emerged from the stables. 'Where are you going? What is wrong?'

CHAPTER TEN

'MATTHEW!' He was looking down at her, his face darkened with emotion. Henrietta recognised anger there, although not with her, she sensed. Behind it was something more: anxiety, apprehension, It was as if he had glimpsed something terrible approaching and was steeling himself to meet it face to face.

She took hold of his stirrup leather in both hands as though her gesture could hold him there until she had her answer. 'Matthew, you must tell me what is wrong. I beseech you. . .'

Matthew's face was blurred in the twilight. His gloved hand reaching as if to caress her cheek turned instead and unclasped her fingers from the leathers.

'I must not linger, Henrietta; I have a long and hard ride tonight if I am to reach London by tomorrow morning.'

Her hands were still caught in his, but at the mention of London her fingers jerked convulsively. 'London?' Her bewilderment deepened. 'Why must you go to London now? It grows dark. . .our people are expecting us at the harvest supper. . .'

Matthew hesitated, and for a moment she thought the yearning in her voice had swayed him. His horse shifted restlessly between his knees, recalling him to his duty. 'Goodbye, wife. I have no time for explanations — Nathaniel will tell you what is afoot.'

The big grey snorted and plunged forward as Matthew spurred him under the archway. The groom, taken by surprise, ran forward and scrambled into the saddle, kicking his own mount after his master, the pack-horse cantering behind.

The beat of hoofs on the hard track carried for a long time on the still air. Henrietta stood in the dim light of

181

the yard staring blankly at the empty archway, her thoughts in turmoil. What could have occurred to send her husband from Winterbourne to London with such urgency? And what was the cause of his scarcely veiled apprehension?

A patch of shadow detached itself from a corner of the stable yard and Nathaniel Cobham barred her way. 'You are in some haste, mistress.'

His sudden appearance made her heart beat wildly with shock. 'Cobham! There you are! What are you doing lurking in the shadows?' Henrietta swept her skirts away from the crabbed figure, making no effort to disguise her distaste.

'But I thought you would desire to know where the master had gone.' His very servility was a calculated insult.

'He is gone to London. Why do you imagine that I, his wife, would not know that? If you have been spying in that corner for the past few minutes you would have heard him tell me.' Perversely she could not bring herself to ask this man she disliked for the information she so desperately wanted.

'I do not spy, mistress,' the clerk responded calmly. 'I attend to my master's business, and have done so since he was a boy. I have his full confidence.'

And I do not, Henrietta fumed inwardly, recognising the gibe.

'Now, would you like to know his purpose in London?'

He was deliberately taunting her, tormenting her with his superior knowledge, but Henrietta's need to know, her love for Matthew, was greater than her pride.

'Thank you, Cobham,' she said with an outward show of civility. She could not afford to let him see his power over her. 'I should like to know the details. My husband was in some haste, as you saw.'

Now he had the upper hand Cobham allowed himself a thin, superior smile. 'He has gone to fight.'

'Fight? Fight whom? Cobham, stop tormenting me and tell me all!'

Any other man would have been moved by the distress in her voice and on her face; by the tumultuous rise and fall of her breast under the patched and worn gown; by her hands clenched in the full skirts. But not Cobham, a man who believed firmly that all women were the agents of the Devil and a barely necessary evil.

This one, this Royalist strumpet with her low-cut gowns and her wanton curls, she was worse than most. For months she had distracted his master from business, defied his authority, prated of her opinions. She was disobedient, wilful, hoydenish and needed watching closely until his master returned — God willing — safe.

'Do you tell me you have not heard that the country is at arms once more? Did you not know that traitor Charles Stuart has brought down the Scottish barbarians on our heads?'

'War! We are at war again? How can this be. . .? I had heard rumours, of course, but there have been rumours abounding these last two years; we have learned to discount them.'

'This is no rumour. A great battle was fought at Worcester seven days past; the news has just reached us from London.'

Cobham was peering at her face in the gathering twilight like a cat watching a mousehole.

'What happened? Who are the victors?' It was incredible; she could hardly comprehend it. The King returned, with Scottish troops, it seemed, and enough force to engage the Parliamentary army in battle. 'I asked you, man, who has won this battle?'

Cobham smiled again, this time with a triumph that gave her the answer. 'The forces of evil were overcome and cast down! The Scottish hordes he had brought down like wolves on the innocent flocks of the righteous were slaughtered by the strong arm of God and General Cromwell.' He could have been preaching to a Puritan congregation, his voice rising in exhortation.

'The King?' Henrietta demanded, ignoring the feeling of faintness that gripped her.

'The traitor Charles Stuart fled the field of battle,' Cobham's lip curled in disgust. 'His capture cannot be far off, then he will be dealt with as was his father. So perish all traitors!'

So, the King was alive, had escaped. The fighting was over. Relief flooded through her; the network of loyal subjects would surely see Charles got safe out of the country. And Matthew, her Matthew, would not have to fight. Why then had he left so precipitately?

'Why has my husband left Winterbourne if the fighting is over?' she demanded. 'What have you not told me?'

'Over? I did not say it was over. The battle of Worcester is won, but armed insurgents roam the countryside; their generals, if determined, could rally them again. God knows when we shall see peace in this benighted land once more.' He shook his grizzled head sorrowfully, the evangelical fervour gone from his voice, an elderly and almost pathetic figure.

'But Matthew. . .why does he go to London?'

'To be where he is most needed. Parliament requires men such as he at this time of peril.'

'Then he will fight?' Henrietta persisted, her head suddenly swimming. The yard was swirling, filled with the noise and clamour of battle, horses screaming, the clash of steel, the smell of smoke and blood. . .

'Mistress, Henrietta. . . Oh, Robert, I do not think she can hear me. She must have struck her head as she fell.'

The smell of smoke was still rank in Henrietta's nostrils. She jerked her head away, an agonising pain lanced through her temples and she was aware of smooth, cool linen under her cheek.

'The Lord be praised!' Alice said tearfully. 'She is alive. Robert — pass me more burning feathers to rouse her.'

'No. . .' Henrietta struggled to open her eyes. The

room was blurred, as were the pale faces hovering above her. She recognised Alice and Robert; the rest were indistinct. 'Alice? Where am I? Is the battle over?'

'Battle, mistress?' Alice turned to Robert, tears coursing down her cheeks. 'She has addled her brain; we must send for a surgeon — send Dick to Aylesbury.'

'She is just confused,' Robert said soothingly, taking Henrietta's hands in his. 'It is all right; the battle is long over and Matthew gone but an hour. He is quite safe. Now, lie still and sip this.' He took a cup from his wife's hand and held it to Henrietta's lips, his arm round her shoulders to support her.

Obediently Henrietta sipped the fragrant, mint-smelling cordial. The room was coming back into focus and she could discern the anxiety on the face of the servants gathered round the bed. Robert gently laid her back on the pillows, but even so she cried out in pain as her head touched the linen.

'Let me see her!' Mistress Clifford pushed aside the group around the bed in her haste. Henrietta realised she must be at the Home Farm, for her aunt was panting with the speed with which she had come to her side. 'Beloved child, my sweet Henrietta. . .why, you are as pale as the pillow!' Gently she probed the thick hair to find the lump where Henrietta's head had struck the cobbles of the yard.

'What happened?' Henrietta managed to ask, wincing even under the delicate touch. 'I can remember Cobham telling me of the battle, then all else is blank. How did I get here?'

'A nasty bump but nothing broken, which is more than I can say for that insensitive clod Cobham when I get my hands on him!' Mistress Clifford waved the gawping servants from the room. 'Out, back to your harvest supper. You too, Robert; tell the people their mistress is in no danger. She needs peace and quiet. Well, go on!' Meekly Robert followed the servants out, leaving his wife and Letty to assist Aunt Susan.

'Letty, soak a pad in witch-hazel for her head. Alice,

find a nightgown. She will sleep here; I do not want her moved until I am sure there is no danger of brain fever.'

'Aunt, I cannot stay; it is Alice's bedchamber.' Henrietta could see the room clearly now in the candle-light, the blurring of her vision and the confusion in her mind both gone.

'Letty and I will make up the spare bedchamber for Robert and myself.' Alice was firm. 'Your aunt is right; to move too soon would be foolish. Sir Matthew would never forgive us if anything were to happen to you while he is away.'

The apple-pickers were singing as they moved among the laden trees in the orchard. From where she sat in the herb garden, propped up in a pile of goose-feather pillows, Henrietta could hear them clearly, follow their progress as they gathered in the store of eating apples.

It was her favourite harvest. The work was less back-breaking than bringing in the corn so all the families of the estate joined in — the men moving ladders and scaling them to reach the topmost fruit, the women filling the baskets with care so as not to bruise the crop. Children scavenged the windfalls, eating as many as they picked, tossing the damaged fruit into barrels for pressing later.

Henrietta sighed and laid her book of poetry aside. Reading was making her head ache again. Since she had been brought up by cart from the Home Farm after her fall two days since she had been confined to bed by her aunt but this morning had finally cajoled her way outside.

Even so, she was not allowed to dress. Instead she wore a loose robe over her nightgown, a blanket tucked round her legs as she sat in a deep armed chair, her feet on a stool. Every half-hour her aunt descended with two male servants to carry her chair further into the shade in case sunlight burned her skin into an unladylike tan or fevered her brain.

The scent of warm brick and stone mingled with the aromatic pungency of herbs and flowers. Bees droned, and, unalarmed by Henrietta's still presence, a thrush was beating a snail against the corner of a stone.

Occasionally she caught a glimpse of the apple-pickers through the open gate, or heard the creak of wagon wheels as the driver moved it to keep abreast of the pickers and their laden baskets. Part of her wished she was in the orchard with them, sitting under a tree, munching the crisp sweetness of an early apple. But her mind felt detached, abstracted from the familiar ritual of the apple harvest, the day-to-day affairs of Winterbourne.

Cobham's news of the battle at Worcester had crystallised the nagging doubts that had been at the back of her mind since Matthew had described to her the realities of war. The King had the right to rule; of that she had no doubt — it was his God-given duty. But did that mean he was always right in his actions? And if men like Matthew, honest, pragmatic, intelligent men, believed the rule of Parliament represented the rule of law, must not there be some truth in it?

If only her head would not ache so, perhaps she could find out what in truth she *did* believe. Henrietta closed her eyes and rubbed her fingers up and down the centre of her brow as though it would help clear the confusion.

Gravel crunched under booted feet — no doubt one of the grooms sent to move her chair again. She opened her eyes, and her mouth, then froze. Matthew stood looking down at her, his face tired, his clothes covered with dust from the road.

With a cry she started from the chair, forgetting the hampering blanket around her legs. Matthew caught her as she stumbled, held her for a long moment without speaking, then pressed her gently back into the chair.

'Matthew! You are unhurt?' Henrietta pulled the rug right around her trembling body.

'As you see. But the same cannot be said for you.' He dropped to the stool at her feet, his eyes on her trembling fingers. 'Your aunt has told me what happened — that you slipped on the cobbles of the stable-yard and hit your head. She assures me you are all but recovered, but looking at you I am not so convinced you should be out of bed. You have dark purple smudges under your eyes. Here, let me look at your head; perhaps we should call the surgeon after all.'

He went down on one knee beside her chair, tipping her gently against his shoulder while his fingers explored the now diminished lump on the back of her skull.

Henrietta closed her eyes, overwhelmed to be in his arms again. He smelled of warm leather; beneath her ear his heart beat strongly, his fingers were warm and sure in her hair. The gentle examination subtly became a caress as he held her. 'What made you fall?' he asked her softly.

'Cobham.' The hateful name broke the moment as nothing else could have. Henrietta pulled back from his embrace to look him in the face.

'Cobham? What are you saying?'

'I did not fall. I fainted. Your clerk took great pleasure in telling me how you had ridden out to war, that the countryside was up in arms again. In my mind I could see you wounded, dying on the battlefield in the mire and the blood. . .' Her voice broke and she could not go on, turning her head away on the pillow to hide her sudden tears.

'Damn the man!' Matthew exploded, taking two hasty strides down the path as if to seek out his clerk and chastise him. 'He knew I had not gone to fight! He sees everything in black and white. His religious views allow him to see no shades of grey. I am sure he did not mean to frighten you, Henrietta.' Despite her tears Henrietta snorted in disbelief. 'His loyalty to me makes him extreme on my behalf. And he is an old man; he served my father before me.'

'In other words you seek to excuse him?'

'No, but he was not solely to blame. I should not have left you as I did.' He raked his hand through dark hair which badly needed trimming. 'I shall be open with you, Henrietta. When the messenger came and told me of the battle I was angry. Angry that it was all starting again just when the country was recovering. And I was here, away from the centre of things, relying on rumour. Your King and all of those misguided enough to support him brought this down upon us.'

'He is your King too!' Henrietta protested. 'Under God. . .'

'Under God and the law, wife. His father would be King still had he acknowledged this truth and been willing to rule in peace.'

'But perhaps *this* King would be willing to accept the rule of law?' Henrietta groped through her own muddled thoughts. 'But he was forced from his country before he could show how he would rule. Parliament will not talk with him; what other choice was before him but to fight?'

'And the sixteen thousand men and boys he dragged with him on to the field at Worcester? What of the widows and fatherless children this day—do they have a choice of anything but grief and penury?'

'In that he was wrong!' He had wrung the admission from her. 'Yet I cannot understand what other course he could have taken.'

'He could have waited in exile until the time was right for negotiation.' Matthew regarded her thoughtfully. 'This nation cannot be leaderless for long; we need our figure-head. But not one who unleashes foreign troops on his people. He will not be easily forgiven for bringing the Scots with him, even by his closest supporters.'

'Your quarrel is with the King, not with me. You knew the battle was over; there was nothing you could do. So why leave in such haste for London? And I felt you were angry with me when you left. Why?' she asked softly. 'In the hayfield you were. . .not angry with me.' And you called me 'love', she thought, but dared not voice it aloud.

'I blamed all supporters of the King—and you were there. And I was frightened for you, for our people, for the future of Winterbourne.' He smiled at her ruefully. 'It was like my mother, the times I was a small boy and came home long after dark. She would be frantic with worry, but when she saw me she would box my ears and shout at me in her relief. I never understood how the one could lead from the other — I do now.'

She held out her arms to him and he came into them, holding her right against his chest, his mouth in her hair. There was nothing said between them; nothing needed to be voiced.

Eventually Matthew disentangled himself. 'Much as I would like to stay here in your arms. . .'

'You are right.' Henrietta was remorseful. 'You must be tired and hungry. You need a bath and a shave; has your man seen to that? I am sure Aunt Susan will have ordered food for you — and then you should rest——'

'Henrietta.' He gently interrupted the flow. 'I keep trying to tell you — we have a guest.'

'A guest!' Henrietta's face fell.

'That is not very hospitable, wife,' Matthew teased. 'And in any case I was not expecting you to entertain him in your nightgown.'

'But I wanted. . . I thought we would be alone.' Henrietta blushed.

'Much as I am flattered by your desire to talk to me alone——' Matthew's teasing tone deepened her blush '—you should be in bed resting. I can entertain our guest myself, with your aunt's able assistance. She has already shown him to his chamber.'

'Who is he?' Henrietta asked, then shivered as the sun went behind a cloud, casting the garden into shade.

'Never mind that now; you should be in bed. What can your aunt be thinking of?' he demanded in uncharacteristic exasperation. Before Henrietta could protest he swept her into his arms, rugs trailing.

As he carried her up the wide staircase Henrietta gave up all semblance of protest, snuggling against the soft leather of his jerkin, breathing in the scent of him. To be held close in the arms of the man she loved, the man she believed was near to loving her, was overwhelming.

In their chamber he laid her gently on the bed,

brushing her hair back from her forehead. 'Now rest, Henrietta.'

He straightened up, but stopped as she caught at his hand. 'You'll go again; I know you will.'

'I am home and here I intend to stay. I shall not leave you again, sweetheart.' Matthew smiled at her. 'And if you continue looking at me like that, wife, I shall be guilty of seriously neglecting our guest.'

'Neglect him for a few minutes, Matthew.' She held out her arms to him, her hair loose against the heaped pillows, her eyes warm and beseeching.

Matthew needed no further prompting. He bent and took her in his arms, his mouth warm and possessive on hers. Henrietta twined her arms around him, holding him even closer, pressing her body against him in a silent incitement to him to stay, shed his clothes, join her in the big bed.

She deepened the kiss, putting all her yearning, all her fears for him into the embrace. Her fingers insinuated themselves into the curling crispness of the hair at his nape and she felt him stiffen and draw back as her fingertips brushed the skin there.

Matthew's eyes were dark pools of desire, and his voice when he spoke husky. 'My wanton wife. . . I am saddle-sore and weary, and you are unwell. Rest now, regain your strength — and I will take myself well away from your lures!'

Warm, happy, reassured, Henrietta snuggled down under the goose-feather guilt and drifted off to sleep. When she woke Letty was moving quietly round the room, drawing the hangings and making up the fire.

'What time is it?' She sat up, rubbing her eyes.

'Nearly suppertime, mistress.' Letty plumped up the pillows behind Henrietta's shoulders. 'What will I bring you? A bowl of broth and some chicken?'

'No, I shall get up; fetch me warm water and the grey gown.'

As she was being laced into her petticoats she asked

idly, 'Have you seen our guest, Letty? I quite forgot to ask Sir Matthew his name.'

Surprisingly Letty giggled. 'Oh, we've all had a look at him, mistress!'

'What can you mean, girl?' Henrietta demanded, bending to tie a garter above her knee.

'Why, in the kitchen they reckon he's the finest looking gentleman ever to come into these parts. So tall, and blond and well dressed. . .'

'Really, Letty!' Henrietta scolded, intrigued despite herself. 'However, since we have such a fine, well-dressed guest, perhaps I too should have a little finery. Bring the amethyst silk and my silver lace instead.'

Half an hour later she paused in the shadow of the hall screens watching the two men as they stood before the fire, wine glasses in hand. Her kid slippers had made no sound on the boards and she was able to watch unobserved as they talked while the servants finished laying the table.

Letty was right; the stranger was a startlingly good-looking young man, almost as tall as Matthew. Thick blond hair curled on his wide lace collar and the firelight danced on his burnished boots. Yet still he looked insubstantial against Matthew's lean, confident figure.

She stepped into the light and both men looked up. Matthew started forward, but the stranger reached her side first, taking her hand in elegantly beringed fingers. He swept a low bow then looked into her face in open admiration.

'Madam! Your most devoted servant! Sheridan, now I see why you linger at Winterbourne. How could you hide such a pearl from London society?'

'To keep her from the attention of such gallants as yourself,' Matthew riposted, not entirely humorously. 'Lady Sheridan, may I present our guest, Sir Edmund Ransome?'

'Sir Edmund.' Henrietta curtsied low.

Matthew took her hand and led her to a high-backed chair by the fireside. 'We did not expect to see you

ARE YOU A FAN
OF MASQUERADE
HISTORICAL ROMANCES?

IF YOU are a regular United Kingdom reader of Masquerade
Historical Romances you might like to tell us your opinion of
the books we publish to help us in publishing the books *you*
like.

Mills & Boon have a Reader Panel for their Masquerade
Historical Romances. Each person on the Panel receives a
questionnaire every third month asking you for *your*
opinion of the books you have read in the past three
months. All people who send in their replies will have a
chance of winning ONE YEAR'S FREE MASQUERADE
BOOKS, sent by post.

If you would like to be considered for inclusion on the Panel
please give us details about yourself below. All postage will
be free. Younger readers are particularly welcome.

Year of birth .... Month ....

Age at completion of full-time education ....

Single ☐ Married ☐ Widowed ☐ Divorced ☐

Your name (print please) ....

Address ....

....

....Postcode............................

THANK YOU! PLEASE TEAR OUT AND POST
NO STAMP NEEDED IN THE U.K.

M/0493/RD

2

Do not affix Postage Stamps if posted in
Gt. Britain, Channel Islands or N. Ireland

BUSINESS REPLY SERVICE
Licence No. SF195

MILLS & BOON READER PANEL
P.O. BOX 152,
SHEFFIELD S11 8TE

Postage
will be
paid by
Mills & Boon
Limited

down. You are in great beauty, my dear, but are you well enough to sup with us?'

It was quite obvious his friend thought her beautiful too: Henrietta was well aware of Sir Edmund's admiring glance.

She saw the guarded look in her husband's face and smiled inwardly, innocently enjoying the first signs of jealousy he had ever shown her. She had no intention of so much as flirting with her guest, but his open admiration warmed her and she was intrigued by Matthew's reaction.

Matthew seated her at the foot of the table with a solicitude tinged with possession. After the men had taken their places she turned to Sir Edmund. 'You have come from London today, sir?'

'Indeed, madam. I undertake a commission for my patron, Lord Hargrave, in Oxford. Your husband gave me his company upon the road and offered me your hospitality for the night.' He took the bread she offered him and added, 'But had I known you were indisposed, Lady Sheridan, I should have gone to an inn.'

'Sir, my husband exaggerates out of concern for me; it was a bump on the head, nothing more. And I would not have missed your company for the world.'

Sir Edmund raised his glass in acknowledgement of the compliment. Matthew's brows rose slightly, but he said nothing. Henrietta caught his eye and smiled demurely. They both knew the game she was playing, and both knew why she was playing it.

Over the chicken talk inevitably turned to politics and the state of the nation. Henrietta realised the two men must have worked together before, as she should have known from Sir Edmund's reference to Lord Hargrave.

'Is there anything else I can tell you of my lord's business before you resume your journey to Oxford on the morrow?' Matthew asked.

'I think not; we had so much time to talk upon the road.'

Henrietta looked enquiringly from one man to the

other. Matthew dismissed the servant from the room with a wave of his hand and lowered his voice slightly.

'You recollect I told you how I served Lord Hargrave during the late conflict?'

'You acted as secretary to his lordship, gathering and sifting intelligence for him.'

'Yes. Now with this latest disturbance in the country he has need of such service again and has asked Ransome to fill this role.'

Instantly Henrietta felt slighted for Matthew's sake. 'Does Lord Hargrave no longer trust you since your marriage to me, the daughter of a known Royalist family?'

'My lord would condemn no one for holding to their beliefs——' Matthew began, but was overridden by his friend.

'Our patron knows Matthew too well to believe anything would turn him from his duty,' Ransome interrupted gently. 'Nor can I believe, having met you, that you would attempt such a thing.'

Henrietta subsided, guiltily aware that in the matter of the letter she was not only going against everything Matthew was committed to, but that she was lying to him also.

'To answer your question, Lady Sheridan, Lord Hargrave believes, as we do, that to heal this nation we must start from its roots, build trust again. Men such as your husband with estates in the country, yet with influence in Town, will be the builders, laying the foundations of a united England once again.'

'Your patron, moderate man as he is, seems not to represent the voice of Parliament from what I hear,' Henrietta remarked tartly.

'You are acute, madam.' The conversation had developed into a dialogue between Ransome and his hostess. Matthew sat back, watching and listening. To Henrietta's anxious eye he seemed tired yet curiously content despite the worry of the King's invasion.

'The invasion of the Royalist army is not all that

concerns us,' Ransome continued. 'Rather it is the growing radicalism in Parliament, the increased influence of the Puritan movement. Your husband must have talked often to you of his fears for freedom of worship and for individual liberty if the legislation we are promised comes to fruition.'

Henrietta rose to fill their wine glasses. Instead of taking her chair again she seated herself on a low stool at Matthew's feet.

'Come, gentlemen. You are both tired. Let us ring for a dish of nuts and drink our wine, turn our thoughts to lighter matters.'

The candles burned down as they talked idly. The firelight flickered hypnotically and Matthew began to stroke her hair, teasing his fingers through the ringlets in an unconscious caress.

Henrietta snuggled closer against him like a warm cat and gazed into the embers, no longer listening to the conversation. For all her contentment she felt guilty; when had she ever allowed Matthew to explain his beliefs to her in the way she had allowed this man, a complete stranger, to do?

CHAPTER ELEVEN

'MISTRESS, should we not stay here tonight?' Letty looked with concern at Henrietta's pinched, pale face framed by the hood of her cloak. Her mistress had not looked well when they had set off from Hertford this morning but now she looked quite faint.

Henrietta paused, one hand on the pommel of her saddle, ready to mount, and gestured to the groom to wait. 'Stay *here*? Letty, what can you be thinking of—look around you. Look at this place! I could not possibly spend the night here and you know I planned to return to Winterbourne tonight. If we do not return Matthew will worry.'

The maid followed her mistress's eyes around the dirty, malodorous inn yard, taking in the cobbles, shiny with rain and horse droppings, the smoke issuing from the broken chimney, the raucous noise of the drinkers in the public rooms.

'I know it is not what you are used to, but you need to rest, mistress,' Letty persisted. 'You have had a long ride from Hertford this morning and this cold rain is set in for the day. You should never have persuaded Sir Matthew you could come home alone when he was called away to London from the wedding.'

Henrietta reached into the folds of her cloak and retrieved a kerchief to mop her wet face, as she had been doing all morning. The October drizzle was insistent, chilling the whole returning wedding party to the marrow, dampening their spirits after the euphoria of the wedding.

When Lord Hargrave's message had reached Matthew on the eve of Aunt Susan's marriage it had taken all her powers of persuasion to get him to leave. The irony of her, a Royalist sending him about his Parliamentary business had escaped neither of them.

'Rest is the last thing I need after that disgusting dinner!' Henrietta grimaced, 'I have never tasted such greasy mutton; it rests heavy on my stomach.' She felt the bile rising in her throat and swallowed convulsively. 'I need fresh air, not that smoke and stench of stale ale.'

The inn was the best Wheathampstead had to offer; none the less the innkeeper was ill used to accommodating the gentry. He had bowed Henrietta and Letty through the crush of damp, smelly bodies in the taproom to a private parlour beyond, leaving their grooms to make shift as best they could after they had fed and watered the horses. The weather had put them a good hour behind; they had intended dining in comfort in the market town of Harpenden.

Henrietta had told herself that she should try to eat the mutton stew, coarse bread and small ale their host had served them. In truth the rich food at her aunt's wedding breakfast the day before had disagreed with her, as most things seemed to these last few days, and the ride had already sapped her strength. She needed to replenish her energies if she was to get back to Winterbourne that day.

'Mistress, will you mount now?' John, her groom, bent his back, hands cupped to receive her booted foot and toss her up into the saddle.

'No, wait!' Letty said. Henrietta was taken aback by her maid's vehemence and sudden authority. 'John, give me the reins and wait over there.' Puzzled, the man complied. As soon as he was out of earshot Letty hissed, 'Mistress, forgive me. . . I know it is not my place to say so, but you should not be tiring yourself so in your condition.'

'My what?' Henrietta stared at her, absently wiping a raindrop off the end of her nose with a gloved hand.

'Your condition, mistress. You are with child, are you not?' Two spots of colour on the maid's cheeks showed how difficult this boldness was for her.

'I must be.' Henrietta stared blankly at the wet mane of her mare standing solidly in the dirty yard. How could she have been so stupid, not realised the thing she had been praying for had happened? 'But Letty—I have been feeling so ill.' Her lack of energy, her want of appetite, the other bodily symptoms—all these she had attributed to the lasting effects of her fall in the yard. Added to that the unsettled state of the country, her sorrow at losing Aunt Susan to be the wife of Lawyer Stone in Hertford and endless depressing rain had all served to convince her she was out of sorts and needed a tonic.

'I had meant to speak to Mistress Perrott, but I thought the queasiness would pass. I never imagined such a joyous thing would make me feel so wretched.'

'And your aunt has had no children,' Letty added shrewdly. 'She would not think to warn you of these early signs. But it was so with both my sisters, and my mother tells me it is more common than not.' She looked around at their surroundings. 'You are right, you could not stay here, but we could go on to Harpenden and stay at the Silver Swan. I have heard Lawyer Stone speak well of it many times.'

'No, we are going home,' Henrietta said firmly, her nausea no longer important. 'John, help me to mount; we leave at once!' Now she knew the truth she desired more than ever to return to Winterbourne, shut the world out, be alone and safe with the child she was carrying and Matthew.

Letty caught John's arm as he came forward and whispered urgently to him. Henrietta, caught up in her own thoughts, did not notice the anxious look her groom cast her, or the extra care with which he helped her into the saddle. Unusually he took the mare's leading-rein and drew his own horse close beside her.

Letty was tossed up behind Peter and the other two armed Winterbourne grooms fell in at the rear of the little procession, one of them leading a pack-horse with Henrietta's bags.

A child, Matthew's child. The thought obsessed her, filled her with awe, lifted her dampened spirits. And once she had shared her secret with him, seen the joy in his eyes, she would be the happiest woman alive.

The road ran along the Lea Valley, past the flooded cress-beds and willows, their stems already bare as they hung over the muddy water. Their horses' hoofs splashed through the puddles, miring the women's skirts and the men's boots as they moved through the empty landscape.

There was no wind; the moisture-laden air hung heavy and cold, dripping from bare branches as the riders ascended the hills into the woods, then dropped down the steep valleyside into Harpenden.

Lights glowed warmly in the windows of the Silver Swan as they rode past the inn yard. 'Will you not change your mind, mistress?' Letty called, looking longingly at the well-kept hostelry.

Mutely Henrietta shook her head. She had hardly heard the question, her whole attention turned inward, listening to her body, the beat of her blood. Her child was cocooned, safe and warm in her womb, however cold and aching she was. She tried to imagine Matthew's face when she told him, remembering all he had said to her on their wedding night as they had looked out over Winterbourne in the moonlight.

She was carrying the future of Winterbourne, the child who would fill the space left by the son he had lost. And she, Henrietta Wynter, was going to survive, was going to bring her child to adulthood as poor Sarah had not.

For the first time Henrietta realised she was in sympathy with Matthew's first wife, could share her feelings. What a fool she had been to be jealous. She could never have given her heart to a man who could easily forget the woman he had been married to, consign her to history without regret or pain.

It was only right Matthew should have fond memories of Sarah, be hurt by the recollection of her death and that of his son. But that need not stop him loving

Henrietta, and in her heart she felt he was beginning to do so.

Her mare stumbled in a pot-hole and John jerked the leading-rein to bring the animal's head up. Henrietta pulled her thoughts back to the present and took up her reins firmly. If she was not careful she would take a tumble, and that she could not afford. 'Thank you, John, but give me the rein. I must concentrate on what I am doing.'

Henrietta dug her heels into the mare's flanks and looked around, assessing their progress. 'What time is it, John?'

'Must be near four of the clock, mistress; the light is dying fast. We will not be on Winterbourne soil till past suppertime.' There was worry in the lean, ruddy face and he glanced about him with unusual sharpness as he spoke.

'What is wrong, John?'

'I would have liked to be home before dark with the roads like this. There are too many masterless men abroad and our horses are weary.' He turned in the saddle and called, 'You two at the back, there — keep a sharp look-out and your cudgels at the ready.'

'Surely there is no danger.' Henrietta began to feel alarm for the first time. John was usually so stolid and unruffled, not a man to imagine boggarts behind every bush, yet now he was on edge, his hand resting on the hilt of his sword.

Her worries sharpened; was the country in such a state of ferment that it was unsafe to travel a day's journey from home? No wonder Matthew had been so reluctant to leave her, even with a reliable armed escort.

'Winterbourne, mistress!' Letty called eagerly at last, undisguised relief in her voice as the lights of the outlying cottages appeared in the darkness.

The village showed no signs of life save for the smoke from the chimneys and the flicker of rush-lights. All doors were shut and barred against the cold and whatever else the night held.

'Who goes there?' They were challenged by the guard on top of the Tudor gatehouse as they approached.

'Your mistress, safe back from Hertford!' John called back, relief at their safe return plain in his voice. One of the grooms spurred his tired horse into a canter to go ahead and rouse the household. Henrietta's spirits rose as the front door opened wide, spilling light on to the gravel before them.

'Where is Alice?' Henrietta asked, surprised to see Martha holding the lantern as John lifted her, stiff-limbed from her saddle. With Aunt Susan now Mistress Stone and Henrietta away at the wedding, Alice had assumed control of the household and Henrietta had expected to see her waiting on the threshold. 'Is she well?'

'Confined to her bed, mistress.' Martha bobbed a curtsy and lifted Henrietta's sodden cloak from her shoulders. 'Pains came on this morning, but then they went away again. Mistress Perrott, she says it's early days yet, but Cook do think——'

'That will do, Martha. Stop gossiping and see to our supper. John, when you have seen to the horses, call at Home Farm and tell Master Weldon we are safe returned.'

The room was swaying; Henrietta still felt the rhythm of the horse after so many hours in the saddle. Her knees felt weak and she clutched at the back of the chair for support.

'Henrietta!' Matthew ran down the stairs and took her in his arms, deep worry etched on his face. 'Thank God you are home safe! I have been cursing myself for a fool for letting you travel from Hertford alone. If anything should have happened to you. . .'

'I was not alone! I had John and Peter, armed to the teeth and watching every bush.' She was touched and happy at his obvious concern for her. She had intended to tell him about the child immediately, but perhaps it would be as well to let his worry abate, or he would never let her beyond the gatehouse again!

Matthew released her, but her feet were so numb with cold that she staggered and almost fell.

'Bed, mistress!' Letty put her arm around her waist, directing a disapproving look at Matthew. 'Martha, bring broth and bread and butter and a flask of the best sack. The mistress has caught a chill on the road.' She lowered her voice and whispered, 'Don't want them gossiping yet a while; it is early days yet.'

'You are so cold, Henrietta.' Matthew stood, chafing her hands. 'Why did you not break your journey at the Silver Swan in Harpenden?' Letty snorted. 'Or at least take a heavier cloak?'

'Oh, it seemed all right when we left; it was such a warm day, I did not expect the weather to turn as it did.'

As she set foot on the first tread of the stairs Matthew added. 'Well, we must get you a heavy winter cloak, a fur-lined one.'

'Oh, no need for that, master; the mistress has a fine one, new last year. Here.' Helpfully Letty lifted the lid of the chest and pulled out the cloak, shaking out its creased folds.

'No! Letty!' Henrietta started forward, but it was too late. The gloves with the message fell nearly at Matthew's feet. He stooped to pick them up, his eyes on her appalled face, puzzlement and a growing suspicion dawning on his own.

He must have felt the message as soon as his fingers closed round the soft kid for his eyes grew hard and steady. 'Come, Henrietta, we will go to our chamber.' He turned to the puzzled servants. 'You are all dismissed.'

'Matthew, what is it?' Henrietta demanded when the chamber door closed behind them. She let the sodden cloak fall from her shoulders and went to warm her hands at the fire, trying to appear unconcerned. Behind her she could feel Matthew's eyes on her back. He was still holding the gloves, the fingers crushed in his own.

Panic was paralysing her mind; she should be saying

something, anything to distract him from the twisted scrap of parchment in the glove, but no words came.

There was a rustle, then a soft thud as the gloves fell to the boards. Slowly Henrietta turned, unable to do anything but face the discovery.

'There is a message in these gloves, madam. But I think you already know that. I now realise you have been at great pains to conceal it from me ever since they were delivered on our wedding-day.' He looked up to meet her eyes. 'What? Nothing to say, wife? Why not tell me to throw it away, that it is but a greeting from the donor of this fine gift?'

Her world was about to fall about her ears and there was nothing she could do to stop it. Matthew smoothed the screw of parchment flat between his fingers and began to read in a cold, flat voice.

'News reached me too late of the marriage you are forced to make against your heart and conscience. Do not despair; it may be many weeks before I can make the journey but I will come to you whatever the dangers and will lift this burden from you.

'Say nothing to arouse your husband's suspicions; show him a complaisant face and pray for our sovereign lord King Charles and for your faithful servant. . .'

'I cannot distinguish the signature. Perhaps you would be good enough to enlighten me.' Matthew's voice was frozen beyond anger, his face rigid as he thrust the offending parchment at Henrietta.

'No. . .no, I cannot,' Henrietta stumbled over the words, breathless with fear. Now Matthew would know everything, realise she was involved in Royalist intrigues, perhaps even plotting the return of the King. And the danger was not only for herself but for Robert and Alice, for young Dick who had carried the message to Oxford, for the whole net of confederates still loyal to Charles.

'Matthew, let me explain,' she pleaded desperately.

'I would like to hear you try.' He crossed his arms across his chest and watched her implacably.

'I. . .' Henrietta realised she had no words to explain away the message. The message was too explicit; there was no possible ambiguity in its expression she could find to divert his anger. Surely now he knew, or could swiftly guess everything.

'I am waiting, wife.' The tightly controlled anger clipped his words.

Henrietta gazed back at him wildly, desperately searching for an avenue of escape where none existed.

'His name—I asked you for his name.'

'I cannot!' The note was signed only with an ornate scrawl which might have begun with a T, but even had she known the name her vow to James forbade her to reveal it.

'Your loyalty is admirable, madam.' A thin mockery of a smile touched his lips but left his eyes as hard as before. For the first time Henrietta's panic congealed into cold fear as she recognised the depth of Matthew's anger. 'A pity you do not regard your marriage vows in such a light—they have worn very thin in scant time.'

With a stricken sob Henrietta dropped her head into her hands, unable to face the anger, contempt, betrayal in his face. There had been much sadness in her short life but she had never had to confront such bitter fury, such ruthless examination. To be interrogated like this by her husband, by the man she loved, was almost more than she could bear.

'Oh, no, madam! Pretty wiles and pathetic sobs have no effect on me.' He crossed to the window, stood with his back to her, rejection in every line of his taut body. The silence stretched on until she thought she would scream, then he said. 'I had not thought myself such a fool, so easily gulled by a chit of a girl. I knew you were hiding something from me, yet on the night we were betrothed you denied you loved another. Let me hear your deceitful lips deny it again now I hold the evidence in my hand!'

The rigid façade of his control was cracking, but, thunderstruck, Henrietta was conscious of nothing but the ludicrousness of the accusation. He believed her to have a *lover*? He thought the letter he held was a love missive from that man?

The accusation was so wide of the mark that it made her smile for one fatal second. Matthew turned and caught it. His fists clenched suddenly at his side. 'So you find it amusing, madam? Perhaps you would care to share the jest with your husband for I confess I fail to see the humour in it.'

'But Matthew. . .' Henrietta struggled to come to terms with the accusation. 'I was a virgin when I came to you in marriage; you know that!'

'All that I know is that you were too cautious to give yourself to him—then. This letter proves your lover is too compromised politically to come to you openly. You have been skilful, playing the loving wife to me. No wonder my arrival at Winterbourne was so unwelcome to you when you were saving yourself for this traitor.' He screwed up the parchment and threw it to floor.

There was no way out of this tangled web without telling him the truth. But to do so would not only break her vow, but would threaten the liberty, the very lives of everyone involved. Matthew was no lukewarm bystander to ignore this intelligence; he believed in the rightness of the Commonwealth, in the rightness of what he had fought for, for what so many had died for. However moderate his view, in his eyes it was the King who was the traitor for he had betrayed his people by ruling above the law and Parliament.

Cornered, Henrietta begged. 'Trust me, Matthew, trust me. . .'

'*Trust you*?' His laughter was bitter. 'Let me remind you what your lover promises: to lift the burden of your unwanted marriage from you. Just how do you expect him to achieve this? A knife in my back one dark night? Or perhaps you are too impatient to wait for his arrival. Something more subtle perhaps, brewed in the stillroom

by yourself or Mistress Perrott to slip into my ale?
Would I sicken and die, eased out of life by your tender
ministrations leaving you a rich and *grieving* widow?'

'How could you say such things?' Henrietta whispered
hoarsely. 'How could you believe such monstrous
things?' He was accusing her of crimes which were
enough to condemn her to the stake. Her lips were dry;
she could hardly say the words.

'I believe the evidence of my own eyes.' He bent to
retrieve the message, folded it and tucked it into his
jerkin. Henrietta realised through the horror that she
was talking to a lawyer, a man trained to probe and
disbelieve. 'You promised to love, honour and obey me.
Well, I was fool enough to believe you were growing to
love me. No matter; a rational man can do without love.
But you have consistently disobeyed me, taken pleasure
in defying me with your defence of the Royalist cause.
And now I find you have dishonoured me — and *that* I do
not forgive, madam.'

A cold hand closed its fingers round her heart. He was
going to leave her. Winterbourne was his, the marriage
was consummated. If he chose to live apart from her,
not see her from one year's end to the next, that was his
right; she could not gainsay it. She was powerless, more
powerless as his wife than she had even been when James
and Francis had been alive.

A sudden hope flared. She had not told him about the
child! Surely he would not leave her when he realised
she was pregnant? Then reality reassured itself; he would
say the child was not his, and how could she ever prove
it? Rather than have him reject it she would keep it a
secret for as long as she could.

'What will you do?' she asked quietly, while inside she
wept. 'Where will you go?'

Matthew smiled thinly. 'Go? I go nowhere, wife. It is
not I who should be slinking away ashamed. No, you do
not get rid of me that easily, however much you desire
it. Winterbourne is mine by law — the only sovereign
power in this land, I would remind you — and here I

remain while it suits me. And you are still my wife, Henrietta, mine to command. I want sons, Winterbourne needs an heir. The country — thanks to your Royalist friends — needs a new generation to heal its wounds.'

The relief he was staying was so great that she almost swooned. When she opened her eyes again Matthew was shrugging his jerkin from his shoulders.

'Matthew, what are you doing?'

'Going to bed, wife, with you, as is my right.' Matthew watched the blush spread up the column of her throat as she comprehended his meaning.

She knew he was using her passionate response to him as a weapon against the unknown cavalier. Henrietta looked up into the implacable green eyes as he drew her unresisting into his arms. It was like stepping into the embrace of a stranger. Instinct told her that nothing she told him, even the whole truth, would convince him of her fidelity, so jealous was he. All she could do was to show him how much she loved him. And if he would not listen to her words she would show him with her body. . .

Three weeks later Henrietta trudged in her pattens through the wet, rank grass to the Home Farm. The rain had turned to fog, lying eerily in the hollows along the trackway, deadening all sound.

Despite his threats on the night when he had discovered the letter Matthew had not come to her bed again. He had moved to the Spanish chamber and spoke to her only when necessary before the servants. In more optimistic moments Henrietta told herself he would not react like this if he didn't feel something for her. But such moments were rare; fighting nausea and depression, Henrietta felt the memory of the happiness they had shared fading daily.

She had not even been able to confide in her beloved friend. Mistress Perrott, believing Alice's child to be in danger of being born before its time, had confined her to bed and forbade all visitors. It seemed now that the danger was less and grudgingly she had agreed that Henrietta could pay a short visit.

The cobbles of the farmyard were under her wooden soles and the buildings looming out of the murk when the air was rent by a shrill squeal of terror. Henrietta's blood ran cold. She stopped in her tracks, her heart in her mouth, unable to tell in the deadening fog where the sound had come from. Then the barn door swung open and in the torch-lit interior she saw a group of men gathering round the great pink carcass of a pig swinging from a beam.

'Mistress?' Robert was walking across the yard towards her. 'You look quite pale.'

'The noise of the pig startled me. I had forgotten the killing would have started.'

'We are doing well; we began a week ago and this one is nearly the last. Well-fatted beasts too; it was a good summer's forage for them in the woods.' He took her arm as they crossed the slippery cobbles to the farmhouse. 'Did the wedding go well? I have had no chance to ask you.'

'Very well. I am just going to tell Alice about it. My aunt was sorry you and Alice could not be there. How is she? I have been so worried.'

Robert looked anxious. 'Mistress Perrott tells me all is well now, although the infant is large.'

'If Mistress Perrott says all is well, you must believe her, Robert. And Alice is healthy and strong.' Henrietta was trying to convince herself as well as him.

'Yes,' Robert said dubiously. 'But she is chafing at being confined to bed for so long.'

'I will go and divert her mind with news of the wedding,' Henrietta soothed him. 'Go and see to the pig!'

'It's me Alice!' she called as she sat on a settle inside the front door and untied the wooden pattens from her shoes. 'May I come up?'

There were footsteps on the stairs and Mistress Perrott appeared. 'Good morning, Lady Sheridan. Now you are here I will go home, but tell her maid to send for me directly when the pains start.' She stooped under the low beam at the foot of the stairs and looked keenly at Henrietta. 'And you — are you well, mistress?'

'Tired, that is all. Are you certain all is right with Alice?'

'God willing she will be delivered of a fine healthy infant within a few days.'

Alice was sitting up in bed, her hair gleaming gold in the subdued light. 'Dear Henrietta!' She held out her arms and hugged her friend as best she could. 'I am so glad to see you at last. Mistress Perrott has been so severe, and Robert has obeyed her every word. Did the wedding go well? Come and sit beside me and tell me all; I am going mad with inactivity.'

Henrietta settled herself at the foot of the bed. 'It was gladdening to my heart to see my aunt so happy. She looked like a young bride, all aglow. She has put all those lonely years of widowhood behind her, all those years of being a mother to me. Lawrence Stone has a fine house overlooking Bull Plain and he has told her to refurbish it from the attics to the cellars as she pleases.'

'Lawyer Stone spending *money*?' Alice's pale brows shot up. 'Are we talking of the same man? Why, you will tell me he has bought a new carriage next!'

'Well, he has not gone that far yet, but give Aunt Susan a few months and I believe we will see even that. Oh, and Alice — ' she leaned forward eagerly ' — he had had his hair trimmed and bought a new suit of clothes. Why, he looked almost handsome.'

'It is good they will be so happy.' Alice sighed sentimentally. 'But we will all miss your aunt sorely.'

They talked some more of the wedding over the glass of wine Alice's new maidservant brought, then Henrietta realised her friend had been scrutinising her face for some time.

'Is there something you want to tell me?' Alice asked gently.

Henrietta blushed. 'How did you know?'

'I can see it in your face. And that dress — the last time I saw you wear it it was loose about the bosom and I was going to take it in for you. Now look at it!'

'I feel so uncomfortable.' Henrietta tugged at the fabric over her swollen breasts. 'Will it be like this all the way through? I feel sick all the time. . .'

'Never mind; it will pass soon,' Alice comforted her. 'Mistress Perrott will give you infusions to take. Sir Matthew must be very happy.'

Henrietta pleated the edge of the coverlet between her fingers. 'He doesn't know. I have not yet told him.'

'He must be blind!' Alice exclaimed, with a laugh, then saw the stricken look on Henrietta's face. 'You are not sleeping together? Why? What is the matter?'

It all came pouring out in a torrent of misery. When she had finished the sorry tale Alice took her hand in both of hers. 'You must tell him the truth. He is a fair man; I cannot believe he would have us punished for this. All of it occurred so long ago and so much has changed.'

'Changed for the worse,' Henrietta said bitterly. 'This new fighting has made Matthew so angry and worried.'

'It will be better soon. Your condition makes you fearful. Robert tells me it is all up with the King's men; Parliament is once more in control. Your husband will be reassured, more tolerant.'

It was extraordinary how confused Henrietta's feelings were. Her love for Matthew was all she cared about, yet her sympathies for the cause remained. Somewhere out there the King was being hunted down like a stag, perhaps to suffer the same fate as his father on the scaffold.

But Matthew was right: the important thing was stability for the country so that her child and Alice's could grow up in peace and never have to choose sides against each other.

When the time came for her to leave she begged Alice not to breathe a word of what had passed between them, even to Robert.

Entering the hall, she dropped her cloak on the chest as Matthew came through the screens, booted and spurred, a saddlebag over one arm. 'Matthew, where are you going?'

'To London on business. It is most urgent, otherwise, as you know, nothing would tear me from your side.'

It was no protestation of love, more a warning. 'Cobham stays, of course?' she enquired coldly.

'Of course. As my eyes and ears. I shall be gone perhaps a week, dear wife.' Through the bitterness she recognised his pain and put out an imploring hand to him, but he shook it off and strode out through the door without a backward glance.

CHAPTER TWELVE

'IT IS good of you to come and stay with me while Matthew is away, Lady Willoughby. These long dark evenings pass so slowly without company.' Henrietta passed her guest a glass of Canary wine and took up her tapestry again.

The older woman had driven up to see her the day after Matthew's departure and, finding her alone, had sent her groom home for her maid, announcing her intention of staying until Matthew's return.

'We have all been dull.' Lady Willoughby took a sip of wine. 'These present troubled times have set all our nerves a-jangling. My husband has driven me quite mad with his prohibitions on travelling. He would not let me stir without an armed escort, even to go these few miles between home and Winterbourne.'

'I know,' Henrietta sighed. 'Matthew left Robert with such strict instructions about the security of the estate that we have all felt prisoners here these past few days. We have seen no sign of the marauding Scots or stragglers from the King's army that the men seem so alarmed about and it is very difficult to carry on the work of the estate with so many men engaged patrolling the house and grounds.'

'I noticed the lad on the gatehouse roof as we rode under this morning. I pray things will settle soon. Surely we will have news of the King's fate, God keep him, before many more days are past.'

'How fortunate the news of the King's return did not reach us in time for Marcus to join his army.' Henrietta shuddered at the thought. 'He brings James so much to my mind, so idealistic, so full of fervour for the Royalist cause.'

'More fool him!' Lady Willoughby interjected unexpectedly. 'Silly boys! What do they hope to achieve by this bloodshed? Matters have passed beyond that now — or would have, if the wives and mothers of this country had any say in the matter,' she added darkly.

After a light supper the two women sat in companionable privacy in Aunt Susan's old parlour reading the broadsheets Lady Willoughby had brought with her and working on their embroidery.

After a while Henrietta put down her work to pull the heavy brocade on its rings clattering across the windows against the dark outside. The night was moonless and cloudy; even the starlight was obscured. From the top of the gatehouse the watchman's lantern shone faintly, a lonely sentinel in the darkness of the November evening.

'You received those broadsheets from London safely.' She settled on a low stool by Lady Willoughby, her amethyst skirts pooling around her on the polished boards. 'Perhaps I will hear from Matthew soon.'

'Do not be concerned.' The older woman rested her hand caressingly on Henrietta's head, responding to her fears rather than to what she had said. 'There has been no fighting recently, only skirmishes and none of those near London.'

Henrietta sat silent, resting against Lady Willoughby's chair, letting her guest's words wash over her. The little flame of hope that Matthew's pain at their parting had ignited flickered and died again, leaving her despairing.

She had been so concerned with Matthew's reaction that the thought of the message itself had been lost. Now, sitting looking at the window-seat above the priest's hole, she wondered about the messenger. He had sent no further word. What if the man had been killed at Worcester? The papers would stay there forever and she could never tell Matthew the truth.

She must have sighed, for Lady Willoughby bent down, tilting up her chin with one thin finger. 'You are asleep where you sit, child! It is time you were in your bed, not drowsing before the fire while I gossip on.'

Henrietta got to her feet, acknowledging that she

would be glad of her bed. 'And you are tired too, Lady Willoughby. It is kind of you to visit me — are you sure your family can spare you to me?'

'You have pretty manners, child.' The older woman got to her feet stiffly and picked up a branch of candles. 'My family are only too pleased to have a few day's freedom from common sense and order!'

Smiling at her guest's robust turn of phrase, Henrietta took her arm as they slowly climbed the stairs. She felt tired and out of sorts; tomorrow she would have to consult Goodwife Perrott; she must not neglect her health and endanger her child because she was so preoccupied with Matthew.

She parted with Lady Willoughby at the guest-chamber door and made her way along the passage to her own room. The gold velvet curtains were drawn across the casements and half around the bed. Letty had turned down the coverlet and run a warming-pan between the sheets. Autumn had well and truly arrived, damp and dark at the end of a summer which the old people of the village spoke of as the hottest in many a long year.

Letty tapped on the door and brought in a bowl of warm water. 'Unlace me please, Letty.' Her maid untied the knots and pulled the bodice lacing loose. 'Oh, what a blessed relief to be out of that.'

'You should have worn a looser gown, mistress. But I suppose Lady Willoughby might have noticed your condition then. Never mind; it is very becoming at the bosom.' Letty was growing pert and confident in her new role of lady's maid now Alice was safely out of the way at Home Farm.

'Becoming it may be, miss, but I shall risk a looser gown tomorrow.' Tiredness and worry sharpened her tone and Letty bit her lip. Unlike Alice she could sulk for days. 'You may go, Letty. Lay my nightgown to warm by the fire. I will finish undressing myself.'

Henrietta fell into a deep, dreamless sleep as soon as her head touched the pillow, cocooned in the four-poster with the curtains drawn tight all round against the draught.

When she woke the room was chill and a light was shining in her face. Confused, she put up her hand to shield her eyes, still three-quarters asleep. 'Who. . .?'

'Henrietta!' Alice's voice whispered from the darkness. 'Are you awake?'

'What. . .what time is it?' Henrietta demanded, struggling to get into a sitting position and gather her wits. 'Alice? What are you doing here?'

''Tis three of the clock. You must get up; he will not speak to anyone else.'

'Matthew?' Henrietta's face lit up. 'He is home?'

'No, not your husband. Robert says it is our man come at last from Oxford.' Alice put the candle down on the bedside table and held Henrietta's robe out for her.

'Where is he?' Gathering the heavy folds around her, Henrietta picked up the candle and followed Alice's swollen figure into the corridor. 'Alice! Wait here; get into my bed and keep warm. You should not be walking about at this time of night. What if you fell? And besides, did Mistress Perrott not tell you to rest?'

'I'll come with you, then when the messenger has gone Robert and I will return home together.' Alice was characteristically obdurate. 'They are in the kitchen yard.'

'Well, take my hand, then. We will go down the back stairs and avoid Cobham's chamber door — that man has ears like a fox.'

The girls crept down the dark stairs clinging to one another, wincing each time a board creaked protestingly under their slippered feet. The wind had risen in the night, moaning and soughing in the eaves and under doors. Twice Henrietta froze, certain she had heard a footstep on the upper landing, but it was only the old house settling for the night.

They reached the store-room at the foot of the stairs, eased open the door and crept along the hall passage, past the sewing-room and stillroom, past the steward's office and the gaping darkness at the head of the cellar steps.

Outside in the yard it was cold. The wind had sent the clouds scudding across the sky and a thin, fitful moon had broken through the darkness. Dry leaves trapped in the corner of the arcade scuttled and eddied, the only sound in the silent yard. The candle guttered and went out.

'Are you sure they're here?' Henrietta whispered hoarsely, her throat dry from nerves and excitement.

'Here.' Robert's shadow freed itself from the privy door in the far corner. He gestured them to join him and as they circled the walls like rats clinging to skirting Henrietta saw a second, heavily cloaked figure standing behind him.

Alice's hand clutched hers convulsively as she glanced round. 'Pray God we are not seen!'

'Robert—take Alice home at once! What were you thinking of, bringing her here with her time so near?'

'I could not enter your chamber, mistress!' His scandalised whisper would have been amusing were not the danger so acute.

'Go wait in the laundry, Alice. The ashes under the copper should still be warm.' She pushed Alice gently towards the door, then turned to face the messenger.

'You wrote to me, sir?' She could not see his face under his hood, but he nodded. 'What is your name?'

'It is best you do not know.' His voice was deep and cultivated. A gentleman, then, by his bearing. 'You have the casket?'

'It is in the priest's hole in the small parlour floor.' An awful thought struck her. 'But you fixed it down, did you not, Robert? How can we lift it without rousing the whole household?'

'I did not nail it, I wedged it. All we need is a thin knife to prise it up, and that I have.' He held up a slim blade that glinted in the muted starlight. 'Come, mistress.'

They crept back, Robert in his stockinged feet, leaving

the messenger with Alice in the laundry. The board was easily freed, although to Henrietta, with her heart in her mouth, every creak was magnified into a crash that would surely rouse the household.

She reached down into the cold, cobwebby gap and with trembling fingers withdrew the casket that had been the cause of so much heartache. If it could just be got safe away perhaps her troubles would go with it.

After what seemed an age they finally regained the yard. Henrietta felt as though she had been creeping about in the dark the whole night long. An owl screeched as it flew overhead and she jumped convulsively, stifling a scream, and Robert, pulling on his boots beside her, nearly fell over with shock.

Finally she was thrusting the casket into the messenger's hands, feeling the responsibility lift from her shoulders as though someone had raised a yoke from her neck. The man secreted it beneath his all-enveloping cloak and Robert stepped into the laundry to fetch his wife.

The messenger took Henrietta's cold hand in his gloved one, brushing his lips over her knuckles. 'Your great loyalty to our sovereign lord the King will not go unrewarded, madam.'

'I want no reward, only that you go quickly and safely. But tell me, is there no news of the King's safe deliverance?'

'Not yet; we wait and pray.'

'Amen to that.' Henrietta stood and watched as he moved into the yard, direct into a patch of moonlight. At that moment the door from the house banged open and Cobham stood there, a horn lantern in one hand, a cudgel in the other.

'Stay where you are!'

Henrietta's hands flew to her throat in shock. Behind her she heard Alice's gasp cut short by Robert's hand over her mouth. After a heart-thudding moment Henrietta realised that only the messenger could be seen in the fitful moonlight. The man threw back his cloak over one shoulder, his hand on his sword hilt.

'No!' Henrietta whispered fiercely. There could be only one end to this: Cobham dead on the cobbles, run through. How could she justify that, explain it to Matthew?

Cobham's grizzled head swivelled as he caught the sound. Henrietta braced herself to step forward, somehow to stop him while the messenger escaped, when behind him another, most unexpected voice broke the silence.

'Wilson!' Lady Willoughby's authoritarian tones echoed round the yard, freezing them all where they stood. 'What are you about, man? As if I did not know!' She was an imposing figure in flowing robe and nightcap, her grey plaits loose on her shoulders. 'Cannot I bring you to a gentleman's house without you sneaking about to despoil his maidservants? What have you to say for yourself? Come, I am waiting!' She folded her arms across her bosom and glared into the darkness.

There was a moment of heavy silence, then, 'I'm sure I'm sorry, ma'am. . .' The man's accent was purest Buckinghamshire. 'But the wench had such a willing eye. . .'

'They all have willing eyes.'

Henrietta realised that for this ludicrous charade to work she must make her presence felt. Alice and Robert, whose presence would be impossible to explain, had melted back into the darkness, but sooner or later even Cobham with his eyes left weak by years of close bookwork, was going to see her in the shadows.

'My thanks, Lady Willoughby.' She stepped into the pool of light cast by the horn lantern and heard Cobham's indrawn hiss of breath. 'The silly wench escaped me. I heard her creeping down the back stairs and followed, but without a candle I lost her in the yard. The next thing I knew, this rogue was standing there, and, not knowing who he was, I dared not show myself.'

Cobham's head swivelled from Henrietta back to Lady

Willoughby. Henrietta knew the suspicion must be in his mind that she was meeting a lover. But how then could he account for the presence of Lady Willoughby? Even Cobham was daunted by her.

'Where is the wench, then?' he demanded, the nearest he dared approach to accusing them of outright lies.

Suddenly a window above them flew open and Letty stuck out her head. 'She's here, mistress, I have her. Flighty slut!' Her voice was shrill with moral outrage. 'I caught her sneaking back in, mistress. Stand still, you baggage!' There was the sound of a stinging slap and an outraged feminine cry.

'Wilson! Get back to your bed in the stables this minute — I shall deal with you in the morning! Henrietta, child, come with me; you must be frozen. I can only apologise for my groom's behaviour. His master will hear of it, I promise. And you, girl — ' She tilted back her head to address Letty who was still hanging out of the window, 'Well done. Lock the slut in her room and Lady Sheridan will deal with her tomorrow as she deserves.'

She put her arms round Henrietta and swept her past Cobham. 'Come along, man, back to your bed. You should know better than to go creeping about like a thief in the night at your age. Lock the doors after us.'

Leaving Cobham speechless in the face of this totally unjust attack, she ascended the stairs, her arm linked through Henrietta's.

At her chamber door she drew Henrietta inside, keeping her voice low. 'I do not know what that was about or who that man was, but he should be safe away by now. Perhaps you will tell me as much as you are able one day, but tomorrow we will be up and off early, before that clerk can cast a rheumy eye over my servants.'

Henrietta threw her arms around her and kissed her cheek. 'You are a wonderful woman, Lady Willoughby! You have saved more people than you know tonight, perhaps even served His Majesty.'

The older woman's eyebrows rose and a spot of colour touched each cheek. 'And you are a surprising young woman, Henrietta—I wish I had you for a daughter. But take care—you will not gull your husband as easily as you did his clerk.'

How fortunate that Matthew had been from home! Henrietta shivered with more than cold as she climbed back into bed. With his false belief that she already had a lover he would not have hesitated if he had found the messenger; the man would be dead by now.

And Cobham was sure to tell him of the suspicious scene. Henrietta could not comfort herself they had fooled him for a minute. He might not know what was afoot, but he would lose no time in telling his master, who would draw his own conclusions.

Could she tell Matthew the truth now the casket had gone? Henrietta tossed and turned, weighing the dangers to the others and her oath to James against the possible reactions of the man she had married.

Henrietta was still undecided when she sat down to dinner next day in solitary splendour at one end of the long table in the hall. She had been tempted to order dinner set in the parlour, it was so lonely here without Matthew or Aunt Susan, especially since Lady Willoughby had gone. But she was mistress of Winterbourne and standards had to be kept up.

The servants were already becoming slack, freed from Mistress Clifford's gimlet eye and Alice's sharp tongue. It would do them no harm to realise their mistress was firmly in charge of the household.

'Martha, that apron is a disgrace. You should not be serving at table in it.'

'There's no guests, mistress,' Martha protested indignantly.

'Well, I do not want to eat with you looking like a wench out of a tavern, and, besides, Sir Matthew may walk through that very door at any moment.'

Martha muttered under her breath, dropped a brief curtsy and took Henrietta's plate back to the kitchen.

'Got out the wrong side of bed this morning,' she said to Mary as they passed behind the screens.

'More like 'cos master ain't there to warm it,' the other maid said pertly, then nearly dropped her platter of fruit in alarm as John, his sword drawn, strode through the front door.

'Mistress, you must go up to your chamber immediately. Lock the door. There is a party of horsemen approaching at the gallop, Royalists by the look of them.'

'This is a Royalist household, John——' Henrietta began, then corrected herself. 'Well, not exactly, but we need have no fear of them. What can they want at Winterbourne?'

'The silver, most like,' John said grimly. 'The men are getting it down the cellar now. You'd best get to your room; I don't want to risk you receiving any insult.'

There was the sound of hoofs on the gravel, then a confusion of voices and colour as half a dozen young men burst through the door. John drew Henrietta behind him and took one step forward, sword at the ready.

'What business do you have at Winterbourne?' he demanded. 'And how dare you burst in upon a lady in her own home?'

'Henrietta!' Marcus Willoughby elbowed his way to the front of the group. 'Since when have I had to be invited in order to visit you?'

'Marcus!' Henrietta sat down with a thump in the nearest chair. Now the alarm was over she realised just how frightening the last few minutes had been. 'What do you think you are doing, and who are these people with you?'

'But you know them all,' he said cheerfully and she realised for the first time that he had been drinking. 'Make your bows, my friends.'

Henrietta did indeed recognise them now—young men of Marcus's age, the young bloods of the county too youthful to have fought in the Civil War, but fervent Royalists for all that. They smiled and bowed, sweeping off their plumed hats in exaggerated gestures of gallantry. They were in their best clothes, silks and velvets decorated with lace and ribbon bows and — like Marcus — were all amiably drunk.

'To what do I owe this pleasure, Marcus?' she demanded frostily, gesturing to John to put up his sword. She ought to offer them hospitality, but was not inclined to do so after their unceremonious entrance. Nor did she want to consider her husband's reaction if he knew they had been there.

'Good news, Henrietta! We bring good news, do we not, my friends?' There was a rowdy chorus of assent which only served to deepen Henrietta's perplexity and growing annoyance.

'If you do not stop talking in riddles, Marcus, I shall ask John to see you all to your horses.'

'The King! The King!'

'Where?' Henrietta looked around wildly, half expecting the gangling figure of Charles Stuart to emerge from the party of young men.

'In Paris. He is safe away; the news just reached us. Bulstrode here brought the tidings and we have ridden to every loyal household in the district to tell them.'

'Thank God,' Henrietta said with profound relief.

'Amen to that,' John echoed her. 'Shall I tell the household, mistress?'

'Yes, bring them here and fetch wine and ale; we must drink to celebrate.' But in her heart she was celebrating something quite different. If the King was safe away over the Channel in France the fighting would end, and there would be no danger of Matthew becoming caught up in it.

There would be peace again, time to rebuild and for her and Matthew to grow together again, await the birth of their child with everything to look foward to.

The dreary weather, the misunderstanding which separated them, her aching, awkward body were all forgotten in a great welling joy.

'There gentlemen, I told you Lady Sheridan would be pleased!' Marcus turned to his friends. 'She doesn't stand on ceremony with old friends. They said you wouldn't want us all arriving unannounced,' he confided tipsily, 'but I knew you wouldn't mind once you knew the cause of it!'

'I thank you, gentlemen, for your consideration in bringing me this news,' Henrietta said with dignity, causing one or two of the more sober bloods to look abashed. 'My husband would wish me to offer you hospitality; my servants are bringing wine now. I hope you will drink to the peace and prosperity of this country before you leave.'

The hint was plain enough, but Marcus and his friends were too intoxicated to heed it. Henrietta sighed inwardly and gestured to the maids to take round the wine. They would soon be gone, leaving her alone to plan for the future. Somehow she would think of a way to explain things to Matthew. . .

There was a sudden vicious rattle of hail against the window panes and the room darkened. 'You had best dine with me, gentlemen, until this downpour passes.' It was the last thing she wanted, or needed, but in the name of hospitality she could not turn them out into the storm. After all, these were the sons of the gentry of the neighbourhood; many of them she had known all her life. 'John, send Letty to attend me and ask Cook to send through food for our guests.'

He did as he was bidden and she turned to Martha. 'More candles, girl, and send Sim with more logs for the fire.'

There was a growing murmur of voices from behind the screens where the servants had assembled from all over the house. 'Come in!' she called, gesturing to one of the maids to pour ale. 'I have good news for you all,' she began, standing at the head of the table. 'The King is safe in France. Peace will return to the countryside once more, you will be able to stand down the guards about the estate. Let us drink to the peace of the nation and the healing of divisions!'

'Amen to that!' several voices called in unison. There

was no mistaking the feeling of relief in the room. Bumpers of ale were downed and the servants returned to their duties, chattering and excited.

An hour later Henrietta looked down the length of the table stifling a yawn. The food was finished, leaving only bones and heels of bread littering the table. Puddles of spilt wine reflected the candle-light which shone on flushed, replete faces. She fervently hoped her unwelcome guests would be inclined to leave now the flow of wine had slowed and the weather improved from downpour to drizzle.

Marcus was seated in Matthew's place at the head of the table. He banged his cup on the table and shouted for silence. 'Gentlemen! We have presumed on the hospitality of our hostess Lady Sheridan for too long and it will soon be night.'

Thank goodness for that! Henrietta thought, absently taking a long drink from the glass of wine she had been toying with throughout the meal. Its warmth hit her empty stomach and she realised with a shock that she had eaten scarcely a morsel.

'A toast!' Marcus continued, lurching to his feet. 'Lady Sheridan!'

The young men raised their glasses and shouted her name, banging on the table enthusiastically.

'Thank you, gentlemen; I wish you a safe return to your homes and —'

'And now we must all stand,' Marcus cut across her. 'I give you the King!'

They all got to their feet, Henrietta among them. She could not stay in her place when such a toast had been called. Suddenly she was suffused with optimism and joy; one day the King would return in peace and she and Matthew and the child she was carrying would be safe and happy together.

Her voice joined with theirs, clear over their deeper tones. 'Our sovereign lord the King! Health and long life to King Charles!'

The front door crashed open. Candles guttered in the

sudden inrush of cold air and the room filled with a swirl of smoke from the fire. Everyone in the room turned as one, glasses and tankards clenched in their hands, words frozen on their lips.

Matthew Sheridan stood on the threshold of his hall, a dark figure silhouetted against the grey evening light. His black cloak hung sodden to the floor, he was bareheaded, his hair plastered to his head by the rain.

The silence stretched on, broken only by the homely crackle of burning logs and the drip of water from his clothes on to the bare boards.

'Matthew!' Henrietta gasped, her hands flying to her throat in disbelief. She had wanted him home so much, had dreamt of it sleeping and waking, but not this terrible figure standing like Judgement in the door.

He took six deliberate, echoing steps forward to confront her as though the young men did not exist. His face was deathly white, his eyes glittering strangely, his mouth a thin, grim line.

'So.' The word dropped into the silence like a pebble into a winter pond. 'So this is how you pass your time when I am away, madam.'

'Matthew, I——'

'Be quiet.' He had never spoken to her like that, with so much contempt and menace in his voice. A muscle jumped convulsively in his cheek. 'Be quiet, madam, until I give you leave to speak. Who are these. . .people? Why are they carousing in my house with my wine, my food—and my wife?'

'Now look here, Sheridan,' Marcus began, blustering. 'You can't talk to Henrietta like that. . .'

Matthew turned slowly to face the young man. With deliberation he threw his cloak back over his shoulder to free his sword arm and with equal deliberation drew the sword from its scabbard. The blade whispered, steel against leather, as he drew it, then held it, its glittering point resting lightly on the table.

'Does anyone else wish to tell me how to address Lady Sheridan in my own home?' he enquired dangerously.

Thomas Bulstrode, perhaps the drunkest and therefore most foolhardy of them all, cleared his throat. 'I. . .'

The blade came up and across with a swish. The tops of the candles in the ornate central candelabra on the table fell, some still smoking, among the debris of the food. An acrid smell rose in the stillness. Matthew raised one eyebrow at Bulstrode, who shook his head mutely, the sweat standing on his brow in great drops.

'I interrupted you, madam. You were, I think, in the middle of a speech on the subject of Charles Stuart?'

'These gentlemen. . .' Henrietta felt her voice dying in her throat; she cleared it and tried again. 'Marcus and his friends came to tell me the King is safe in France. We are all very relieved that the fighting is over.' She could see the whole scene through his eyes. His wife, the sole woman in a group of drunken youths; the King's health being celebrated; her own voice tipsy with wine and relief, speaking what to him was treachery and disloyalty.

'Gentlemen.' With an effort she pulled her eyes from Matthew's cold face and turned to the aghast young men. 'I must bid you goodnight and a safe return home. My husband, as you can see, is wet and tired and I would crave your indulgence.'

'Henrietta——' Marcus began, then broke off as Matthew's sword-point lifted again. He swallowed convulsively but carried on, possibly the bravest thing he had ever done in his life. 'Lady Sheridan. We thank you for your hospitality, especially as we arrived unannounced and forced our presence on you. My mother will be delighted to hear of Sir Matthew's safe return. We bid you goodnight.'

Henrietta knew what he was trying to do and was grateful for his courage. She smiled gently. 'Goodnight, gentlemen.'

Matthew did not even turn as the door closed behind the last subdued youth. He shrugged the heavy cloak from his shoulders, letting it drop in a sodden heap on the boards, lifted a rummer of sack and drained it in one draught, the sword still in his hand.

He stood for a long moment, his eyes on the empty glass, then dashed it into the fireplace with a terrible violence.

Henrietta moved swiftly behind one of the heavy oak chairs. It had never occurred to her that Matthew might strike her in any circumstances, but she knew most husbands would think nothing of doing so to a wife who gravely displeased them. And she was frightened for the child she was carrying.

That fear must have shown on her face; Matthew sheathed the sword and stepped away from her. 'You do well not to underestimate my anger, wife, but I do not strike women — even those who are disloyal, disobedient and flagrant in their flouting of the law.'

Henrietta stared at his face, its lines chiselled in the leaping firelight. The dark shadows under his eyes spoke of little sleep, the tendons of his throat were taut. He seemed thinner and she spoke without thinking, full of love and worry for him. 'Matthew, you have not been looking after yourself.'

'Do not peddle your soft words, Henrietta. Should I believe you care how I am? I did once, and told myself I was a fool for it.'

'I do care, Matthew! I *love* you. . . I believe I have always loved you!' It was a cry from the heart, her heart that was breaking.

'Love! Do not defile the word by using it to lie to me. It will not work, Henrietta. Do you know what I have been doing, these days in London? I have been listening to the voices of those extremists who feel justified in their extremes by the damage done by *your* King and his heedless supporters. I have been attending to the affairs of people who have lost husbands and sons at Worcester. And when I return home to my lands and my people and my wife I find her flouting everything I believe in, undermining everything I have worked to achieve.'

He swung away and stood, his back to her, one hand

clenched on the stone mantelshelf, staring down into the heat of the fire. 'Do not tell me you love me, Henrietta. I cannot believe you. I believed it once, fought against the evidence of my own eyes when I saw that letter. But I have been away — away from you — where I could think clearly.'

If he rejected her words of love she would have to show him how she felt. Henrietta moved slowly to his side, but he continued to stand there, his face averted. She touched his sleeve compelling him to turn and face her, and she saw his eyes dark, not now with anger but hurt and pain.

The tears slid slowly down her cheeks and she reached up a hand to stroke the hollows under his cheekbones. His skin was dry, taut, burning to her touch, and she felt a pang of alarm. Her other hand touched his forehead.

Matthew flinched away, shaking her off. 'Do not touch me! Do not think you can seduce me with your body as you have done before, you jade. You know I cannot resist you. . .' His eyes were bright, fixed on her face, then he staggered, clutched helplessly at the table, and fell full-length, unconscious, to the boards at her feet.

CHAPTER THIRTEEN

His forehead burned hot and dry under her palm. 'Matthew, my love!' Henrietta lifted his dark head on to her lap and smoothed back the wet hair from his temples. 'Matthew, speak to me! Wake up. . .oh, what can be wrong with him?'

She could see no wound to account for his collapse, no rash or mark on his pale skin. 'Martha! Letty! Come quick,' she cried, distractedly stroking his face, the tears running down her cheeks unchecked.

The two girls arrived together, breathless and frightened, followed by John. 'Mistress, what is it?'

After one quick glance he fell to his knees beside her but made no move to touch the unconscious man. 'Mistress, have a care; he may have the plague.'

Henrietta stared at him aghast. 'The plague?'

"Tis always rife in London Town,' the groom responded grimly, scrutinising Matthew's face without touching him. 'Does he have a fever?'

'He is burning up. We must get him upstairs to bed; Martha, prepare the chamber quickly. Fresh sheets and light the fire. . .'

Martha pulled her skirts back, her lip quivering. 'I'll not stay, mistress, not if he's got the plague. You come away, mistress, leave him to die — there's nothing you can do, God save us all!'

'You wicked girl!' Henrietta rounded on her furiously. 'You do as I tell you or you leave this household tonight with no character. The master is not going to die, neither has he got the plague.' She spoke with more assurance than she felt, never having seen the dreaded disease which all men feared above everything. 'John, help me get him to our chamber.' The groom stood up and made for the door. 'John — I beg you, do not leave me — Letty and I cannot manage by ourselves.'

'I'll not leave you, mistress, never fear, but I'll need another of the lads to help carry him.' He paused beside the tearful figure of Martha. 'And you, silly wench, get about your business as your mistress tells you or I will give you a beating to remind you of your duty.'

Martha fled upstairs with a wail of dismay, leaving Henrietta and Letty kneeling white-faced over the supine figure. 'It is not the plague, is it, Letty?' Henrietta begged. 'You have seen it, haven't you?'

'My uncle died of it in Aylesbury and my mother told me of the signs.' Her fingers hesitated over Matthew's shirt front, then with a visible effort of will she unlaced it, pulling it open to reveal his chest. 'There are no swellings, mistress.' Emboldened, she insinuated her fingers under his arms. 'This is where they begin, but I can feel nothing.'

'Then it is not the plague?' Henrietta cried with relief.

'Mayhap not.' Letty bit her lip in an effort to remember the symptoms. 'What is his breathing like?'

Henrietta put her ear to his chest and listened to the rasping intake of breath. 'It is not right, Letty; his lungs must be afflicted. We must send to Aylesbury for the surgeon.'

'We have not time!' Letty pulled her mistress upright. 'And if it is the plague the surgeon can do nothing, even if he were willing to enter the house. Mistress Perrott will know what to do.'

'Run and send Sim,' Henrietta urged, falling to her knees again and cradling Matthew in her arms. His face in the firelight was drawn and thin, his eyes sunken. How had she missed it when he had first come in? How had she not seen how ill he was? His anger had given him the strength to stay on his feet — but what had given him the strength on the journey from London to Winterbourne?

'My love, my love, don't die; please don't die,' she

whispered over and over like a litany. 'I need you, our child needs you. . .'

It seemed an age before John and Tom appeared and carried the still unconscious Matthew upstairs between them to the master bedroom. Martha had worked quickly, more out of fear than duty; the fire burned brightly and the bed was crisp with fresh linen. The maidservant backed from the room as they entered, a handful of pot-pourri held to her nose.

'Put him down,' Henrietta ordered. 'John, help me undress him. Tom, get Cook to heat bricks and wrap them in flannel; his hands are freezing.'

John pulled off the muddy riding boots, swearing under his breath as he cut himself on the spurs in his haste. 'His feet are cold too, mistress.'

Henrietta raised her eyes to look at her groom across her husband's semi-clad figure. 'He is so pale and drawn, John.'

'If this is the plague it will be all over for better or worse in five days. That being so we will soon know if he is afflicted.'

They both stood looking at him in silence, listening to the laboured rasp of his breathing. 'Could it be the pneumonic fever?'

'More than likely, mistress. You must keep him warm and hope that the fever breaks.' He stroked his chin, considering. 'Shall I send for the surgeon? If we tell him it is not the plague he might come.'

'To cup him and take away what little life blood still runs in his veins?' Henrietta had no great trust or regard for surgeons except for dealing with simple breaks or cuts. Her aunt had brought her up to understand and use the country remedies and the wisdom of the local wisewomen and their plants and simples. 'Sim has gone for Mistress Perrott; they will not be long, God willing.'

By the time they had wrestled Matthew's limp body into a nightshirt and tucked him between the covers Letty had fetched the first of the hot bricks.

'Where is Martha?' Henrietta demanded sharply.

'Nursing her boxed ears in a corner of the kitchen,' Letty was grim. 'I found her wailing about how the master had the plague and how we'd all be locked up in here by the constable with a plague cross on the door until we're dead.'

'Have the servants all run away?'

'No, they have more sense.' John opened the door. 'I'll go down and talk to them, but Cook has the wit to disregard anything that tale-carrying wench would say.'

Henrietta wrung out a cloth in the water-pitcher and began to sponge Matthew's forehead gently.

'He looks so white, mistress,' Letty whispered.

'It is just the sheets,' Henrietta said stoutly, wishing in her heart she believed it. She was very much afraid but some instinct told her not to admit it, even to herself.

'What have you done to him, Jezebel?' a voice hissed from the door. Both women jumped, spinning round to see Cobham standing just within the room, watching them with hatred burning in his eyes.

'Cobham, hold your tongue! Your master has a fever and if you wish to help him you will go away and leave him in peace.' Henrietta turned back dismissively to the bed, but the clerk did not move.

'You. . .you are to blame for this with your potions and your philtres.' He sidled up to the bed, stabbing a bony, accusatory finger in Henrietta's direction.

'What are you talking about, man?' Henrietta wrung out a fresh cloth and laid it on Matthew forehead. 'My husband has only just returned, with a fever, as you see. How can anyone in this household be responsible for his condition?'

'Harlot! You wish him gone so you can continue your wanton life. . .distance is no barrier to a witch's arts.'

'Get out!' Letty shoved the wizened clerk with such force that he staggered and was out of the door before he had a chance to recover himself. She slammed it and turned the key.

'Thank you, Letty; we have no time to spare for Cobham's ravings. I think age must be turning his brain.'

They were distracted by Matthew moving his head restlessly on the pillow. He moaned softly and Henrietta motioned urgently to Letty for some water. 'His mouth is so dry; if only I could get him to drink!'

'He is insensible, mistress; you will only choke him if you try and force him to drink,' Letty pointed out.

Henrietta contented herself with moistening his cracked lips with a kerchief dipped in the water. 'Where is Mistress Perrott?' she fretted.

Suddenly there was a great clamour in the corridor outside in the midst of which the wisewoman's voice could be heard raised in anger.

Henrietta wrenched the door open. 'Be quiet all of you! Your master is sick. What is happening here?'

Mistress Perrott stood halfway up the stairs holding a covered basket tightly against her chest, her face flushed and angry. Cobham barred her way at the head of the stairs, a rusty black figure, arms outstretched like a scarecrow, defying her to pass him.

'I shall not let you near him, witch!'

Henrietta gasped at the word and beside her Letty automatically stretched out her hand, making the sign against the evil eye.

'Bewitch me if you dare, daughter of darkness; I am under the protection of the Lord—your spells will have no effect on me. But approach my master at your peril!'

Henrietta's frayed temper snapped as she realised that servants were gathering in an excited knot at the foot of the stairs, the word 'witch' passing between them in vehement whispers.

'Cobham, be silent, let Mistress Perrott pass! We all trust her in this household with our lives.'

'She shall not; you are in unholy alliance with her and the Devil. You have bewitched my master, now you will kill him. Whore! Jezebel! Salome!'

Henrietta stood aghast, unable to deal with the intemperate outburst. The clerk's hair was awry, spittle foamed at the corner of his mouth and his fingers were clenched into claws with his hatred. To her frightened eyes he seemed possessed himself.

Heavy footsteps sounded on the treads, and John and Tom pushed past Mistress Perrott and seized Cobham, one on each arm. 'You don't speak to the mistress like that, you canting Puritan!' John's amiable face was choleric with fury. 'And Mistress Perrott saved my youngest when he had the flux last summer.'

'You are all damned!' Cobham shouted at the frightened servants below. 'I'll have the witch-finder on you. This whole village——'

Tom slapped his free hand over the clerk's mouth, cutting the flow off abruptly. 'What shall we do with him, mistress?' Above the gagging hand Nathaniel's eyes bulged.

'Put him in his room and turn the key in the lock until he has calmed down.' Henrietta pushed past them and down the stairs to the wisewoman. 'Mistress, forgive us. The man is deranged with worry for his master. We have much need of you; I fear for my husband's life.'

As Nathaniel was dragged struggling down the corridor Henrietta ushered the older woman into the bedroom. Matthew seemed unchanged; the commotion outside had not roused him.

Mistress Perrott laid a hand on his forehead, then lifted an eyelid, gazing into the unresponsive pupil for a long while. Then she pulled back the sheets and opened his nightshirt, running knowledgeable fingers over his chest and under his arms. Finally she put her ear to his chest and listened.

'It's not the plague. It may be marsh fever, or a chill settled on the lungs. Has he been very cold and wet for a long time?'

'I don't know. He has not been gone very long. . .but he has been in London. Can we be certain it is not the plague?'

'He has not the signs.'

Henrietta felt some relief that her worst fears were

unrealised. 'But he is so pale and drawn — not like the vigorous man who left Winterbourne so recently.'

Mistress Perrott pulled back the covers. 'No. He may have been over-tired, starved of good nourishment. He has not been taking good care of himself. Then any fever would take hold fast. He is in great danger, Henrietta; I will not hide it from you. His lungs are much congested and the fever strong.'

'What can we do?' Henrietta asked in despair, holding on to Matthew's hand tightly as though her touch could bring him back.

'We must break the fever, or there is no hope. Keep him warm as you are doing, cool his forehead with damp cloths and moisten his lips. I have an infusion of borage here; pour boiling water on it and hold it close for him to breathe. And pray to God to spare him,' she added grimly.

She unpacked the bottles and packets from her basket and turned back to the door. 'I will come again in the morning.'

'You cannot go!' Henrietta took her arm. 'I need you!'

'There is nothing more I can do for him that you cannot and Mistress Weldon is in need of me now. Sim caught me as I was leaving to attend her. Her time is near, and it will not be easy.' The older woman hesitated, then touched Henrietta's cheek comfortingly. 'He is fit and strong despite what has happened recently. He has much to live for; when he is conscious and can understand you, tell him of the child. And save your strength; look after yourself for his sake as well as for your own.'

'Had you told her about the child?' Letty asked as the door closed behind the wisewoman.

'No, she must have guessed as you did. Letty, are you afraid to help me? You heard Mistress Perrott say it was not the plague.'

'Not I, mistress. I will be here, and so will all the others. They are loyal to you, mistress, no matter what nonsense that clerk spouts at them.'

★ ★ ★

'I fear he is not better, Henrietta.' Mistress Perrott straightened up from the bed, smoothing the covers back across Matthew's chest. 'And two days have passed since he collapsed. Has he shown no signs of wakening?'

'None. He is restless from time to time, but that is all.' Henrietta looked up from the low stool beside the bed, still holding Matthew's hot, dry hand in hers. 'But he is not worse — surely there is some hope in that?'

'I fear not, child. Insensible as he is, he cannot help himself or fight the fever with his will.' The wisewoman touched Henrietta's shoulder, her face compassionate. 'You must prepare yourself for the worst; he could slip away from us at any time.'

'No! I will not let him! He has everything to live for — I will not let him die.' The unshed tears stood in her eyes, but she would not let herself give way and believe what the older woman was telling her.

'Send for Lawyer Stone. You need a man here to advise you.'

Henrietta knew what Mistress Perrott really meant: Matthew was going to die and his lawyer should be here when it happened. She shook her head in denial of the thought, then realised how comforting it would be to have the old man by her side. And if Mr Stone came Aunt Susan would surely be with him. News of Matthew's illness had not been sent to Hertford; there had been no time to think of that. But the thought of Aunt Susan who had always made things right in the past coming to comfort her was so overwhelming that the tears spilt over and finally ran down her cheeks.

'I will send Letty to you.' Mistress Perrott patted her shoulder. 'Then I must go to the Home Farm.'

'Alice!' Henrietta realised with a guilty start that she had not spared a thought for her friend. 'Is she safe delivered?'

'A fine healthy daughter, the same night your husband returned. But it was a difficult birth; she is very tired. I am concerned for her.'

'Of course you must go.' Henrietta scrubbed the back

of her hand across her eyes and got to her feet. 'Give them both my love and tell Alice to rest. Does she know why I cannot come to see her?'

'I told her something of your husband's illness yesterday. I will say I have asked you not to come yet in case of contagion; she must not be worried.'

Letty arrived as Henrietta finished a brief note to Lawyer Stone. She made no attempt to hide her fears or the seriousness of Matthew's illness. 'Take this to John.' She pressed Matthew's signet-ring into the soft wax, then handed the sealed letter to the girl. 'Tell him to send a groom to Hertford with all dispatch.'

Letty took the letter with a solemn nod and hurried from the room. Henrietta stood with one hand on the hangings looking out over the orchard at the lowering purple sky. There was snow heavy in the clouds and the first silent flakes drifted past the panes as she watched.

Although it was only morning she pulled the hangings closed, shutting out the bleak coldness, and put another log on the fire.

Then she settled on the stool and laced her fingers in Matthew's lax ones again. All she could do for him now was to stay with him and hope that even though he was unconscious some part of him was aware of her touch, of the strength of her will and her love.

It was early the next evening that the crunch of snow under coach wheels alerted her to the arrival of Lawyer Stone. Henrietta tugged open the hangings and saw to her immense relief the old lawyer handing her aunt out of the coach in the light spilling from the front door.

She hesitated by Matthew's side, caressing his unresponsive cheek, then wrenched the door open and ran to the head of the stairs. 'Aunt!' Despite herself her voice broke and she could not go on.

There was a flurry of skirts on the stairs, then her aunt was enfolding her in her arms, her cold cheek pressed against Henrietta's flushed one. 'My darling child, how is he?'

'Come and see.' Henrietta tugged her aunt's gloved

hand. 'Tell me what to do! Mistress Perrott says he will die, but we will not let him will we? Not now you are here. . .'

Susan looked at her niece and saw not the woman but the six-year-old Henrietta, frightened over some calamity or wakening from a bad dream and trusting her aunt to chase away the horrors. Her face was drawn and white and there were black circles of sleeplessness under her eyes.

'Do not worry, child, I am here. We will look after him together. . .' Her confident voice died away as she saw Matthew for the first time. She struggled, but was not quick enough to mask her dismay and shock from her niece.

'Aunt?' It was a hoarse supplication, then Henrietta forced herself to face the reality. 'You think he is going to die too.'

'It is in God's hands.' The older woman took her by the shoulders and gravely looked into her eyes. 'We will pray, all of us. Now, go to your room and rest. Send Letty to me. If there is any change I will call you; you will do your husband no good by making yourself ill.'

She dropped her cloak and hat on the chair and pushed back her cuffs. 'Trust me with him, child; I know how much you love him. Now go!'

From her chamber window Henrietta could see the light escaping from around the drawn hangings in the master bedroom. The snow swirled thickly in the courtyard and the whole night was muffled and silent. If she had left it any later to send for them they would not have got through from Hertford.

Her aunt was right; she needed to rest. Letty had laid her nightdress to warm by the fire, but Henrietta ignored it. She had had scant sleep, and that crouched by Matthew's side. She would just lie on the bed and close her eyes for a while. . .

It was cold when she woke, the room full of white light reflecting off the snow outside. The fire was a mass of soft grey ash and the candles had guttered and gone out in the sconces.

'Matthew!' Henrietta started up off the bed. How could she have slept so long? There was a tap at the door and Letty opened it cautiously.

'Mistress—I thought you had gone to bed.' She looked at Henrietta's crumpled gown and dishevelled hair in dismay.

'Letty, is he. . .all right?' She hardly dared ask.

'Unchanged. Mistress Stone has not left him all night. No, there is no need for you to go to him yet.' She put a restraining hand on Henrietta's arm. 'I will bring you hot water and a fresh gown, then you can break your fast with Lawyer Stone.'

The old lawyer stood up as she joined him in the small parlour. The servants had laid a table there by the fire to escape the draughts in the great hall and he was toying with bread and bacon.

'My dear girl.' He held out his arms and she walked into his embrace. He hugged her so tightly that he almost squeezed the breath from her and she realised how worried and concerned he was. 'Now sit down here by the fire, and eat this.'

He cut her a slice of bacon and buttered bread, pushing the plate into her unresisting hands. 'Eat up— you need your strength.'

To her surprise Henrietta was hungry. The bread and meat might have been sawdust for all the taste they had, but still she finished them ravenously, washing them down with a mug of small beer.

'That is much better; there is colour in your cheeks again,' Lawrence Stone said approvingly. 'In your condition you must take great care of yourself.'

'You know? Did Letty tell you?'

'She thought we should hear of it straight away. She is a good girl, that one, a good head on her shoulders.' Suddenly his bluffness fell away, and he began to fiddle with his ale mug, his eyes averted. 'There are things we must talk of Henrietta. I know it is painful for you. . .'

'You mean, what I must do if Matthew dies?' Her voice was quite steady and she met his eyes direct. 'There is no need; he is not going to.'

'Henrietta, you must not deceive yourself. I admire your courage, but we must face the facts of the case. . .'

'No, I *will not* accept that Matthew might die.' Henrietta stood, one hand on his shoulder. 'I know you mean well, but I cannot give up. Oh, if only he were sensible long enough for me to tell him I am carrying his child, it would be enough to save him!' She paused at the door. 'I shall go to him now and relieve my aunt; she must be very tired.'

Susan was holding a sponge to Matthew's lips, patiently attempting to coax a few drops of liquid between them. The pungent aroma of spirits met Henrietta's nostrils as she closed the chamber door quietly behind her.

'How is he, Aunt? Has there been any change?'

Her aunt straightened up, one hand in the small of her back. In the searching morning light she looked every one of her forty years. 'No change; then again he is no worse. You look better, my dear.'

Henrietta kissed her aunt's cheek and took the sponge from her hand. 'I slept too long,' she reproached herself. 'Thank you for staying with him. Your husband is breaking his fast in the small parlour; why do you not join him and then go to bed?'

'I shall, child.' Susan took her niece's cold hands in hers. 'I am overjoyed to hear you are with child; pray God Matthew lives to share your joy.'

Henrietta managed a brave smile. 'He will.' But as she looked at the still figure lying in the big bed all her hope ebbed away, leaving her desolate, sure she had been deceiving herself.

For the rest of the day she hardly left his side, seated at his bedside on a low stool, holding his hand, talking to him of all the things she had never said, all her plans for the child he would never see.

As the evening drew in Letty came in to make up the

fire again and draw the hangings closed. Her aunt tried
to persuade her to go downstairs and eat, but Henrietta
refused in case Matthew woke to find her not there.

'Go to bed, Aunt; I will sit with him tonight.'

Mistress Stone opened her mouth as if to protest, then
her eyes took in Matthew's waxen face and the quiet
desperation in Henrietta's eyes and with a last kiss she
left, closing the door behind her.

Towards midnight Henrietta dozed, her head dropping sideways to lie on the coverlet beside their clasped
hands. She woke to the sound of a log falling in the grate
and was instantly aware of a gentle touch on her hair.

CHAPTER FOURTEEN

FOR a second Henrietta thought she was dreaming, but the moth's touch became firmer and she was suddenly aware that the rhythm of Matthew's breathing had changed to a deeper, more regular pattern.

Hardly daring to hope, she raised her head and found herself looking into Matthew's eyes. Sunken and shadowed as they were, they still held a glimmer of vitality; as he saw her face his lips moved in a painful half-smile.

'Henrietta. . .' His voice was the merest thread of a whisper.

'Don't try and talk!' Her heart soared in her breast as she mixed brandy and water, splashing it in her eagerness. She supported his shoulders and held the cup to his mouth. 'Try and sip this slowly; you must be so thirsty.'

Matthew managed to drink most of the cupful in slow, difficult sips. It was only when he had finished and she laid him back against the pillows that Henrietta dared let him speak.

'What happened? How long have I been here?' he croaked.

'It is four days since you arrived home, racked with fever and wet through. You collapsed in the hall and have been insensible ever since.' Henrietta chafed his hands between hers, willing her strength and life back into him.

'I remember riding. . .being cold and wet, wanting to be at home with you. . .but that is all.' He put a shaky hand to his forehead as though to rub away the fog in his mind. 'And yet I seem to recollect your face. . .you were fearful. . . I had frightened you.'

'I was frightened because you were so ill,' Henrietta

said soothingly, afraid that he would become agitated in his weakened state if she reminded him of the scene of his homecoming. 'You have had a fever of the lungs. How do you feel? Have you pains anywhere?'

'My chest is sore,' he managed to rasp. Henrietta nodded; that was what Mistress Perrott had told her to expect. 'And I feel so. . .weak.'

'Could you manage some broth?'

Matthew moved his head slowly on the pillow. 'No. . .more water. I am so thirsty.'

When he had drunk again Henrietta bathed his face gently, the cloth rasping through the growth of beard over his hollow cheeks. 'Try and sleep, my love.' She brushed her lips softly across the back of his hand, dropping unconscious tears on his skin as she did so.

'Wait.' He touched her cheek. 'What did you call me?'

'My love.' She managed a smile through the tears of relief. 'You are my love. I have never loved anyone more, nor ever will in my life.'

His eyelids drooped, he was almost asleep again, but his lips managed to form the words, 'And I. . .love you too. . .'

'Matthew.' She had to tell him the wonderful news she had kept in her heart. 'Matthew, I am carrying your child. . .' But he was asleep, a touch of colour on each cheekbone. His breathing was steady despite a painful rasp with each indrawn breath and his skin was warm and damp, the fever broken.

Henrietta dropped to her knees beside the bed, hid her face in the covers and said a heartfelt prayer of thankfulness. He was going to live; of that she was certain beyond doubt. And—her heart leapt as she got to her feet again—he loved her; he had said so.

The moment of still thankfulness burst like a bubble of joy and she lifted her skirts and dashed to the head of the stairs.

'Aunt! Lawyer Stone! Letty! Come here!'

Doors were flung open all along the corridor. Aunt Susan her robe dragged on anyhow, her plaited hair flying, rushed to her side followed by her husband, his face a picture of concern.

'Henrietta. . .what is it? Surely he is not. . .'

'No!' She hugged her aunt joyfully. 'No, he is alive! He has woken and spoken to me. Oh, Aunt, he is going to recover!'

'Thank God!' exclaimed Letty, and the group of servants filling the corridor behind her chorused,

'Amen to that!'

John, emerging from Robert's old room, elbowed his way to the front. 'Mistress? What's afoot?'

'The master has woken,' Letty said, and suddenly burst into tears, flinging herself into his arms.

John shot Henrietta a startled glance, although he tightened his arms around the sobbing girl.

'Take her away and comfort her; she is over-tired from helping me these past days.' Henrietta smiled at her head groom. At least this would put a stop to Letty playing propriety with him!

'I will sit with him now, my dear,' her aunt began, propelling Henrietta towards her old room. 'You must rest; he will need you tomorrow.'

'Indeed I will not,' Henrietta declared roundly. 'I thank you, Aunt, but I shall sleep in our chamber with my husband. All of you, please go back to bed; I am sorry to have roused you, but I had to share my good news.'

Back in Matthew's chamber Henrietta slipped quietly out of her clothes and into her nightrobe, then climbed into bed alongside him. He was lying in the middle of the bed, but she curled up happily, one arm protectively around his waist.

She was woken by the bed dipping beside her and a muttered imprecation. Matthew was struggling to sit up.

'Lie still, my love,' she urged, hopping out of bed and hastening around to help him. 'There.' She plumped the pillows behind his shoulders, biting her lip with sudden anxiety as he was racked by a rattling cough.

A tug on the bell-pull brought Letty at the run. She

peeped round the door, her face breaking into a smile of pure pleasure at the sight of her master sitting up in bed.

'Broth, Letty, and some good red wine,' Henrietta ordered before turning back to look long and lovingly at the man who had been restored to her. 'Matthew, how much do you remember of last night?'

'I remember telling you I love you. And I do, Henrietta, with all my heart.' His eyes, no longer bright with fever, were steady on her face.

So she hadn't dreamt it, nor had he spoken in delirium. 'Why did you not tell me before?' She sat on the end of the bed, pulling a blanket around her shoulders. 'Matthew, I have been so unhappy.'

'And so have I. We must speak of this, Henrietta. But come back to bed, love; you will catch a cold.' He held out his hands to her, but she shook her head.

'No, I need to see your face while we talk! Matthew, please tell me, why have you not told me how you felt before?'

'I was going to tell you when I came back that day after you had fallen in the yard, but you were unwell and we had a guest in the house.'

'But Ransome was not with us always. So many times I have felt we were about to reach each other but something always came between us again.' The shadow of all that time wasted on misunderstanding and unhappiness showed on her face.

'I tried to tell you how I felt.'

'I remember everything you have ever said to me,' Henrietta replied steadily. 'And you never spoke to me of love.'

'I was angry with you,' he said wryly. 'I thought you despised me and my beliefs, enjoyed flouting my advice not to espouse the King's cause so openly. And I was angry with myself for falling in love with such a wilful woman.'

'Oh, my love, if only we could have spoken of it.' Henrietta shook her head despairingly. 'It took me a long time to realise, but I know now the King was wrong to continue to ferment division among his people. But Matthew, although I love you, I cannot say I support Parliament and General Cromwell, because it would not be true and I cannot lie to you.'

'Come here to me, my love.' Matthew held out his arms and this time she came into them willingly. After a long moment he spoke again, his words muffled by her hair. 'I have never sought to turn you against your conscience, Henrietta, but I judged you too harshly. How could you be expected to understand the politics of this troubled nation if all you have been brought up to know is one position? And to have lost your father and brothers as you did. . . I was too harsh——' He broke off, coughing.

Henrietta freed herself and lifted the cup of wine to his lips. 'Hush, drink this. Do not tire yourself with talk; I understand.' She brushed the damp tangle of hair from his forehead. 'I love you so much, Matthew. While you have been away I have thought so much about what you believe, of the dream you have for a secure future for our child.' Unconsciously her hand rested over the child in her womb.

His face was transformed by joy. 'Then I did not dream the words as I fell asleep last night? You are with child?'

'Yes. It is due in the late Spring.'

He lifted her hands and kissed them. 'Henrietta——'

Letty's entrance cut across what he had been about to say. Henrietta took the tray and refused to let him speak until he had drunk as much as he could manage of the rich beef broth.

At last he lay back, the colour stronger in his face, his eyes brighter, more alert, his voice steady. 'And you, wife, why did you not tell me you loved me before?' He watched her face, the blush spreading over her cheeks, her downcast eyes. 'Surely it was not so very difficult?'

'Matthew, I am so ashamed of it, but I was jealous of Sarah, convinced you still loved her. . .' Her voice trailed away.

'Sarah? But she has been dead these past six years!'
He sounded genuinely bemused.

'Your face when you spoke of her. . .the pain in your
eyes when you recollected her death. You spoke of her
so often,' she whispered, her eyes still cast down.

'Henrietta, look at me.' He tugged her hands and she
met his eyes reluctantly, still ashamed of her jealousy.
'Listen to me. I loved Sarah; we grew up together
knowing we would eventually marry. It was our fathers'
wish for us. We were friends first, lovers second, she
and I. She was gentle and meek and obedient—not at all
like you, Henrietta.' She gasped indignantly, then looked
up and saw the smile in his eyes.

'I loved you the first time I saw you, so proud and
haughty, so passionate inside. Sarah and I never crossed
words; ours was a steady marriage. But until you I never
understood what passion between a man and a woman
truly was.'

'You made me feel so wanton. . .so unmaidenly,' she
confessed, blushing still deeper.

His grin was almost like the old Matthew. 'You make
me very eager to be well and strong again, wife!' He
tipped up her chin and gazed long and lovingly into her
brown eyes. 'Kiss me.'

Henrietta let her lips rest gently against his, her arms
round his neck, their hearts beating together. The long,
tranquil moment stretched on; she wondered hazily how
it was possible to be so happy, so at peace.

But there was still her secret lying between them. She
must face it; to be true to Matthew she must be untrue
to her brother, break her oath and trust in Matthew's
moderation that what she told him would not hazard the
safety of Robert, Alice and the others.

'Matthew, there is something I must tell you. I know
you have been suspicious that I have not been open with
you, that I have kept a secret from you. And there is the
letter. . .Now we have found each other there can be no
secrets between us——'

'Do not tell me.' He broke across her confession. 'I

know that you love me and no other. I trust you, Henrietta.'

'But I must tell you,' she implored. 'I would have told you sooner but I had sworn an oath.'

'No. Enough—you must not break an oath for my sake.'

The door crashed open behind them, startling Henrietta so much that she nearly fell from the bed. Nathaniel Cobham stood on the threshold, hair and clothes awry, face wan from four days' enforced seclusion.

'Master Matthew! Thank the Lord you are alive!'

Matthew's brows shot up. 'Nathaniel! Do not distress yourself so—I am much restored, thank you. Come in and shut the door.'

'Have you drunk anything that witch has prepared for you?' Cobham demanded, white-lipped. 'Pray God I am not too late.'

'Have you taken leave of your senses, man?' Matthew demanded, struggling to raise himself in the bed. 'How dare you address your mistress in those terms?'

'Ask her why she has kept me prisoner these past four days!' the clerk demanded. 'I was dragged from your side by her louts, thrown into my room. . . I would be there still if it were not for the stupidity of the dolt guarding me.'

'Henrietta! Is this true? Have you ordered Nathaniel incarcerated?' Matthew looked at her, uncertain whether to believe the clerk's ravings or not.

'He accused Mistress Perrott of witchcraft when she came to help look after you. Matthew; he acted like a man demented. The servants were terrified; I had no choice.'

'She lies!' Cobham blazed, one bony finger raised in accusation.

'Nathaniel, I will become seriously displeased if you continue in this intemperate manner. It should be obvious to the dullest wit that I am mending—and that due to my dear wife's care.'

'Your *dear* wife! That Royalist whore——'

'Henrietta, ring for John; you are right—his brain is turned. . .'

'Hear me out. Ask your dear wife about the man whom I found meeting her in the yard in the dead of night while you were away.' Matthew shot Henrietta a puzzled glance, his eyes narrowing as he saw the colour drain from her face. 'She met him in her nightrobe, was conducting him to her chamber when I discovered them. She and that old crow Lady Willoughby hatched some pretence of a groom and a servant wench, but he was no groom. I saw his clothes, his sword. He was a gentleman.'

'Henrietta? Tell me he lies.'

'I cannot. There *was* a man here, but he was not, is not, my lover.'

'Then he did not come to meet you?'

'Yes. . .no. . . I cannot say. Matthew, believe me, I have done nothing to harm you.'

The silence in the room was palpable as Matthew's eyes moved from his clerk's features to his wife's and back to Cobham again. Henrietta felt a welling black despair enfolding her; all their new-found love was being poisoned by the clerk's suspicions.

'I know of this already. You tell me nothing new, Cobham.' Matthew's calm pronouncement was so unexpected that both Henrietta and Cobham gasped. 'You are overwrought by worry for me. For that reason, and that reason only, I forgive your wild accusations about my wife. When you are calmer you must apologise to your mistress yourself. Now go to your chamber and compose yourself.'

Stunned into silence, Cobham shuffled from the room, a shabby, diminished figure in rusty black.

'Matthew. . .thank you for your trust,' Henrietta began, stumbling over the words. 'But he was telling only the truth—there was a man, I was trying to tell you.'

'And I told you, wife, that I do not ask you to break

your secret, but it is best I do not know.' He lay back against the pillows, his face suddenly grey with fatigue.

'We will talk of it later.' Henrietta was too concerned for his health to persist. 'Cobham must go; I will not have him carrying on so — he sets the entire household on its heels! I wonder you tolerate him.'

'He was not always so, but there has been much tragedy in his life. His family were all killed in a fire; his sorrow only served to increase a narrowness which was always part of his character and beliefs. But he had been a loyal servant to both my father and myself — could you bring yourself to disown Alice if she too became difficult with age?'

'No, of course I could not. Sleep now, my beloved, and I will sit by you.'

'You too are fatigued. Go to your own chamber and rest, Henrietta. There is the child to think of and you are too precious to me to risk your health.'

When Henrietta woke the shadows were long in her room despite the brilliant white of snow outside and the house was quiet. The realisation of her happiness sent her almost running down the corridor in her haste to return to Matthew, to be in his arms again, to share more confidences, more words of love.

The bed was empty, his clothes gone from the press, his boots from beside the chair. Henrietta's hand flew to her mouth; where had he gone, why had he gone? Had he had second thoughts in the hours they had been apart? Had Cobham come back and filled his mind with poison?

Henrietta ran down the stairs calling for Letty, for her aunt. John emerged from the kitchen corridor, a mug of ale in one hand. 'Mistress, what is wrong?'

'John! Have you seen your master? He is gone from his room.' She was too distraught to beat about the bush.

'Why, yes, mistress. He asked for a horse to be saddled a good hour since.'

'You let him go out in this cold? John, it could be the death of him!'

'He seemed well enough, mistress, and he was dressed for riding.' The groom's normally civil tone held a touch of indignation.

'I'm sorry, John; of course you could not have stopped him. But where has he gone?'

'North, up the green lane. The short cut to the Oxford road by Home Farm, I supposed.'

Henrietta dragged her cloak from the chest, thrusting her slippered feet into wooden pattens. 'I must find him; he was too weak to ride far.' She almost pushed past John in her hurry and ran across the slush of the yard towards the bridge.

The hoofmarks were clear in the untrodden snow beyond the moat. After a few yards Henrietta had to stop to knock the accumulated snow from her pattens; as she straightened again she heard the muffled, plodding step of an approaching horse.

He must have fallen and the horse was returning without him. Her heart knotted with fear; even now he could be lying in a drift, the life's heat seeping from his body. Henrietta broke into an unsteady run as the grey horse rounded the corner of the lane. Even in the gathering gloom she could see the figure almost slumped over its neck.

'Matthew!' At her cry he looked up and straightened in the saddle. 'What are you about?' She snatched the reins above the bit and tugged the horse towards the house.

He tried to speak but managed only a hoarse, painful cough. At that moment John reached them and swung up into the saddle behind his master, kicking the horse into trot.

By the time Henrietta had reached the hall Matthew was wrapped in blankets in the big chair before the fire, recovered enough to wave away offers of broth and hot bricks.

She sent the servants away and knelt in front of him. 'Matthew, why were you leaving me?'

'Leaving you?' He was taken aback by the question, the tears standing in her eyes. 'I was not leaving you.'

'But you were on the road to Oxford. . .'

'I was at Home Farm, speaking with Robert and Alice. They sent me a message.'

'*Home Farm!*' All her worried and doubts vanished in a surge of relieved anger. 'You should not be from your bed, let alone riding in this cold to the risk of your very life! What message could be worth that?'

He held up both hands to fend off her attack. 'Peace, Henrietta! I had not taken you for a nagging wife.' There were dark shadows of fatigue under his eyes, but his face was softened by laughter.

'Nagging! Matthew, I believed you had left me, that you had thought again on what Cobham had told you. . .'

'My poor darling.' He touched her cheek, catching a tear as it slid from the corner of her eye. 'I was wrong to tease you, and thoughtless to leave without letting you know. In truth, I am weaker than I knew; I had hoped to be back before you woke.'

'But why did you go?'

'Letty had told Alice of Cobham's accusations. She is still confined, but she was determined I should know the truth. As she told me, she was bound by no oath as you were and has revealed all she knew of the casket and the messenger.'

'She dared do so?' Henrietta knew the risk Alice and Robert had taken. One word from Matthew in the right quarter and their lives would have been forfeit.

'They dared because of their loyalty to your family and their love for you. And, like me, Robert wants to put the past aside and build a new future for our children. Forgive me, my love, for ever having doubted you.' He took her hands in both of his.

'There is nothing to forgive. And I was breaking my marriage vows in deceiving you.' She met his eyes and found such warmth in their green depths that she was shaken to her heart.

'You have had so much to bear. How could you stay so strong when you stood to lose everything — our love, Winterbourne, your people?'

'I had no choice. Loving you as I did, I could not lie to you so I chose silence. I thought once the papers were safe away and I was quit of my bond I could find a way to explain to you without involving Robert, Alice and the others.'

'Loyalty must be in the air at Winterbourne. I will try and be worthy of it — only say you forgive me, my love.'

'Of — of course I forgive you,' Henrietta stammered, unable to believe it was all coming right at last. 'But you will not be angry with Robert and Alice for helping me?'

'Never, for such loyalty. We all want the same thing, my love — peace and a future for our children.' He stretched out an arm and caught her to him, holding her so fiercely that she wondered where he had found the strength.

She drew back so that she could look into his face. 'I am at peace with you, Matthew. And you, my love, are you at peace with me?'

Matthew's eyes smiled into hers. 'Now and for always. Nothing will ever part me from you, Henrietta, my own true love. I have come home here to you and Winterbourne — it will take greater powers than Kings and Parliaments to part us again. . .'

The other exciting

MASQUERADE
Historical

available this month is:

FOUR IN HAND
Stephanie Laurens

Unexpectedly inheriting the dukedom of Twyford from his uncle, Max Rotherbridge was stunned to discover he had also inherited wardship of the four Twinning sisters.

The eldest, Miss Caroline Twinning, was the embodiment of all his dreams, but even rakehell Max knew that as her guardian, she was the one woman he could not seduce. And who better than a rake to ensure that other rakes did not succeed in compromising the sisters? Max knew his life would never be the same!

Look out for the two intriguing

MASQUERADE *Historical*

Romances coming in May

HERITAGE OF LOVE
Sarah Westleigh

Life was hard in the Devon fishing village where Charlotte Falconer tried to keep her vulnerable family afloat, but it was her mother's death that caused a real catalyst, when Charlotte discovered she was not the child of the man she had always called father!

Victorian social mores were strict, and she had no expectation that her real father would ever acknowledge her. What she couldn't guess was that the secret relationship would cause untold damage between her and Francis Longford, an intriguing American businessman, who found Charlotte's warmth and sincerity charming, her attitudes so different to those in his own circles . . . until he overstepped the mark and alienated Charlotte!

ALL OF HEAVEN
Petra Nash

Miss Cecilia Avening was determined not to apply to her grandfather, the Earl of Syreford, even though at 19 her future was uncertain. Required unexpectedly to help Lord Marcus Inglesham with his three excitable nieces as they journeyed to London, Cecilia found the children were not about to let the acquaintance drop, which meant continued contact with Marcus. But he was considering the ladylike Miss Chadfield as his future wife, and a lowly governess surely had no place in such circumstances?

Also available soon in Large Print

TWO HISTORICAL ROMANCES

&

TWO FREE GIFTS!